HUNTING EL DESPIADADO

ALSO BY CHRIS MULLEN

Rowdy Series

Rowdy: Wild and Mean, Sharp and Keen

Rowdy: Redemption

Rowdy: Dead or Alive

Rowdy: Rescue

Rowdy: To Catch a Killer

Rowdy: Return

Cass Callahan Series

Dead Land

Kill Order

Hunting El Despiadado

HUNTING EL DESPIADADO

CASS CALLAHAN
BOOK THREE

CHRIS MULLEN

WOLFPACK
PUBLISHING
— EST 2019 —

Hunting El Despiadado
Paperback Edition
Copyright © 2024 Chris Mullen

Wolfpack Publishing
701 S. Howard Ave. 106-324
Tampa, Florida 33609

wolfpackpublishing.com

Paperback ISBN 978-1-63977-385-5
eBook ISBN 978-1-63977-384-8
LCCN 2024932361

To those who hunted with me, and continue to watch my six

HUNTING EL DESPIADADO

CHAPTER ONE

I stood on the concrete steps outside the FBI El Paso Field Office, a gritty taste still resonating in my mouth from images of weeping faces, of caskets, and burials of which I had attended way too many over the past few weeks. I felt as dark as the shadow that had fallen over the small border community of Brewster, Texas, but I was here, on the doorstep of Special Agent Thomas Zuñiga, ready to hunt down the man and the cartel responsible.

Looking across the busy Borderplex into Ciudad Juarez, Mexico, I felt as if eyes were watching me, studying my features, predicting my next move. *Fuck 'em*, I thought. The Camargo cartel was embedded deep in the veins of the state of Chihuahua and was threatening expansion which in its own right could start a territorial war between competing cartels. That was their problem.

Kill Hydra, our secret FBI kill squad, was also a problem they were going to get to know pretty damn well, and soon. That is what brought me to El Paso and stopped me from going rogue into Mexico Lone Wolf McQuade style, although I still felt that intense spirit of an angry Chuck Norris. When Agent Zuñiga first approached me about joining his *Kill Hydra* team, I dismissed the idea as if it had been an insult. Now, he was about to find out that I was prepared to take his mission to a whole new level. Mythology says, chop one head off a Hydra, two grow back. Let's see how well it does with a gun in its ear and a grenade shoved up its ass.

Kill Hydra was an unofficial operation with parameters determined from headquarters on a situational basis. But when the bullets fly and big brother is tucked safely behind a desk, I intended to stretch the limits and end the reign of terror that was the Camargo cartel.

And then there was Carlos Ruiz-Mata. The killer. The bomber. *El Despiadado*. I hated the man and the thought that he lived and breathed as if he were free. Untouchable. Since disappearing into Boquillas, Mexico he had slipped off the radar and become a ghost. But no man can truly disappear. He could hide. He could move around from safe house to safe house, but I do not think that he had any concern for the consequences of his actions in Brewster. In fact, I wanted him to feel safe; to feel untouchable. He had crossed borders, attacked my son, killed my friends, destroyed the sheriff's office, and was now on siesta somewhere south of the Rio Grande. The more comfortable he was, the easier it would be to hunt him down. I was just the man for the job and had all but one team member in place.

I looked at my watch, then glanced around the parking lot. A trickle of sweat dripped down the back of my neck. Even in late October, the West Texas sun was relentless. I saw an old Chevy Silverado pull into the lot. Its engine grumbled with attitude much like the driver I knew behind the wheel.

With a squeak of the brakes, the truck hovered over two parking spots, its front end angled to one side of the line. I could see a patched dent in the rear driver's side door. A white bumper sticker with large black lettering had been carelessly, yet purposefully placed on the tailgate at eye level so that any driver following too close could read the message. *Come Any Closer, I Will Shit in Your Mouth.*

The driver's door swung open. A large man, built more like a construction worker, stepped out—forearms like jackhammers, shoulders like the broad side of an elephant, steel jaw and chin, flecked gray hair, and the bulge of a beer belly that acted more like a protective barrier than flabby obstacle when the shit hit the fan.

It was Ray.

Ray Tucker, my former *Dragon Company* lieutenant, Houston Police detective partner, good friend, and royal pain in the ass was my personal, no-questions-asked, addition to the *Kill Hydra* team. I wanted somebody I knew I could trust watching my back, somebody who would not hesitate in a fight, somebody who had skin of his own in the game. Ray was my son Spencer's godfather. When I told him what had happened and what I was planning to do, it took all of two seconds for him to agree to be on my team.

"Just tell me we ain't bringin' any beaners back with us. Gonna roast 'em all for hurting Spence!"

"Hooah," I told him, and that was it.

I watched as Ray walked over to meet me. He took his time, almost sauntering across the concrete and up the few steps. Stopping in front of me, he reached for his sunglasses, pulling them off his nose with a slow, cinematic swipe of the wrist.

His blue eyes had a psychotic twist in them, reminding me of how the White Walkers in Game of Thrones looked at their helpless victims as they lay spread across a gruesome battlefield of newly recruited dead.

He opened his mouth to speak, then paused to offer me a hand. We shook once, but he did not let go. Instead, I found myself being pulled forward into an inescapable bear hug, wrought with slaps to my back, and deep laughter of an old friend.

"Let's go bag us some bad guys," Ray said.

He let go of his ironclad grasp to the relief of my lungs and caving chest cavity.

"Slow down, killer," I said. "One step at a time. First, let's get you caught up to speed. Need you to meet Special Agent Thomas Zuñiga. This team is his baby. We're here to make a man out of it."

"Head Honcho, huh? This cat better be pretty damn special."

"He is. Can't say as much about all of 'em, but I trust Zuñiga."

Agent Zuñiga showed no resistance when approving Ray's addition to the team, but he must have had some hidden reservations because he hinted at the possibility of an extra man of his own to be included. It was unexpected, but over my years of law enforcement work, the unexpected became the norm, especially when faced with a joint operation between three letter agencies.

"Trust," Ray said, laying a hand on my shoulder. "That's a hard thing to come by. Hope you're sure about this one."

"Come on," I said. "They're waiting."

Ray let go of my shoulder and smirked. He was a hard ass through and through, yet I could see genuine emotion behind his steely blue eyes.

"I missed you, Cass."

I had known Ray for a long time. During our time in the Army, we had seen the unimaginable effects war had on a nation, on its people. We walked through the rubble, past shattered lives and damaged souls on a Middle East tour while the whole world watched and waited, all the while wondering what the United States military would do next. We were the faces of safety to some and the wanted heads on a collection sheet to others. Through the smoke and fires, the missions and furloughs, Ray and I became brothers. We shared the same layers of mental scar tissue. We understood the gravity of our missions. It was what kept us close. It was a bond born from fire, and one that held firm like the roots of a hundred-year-old oak. We each had our ways of dealing with the nightmares and the victories, but one thing remained constant —trust.

When we traded in our military fatigues for civilian clothes, we were reunited on the streets of Houston, charged with a new duty—*To Serve and Protect*. We rose quickly through the ranks and were partnered up as detectives. Our tasks were simple, get the job done. And we did, every time. I loved it. I knew Ray loved it too, but his no filter attitude set him back a time or two. He took issue with authority, and in true Ray fashion, voiced his opinions for all to hear regardless of who was in the room or in whose face he was standing nose to nose. He had been busted down to patrolman more than once, "served my time," as he would say, but we always bounced back. Our history together made us effective, and the big brass knew it. Our military experience helped tamp out the shock and surprise of urban violence when the blacktops and sidewalks back home presented horrors like those we survived abroad. The bullets were just as deadly, the screams of pain or anguish just as piercing, and blood spilled in the same life-sucking streams of red.

Side by side, Ray and I walked into the El Paso FBI Field Office where Special Agent Zuñiga was waiting with the rest of team *Kill Hydra*. Plans were in motion, and the hunt for *El Despiadado* was about to begin.

CHAPTER TWO

The barrel of Flint's Winchester .308 glimmered in the afternoon sun. Its weathered and worn walnut stock pulled snug against his right shoulder pocket. The rear aperture and the steel sight post at the end of the barrel aligned and aimed at the subtle movement down range. His breath was shallow. His finger rested along the curved trigger shoe. In position and ready to fire, he waited.

Cattle lowed in the distance. The small herd fragmentation was Floyd Huckabee's. They had split off from the main herd that roamed the open expanse of the CR under a grazing agreement between the Flyin' H and the Callahan Ranch. In larger numbers, cattle were less vulnerable to predators, but this small group of drifters had wandered off far enough to gain the attention of a pack of unwelcome guests.

Flint's keen eyesight followed the movement with the .308 poised and ready to fire.

"I count four," he said in a gravelly whisper. "We shoot together. Got it?"

"Got it," Raven said.

Perched atop Tucker, a horse named by Cass for his

longtime friend, Ray Tucker, Raven steadied her aim. She held a Remington 700 CDL bolt-action rifle in her hands. It was a beautiful piece of weaponry, renowned for its impeccable accuracy, and it fired a .243 caliber round—an ideal choice for Raven, given her beginner status. With the addition of a Vortex Viper 6.5-20x50 PA riflescope and a detachable magazine capable of holding four additional rounds, Raven wielded true power, and she did so with ease.

Raven, once an elementary school teacher, had begun to transform herself beyond any expectations either she or Cass had imagined since moving to West Texas from Houston. The circumstances of the move revolved around healing and fresh starts for both her and Cass, but they both learned quickly that life throws curve balls every day, even in the barren terrain of the Trans-Pecos.

During her limited time on the Callahan Ranch, or CR as they called it, Raven had found herself again, but discovered a strength hidden deeper inside of her and a drive to become more than just a lawman's wife. Following the attempt on her life by the sicario known as *La Sombra Negra*, Raven emerged with a toughness and grit one only found within themselves when forced to walk through fire. Her determination to never be put in a position again where her life hung in the balance filled her with a drive to become more than she ever thought before. Now with Cass gone, she aimed to become an all-encompassing addition to the ranch that bore her family's name.

Raven closed her left eye, peering through the scope with her right. Like a seasoned professional, she panned the rifle until she found her target aligned in the crosshairs and controlled her breathing.

"Ready," she said, her aim unwavering, the rifle as steady as if it were locked in place.

"Good. Like we practiced," Flint whispered. "On my count."

Raven's heart pounded.

"Three..."

Her finger pressed against the trigger, ready to fire, to protect, to kill.

"Two..."

Tucker stood still beneath her, head lowered and gaze remained fixed forward as if she knew why they were there and what was to come.

"One..."

Raven let out a short breath, then held the rest inside.

BLAM!

A synchronized blast echoed out as the two rifles erupted in a flash of heat and force and bullets. Not waiting for a second count, Raven reached for the bolt handle, lifted and slid the action to the rear, and ejected the spent .243 casing. With one fluid motion, she then pushed the bolt handle forward and locked a new round in place.

Their target had been a pack of feral dogs. While images of childhood furry friends came to Raven's mind, she knew that these animals were nothing like the house pets she had loved throughout her life.

The first two shots hit their target as if painted by a tactical laser, killing two of the dogs in a violent mix of flying bullets and snarling teeth. Flint's second shot was just as effective, killing a larger canine closing in on a small calf, but Raven's shot missed its mark. The remaining feral dog ran from the herd and the bullets and its wild, dead pack, disappearing in the brush well beyond the perimeter of the grazing cows.

Flint lowered his rifle. Raven swept hers side to side in search of a new target. A few of the cattle had been spooked by the commotion but settled back into their nonchalant milling and standing about. To Raven, it reminded her of kids on a playground, grouped together and killing time until recess was over.

"Easy there," Flint said. "Job's done."

Raven lowered her rifle and slid it into the sheath on her saddle. She glanced at Flint, a swirl of emotion revolving in her eyes.

"You okay?" he said.

"Yeah." She felt an exhilaration surge through her body, tingling her fingertips, her thighs, the nape of her neck. It was a new feeling. A good feeling. And, she liked it.

"Good. Help me move these cows back to the herd. Just follow my lead and you'll do just fine."

Flint gave his horse a kick and rode ahead toward the cows. Raven held back just long enough to give Tucker a rub on her shoulder. She lifted and turned her head, then made a pleasurable huff.

"You're a good horse, Tucker."

With gentle heels, she nudged Tucker's ribs, then clicked her cheeks, signaling the horse to walk on.

Under a cloudless West Texas sky, Raven got her first real taste of ranch life beyond the confines of the house and barn. Watching Flint work, she copied his whoops and hollers, riding drag as they moved the cows along the terrain like the cowboys of old. When the herd was reunited, they returned to the carcasses of the dead, feral dogs.

"What now?" Raven asked.

Flint looked at her, a smirk escaping the corner of his mouth. "Barbeque."

To his surprise, he watched as Raven dismounted her horse, dropped the reins, and began dragging one of the smaller carcasses closer to the larger one. Without looking at Flint, she walked to the last dead animal and pulled it over in the same manner. This one was larger and took more effort, but she did not once complain or ask for help. With a grunt and a heave, Raven lopped the body across the others crossways, then stood up and dusted her hands on one another. She gave Flint a no-nonsense glare.

"You just gonna sit there or are you gonna fire things up?" she said, her voice commanding.

"Well, shit," Flint said under his breath.

Raven placed her hands on her hips and waited.

Flint smiled at her. "Yes, ma'am."

CHAPTER THREE

The sway of *Peniel's Eden* over the gentle waves and the fresh salt air that filled Carlos Ruiz-Mata with each relaxed breath lulled him into a trance as he lounged on deck of his thirty-seven-foot sailboat off the coast of Guaymas, Mexico. The sun overhead shone with a radiance that warmed the decking beneath his feet and caused a red glow to appear behind his eyelids while he rested. The clear, calm waters of the Sea of Cortez offered solitude and respite and was an anchor's paradise. It was a place where *El Despiadado* remained dormant, leaving Mata to enjoy the savory pleasures of life—fine wine, gentle breezes, painted skies at sunset that cascade in a sfumato of warm hues, and abundant marine life ripe for fishing or weightless observation in a Shangri-La of aquatic serenity.

But not all was always calm on board *Peniel's Eden*. Even in a secluded place such as this, Mata was left to face the horrific memories for which he had been responsible. He and *El Despiadado*. The restful nature of this retreat was no stranger to Mata after completing a mission for the Camargo cartel. It had become a tradition of sorts that allowed him time to deal with what he had done in a way that both healed him and scarred him further. Left alone to face his demons, Mata was in a constant internal battle of good and evil. Regardless of who he was, at any given time, Carlos Ruiz-Mata was still his father's son, his mother's son, and he was damned to face life, and eternity, repenting for all the terrible things he had done.

Ice clinked in a spent glass where a splash of Casa Dragones had once been. The frozen remnants melted and fell away as its delicious climate transformed into the dregs of watered-down tequila. Sweat dripped from the glass forming a ring of moisture around its base as it sat on the teak wood deck, forgotten.

A cell phone resting on the deck near the tequila glass buzzed to life. Mata stirred and sat up. He wore white Bermuda shorts and an unbuttoned, loose-fitting camp shirt. The vibrant tropical print of the shirt pulsed with life in the afternoon sun. His skin was dark, and the tattoos that covered most of his torso looked blacker than ever.

Beneath him, the demanding buzz of the phone continued. Mata leaned over and picked up the sweaty, spent tequila glass. Holding it, he huffed once, then looked to the waters beyond the edge of the boat. He stood, and with a dismissive flip of his wrist, tossed the glass overboard. The phone continued to nag as Mata walked down the steps that led into the central saloon of *Peniel's Eden*.

He stopped before closing the hatch and reconsidered answering the call, for he knew who was on the other end of the line.

CHAPTER FOUR

"Mr. Tucker," Agent Zuñiga said, his eyes studying my longtime partner. "I understand that you and Agent Callahan have quite the history together."

Ray sat across a metal table from Zuñiga in a conference room in the FBI El Paso Field Office. I sat next to Ray looking at photographs of Carlos Ruiz-Mata and his cartel cronies. Introductions had been cordial, but it seemed that Zuñiga was searching for more information about Ray than I had already provided.

I looked up when I heard the question, knowing fair well that this could go one of two ways. Ray could show his man-of-few-words subjective side, or...

"What the fuck is that supposed to mean?" Ray blurted out.

...or that side—the belligerent, don't waste my time, has issues with authority Ray.

The room sucked his words up and spit them out leaving a cold silence about us that could have frozen raw meat. I glanced at Zuñiga. He caught my eye contact, then curled his pursed lips into an all-out smile that ended with a laugh.

"Just as I expected," Zuñiga said. "But I like that. I like that."

He nodded his head at me, then reached below the table and pressed a button that frosted the windows and activated a hidden video screen that descended from above the ceiling tiles. The screen flickered to life with images of two men. Lines of text were displayed beneath each picture that included name, approximate height and weight, age, physical features, known accomplices, last known whereabouts, and aliases used by each. Before us, larger than life, were the images of Arturo Mendez, also known as Señor de la Droga, and Carlos Ruiz-Mata.

The sight of them was fuel enough to burn my insides. I clenched my fists under the table, digging my nails into my palms. I had seen Mata before. I stood face to face with the man. The son of a bitch bought me coffee, for Christ's sake. And, to add insult to egregiousness, I actually shook his hand having no idea who he was at the time. It was a regret I would always live with having learned that shortly after our meeting, he killed three deputies, one office worker and detonated explosives that destroyed that South Brewster County Sheriff's Office. As the investigation continued, we discovered that he had also killed my good friend and Deputy Javier Santos, attacked my son and killed another teenage boy, and is suspected of killing an older man inside a stolen church van. All in all, he wreaked havoc on my West Texas hometown and I wanted his head.

I was familiar with Arturo Mendez only from recent surveillance photos that Zuñiga had shared with me. This was the first time I had a good, close-up view of the man. He had long, jet-black hair pulled back into a ponytail. His face was rough, pitted with scars and wrinkles like he was a poor man's Danny Trejo. He kept his mustache trimmed close to the skin, curling it down as if he abhorred everything. Even the sagging patches under his black eyes seemed to be filled with dark history just waiting to be spilled.

Ray leaned over to me. "That's one ugly moth-erfucker."

"Carlos Ruiz-Mata and Arturo Mendez," Zuñiga said. "Also known as El Despiadado and Señor de la Droga. These two men have disrupted the drug scene in Mexico over the past few years and have made quite a name for themselves along the way. As you are already aware, Mendez gives the orders. Mata makes sure nothing stands in the way. That's how you came to know him. The infor-mation on the USB drive, the one you failed to hand over to me, I might add, must have held information vital to the cartel."

"It was vital, all right. It held names, dates, contacts, coordinates, shipping logs, manifests, delivery schedules, and a list of everyone they had in their pocket along with information about their families from grandparents to their children. No one was off limits."

I reached into my jeans pocket.

"As for never giving you the drive, well, you know why I held onto it. You follow through with your end of our deal?"

"What deal?" Ray said.

Zuñiga leaned forward and folded his hands on the table.

"We had a deal to help an undercover get his family out of harm's way. Your friend here withheld evidence from the FBI and used it as a bargaining chip to ensure I delivered on promises I had made."

Zuñiga looked me square in the eye. I leaned back in my chair and listened as if I was being lectured in the principal's office.

"Good for you, Cass. Woulda done the same."

"Glad the two of you are on the same page. Trouble is, the drive was destroyed in the explosions in Brewster and now we have no further information than the recollection of your comrade in arms here."

Ray scowled at Zuñiga, taking exception with the statement.

I leaned forward, withdrew my hand from my pocket, and dangled a neon green USB drive affixed to a key chain in front of Zuñiga.

"It's a good goddamn thing that Raven made a copy before I brought it to the office. Didn't find out about it until after the attack in Brewster."

I slid the drive across the table.

"I knew you hit a home run with her, Cass," Ray said, slapping me on the back. "Raven's one hell of a woman."

Zuñiga picked up the invaluable piece of plastic-wrapped tech and smiled.

"I have to say I must agree with Mr. Tucker. And, for the record, Balde Ramos's family was extracted one week ago today. Everyone is safe and sound and has been relocated under witness protection. The cartel will never find them."

"Ramos?" Ray asked.

"Tell you later," I said.

"Now, if I may return us to the matter at hand," Zuñiga said, redirecting his attention to the screen.

Before he had a chance to resume his briefing, an intercom buzzed and a voice I had hoped not to ever hear again asked to be let into the room.

"What the hell?" I said, but I was too late.

Zuñiga must have pressed a different button because the screen stayed in place and the windows remained frosted, but an electrical click sounded out as the door unlocked. Just as I thought, Special Agent Dylan Sharp entered the room, followed by a second man dressed in a suit and sporting a drill sergeant's crewcut.

"You son of a bitch," I said.

"What?" Sharp answered, acting surprised. "You miss me, Callahan?"

CHAPTER FIVE

I watched as Agent Sharp made himself at home next to Zuñiga. The man with him sat at the foot of the table. I could sense the friction and almost feel the heat when his eyes met Ray's. Sharp boasted a smugness about him, another quality I loathed in him. His nose remained a crooked reminder of how distrusting and inappropriate Sharp had acted when we first met as well as a satisfaction that it was my fist that helped mold its new shape.

The room became still. Ray was locked in a stare-down with Sergeant Crewcut, and I was imagining all the deliberate things I wanted to do and say to Agent Sharp. I was sure he felt the same, but it seemed for the moment that he had the upper hand. His very inclusion in this meeting was the first jab. Score one for the dickhead.

"Gentlemen," Zuñiga began. "No need for posturing. We're all on the same team here."

"Wait one minute," I said, my voice bellowing with objection. "You never said anything about Sharp being included on this mission."

"Sorry to wreck your party, Callahan. Get used to my being around. But don't worry, I'll give you a bite of my burrito once we get south of the border."

Fuming, I jumped from my seat and lunged across the table at Sharp. He dodged before I could grab his collar and yank his head onto the table. Papers flew. Ray stood, knocking his chair to the floor. His forearms bulged over his clenched fists. Sergeant Crewcut rose and placed his palm against Ray's chest. That was a mistake that could have escalated and ended our meeting at the same time.

Ray looked down at the hand on him and, of all things, smiled. "Don't need that hand, hoss?"

Zuñiga's face contorted with disapproval and slammed his fists on the table. The loud metal clang and resounding echo in the small, soundproof room grabbed everyone's attention. "Everybody, sit!"

"Tell your dog to get his paw off before I make him beg me to let him go," Ray said. His voice was low and direct, while his eyes bore a hole into Sergeant Crewcut's glare. I heard his knuckles crack as he flexed his fist.

"Agent Crank. If you will?" Zuñiga motioned for him to lower his hand.

It took a moment for the hot air between Ray and Sergeant crewcut to diffuse, but the two mountainous men entered a stay of action when Agent Crank lowered his hand and took a seat.

Zuñiga turned his attention to Ray. "Mr. Tucker. Your turn."

Ray looked at me and rolled his eyes, then gave me a subtle wink. He would always have my back, and this extra show of force announced that to the entire room.

Agent Sharp, in true form, was more mouth than action. I saw the stern look Zuñiga flashed at him. A submissive yet irritated expression crept along his pointy face, but he returned to his seat as well.

I turned to look at Zuñiga. When our eyes met, I sensed a hint of distrust, but I filed that away with all the other bullshit logs I kept stored in the far reaches of my head. Fact was, I felt the same about him.

"Shall we get back to it or let the cartel off the hook?" he said.

"No more surprises, Zuñiga. That includes personnel," I said.

"Fair enough. Now, if you will take your seat we can continue." Zuñiga waited for me to sit first. I lowered into my seat, coming eye to eye with Agent Sharp once again. I knew we were on a collision course to butt heads, but round two would have to wait, for now.

Zuñiga remained standing and addressed his dysfunctional *Kill Hydra* team.

"Since it is clear you each have your own way of introducing yourselves to one another, allow me the opportunity to simplify things for you." He pointed at each of us as he called our names. "Special Agent Dylan Sharp, FBI. Agent Max Crank, FBI. Detective Ray Tucker, Houston PD. Special Investigator and Kill Hydra team leader Cass Callahan."

Sharp's eyes widened at the announcement but lost the chance to object when Zuñiga continued without pause.

"Men, you are no stranger to the conflict at hand. We are facing a formidable adversary in the form of the Camargo Drug Cartel. Arturo Mendez and Carlos Ruiz-Mata are ruthless, relentless, and need to be taken down. The Camargo cartel is known for its network of hardened criminals, and its unrelenting pursuit of power and profit. They've left a trail of violence and destruction in their wake, both within our borders and beyond. We know that all too well. This team, *Kill Hydra*, is not merely about bringing justice to those who think themselves untouchable but will play a huge role in the toppling of a growing empire. It's our job to cut off its head and not let any more grow back in its place.

"This is a covert mission shrouded in secrecy. The dangers are real, and they are substantial. Once you step foot into Mexico, you will be on your own. In this world, 'trust no one' is a guiding principle. That includes local authorities. The cartels have infiltrated every level of government and its corresponding agencies, including the state police and the Mexican National Army. Be vigilant, operate in the shadows, and above all, watch each other's backs. We will only achieve success if we remain a team."

Zuñiga tossed each of us a manila folder. Ray shuffled in his seat. It was clear he had something on his mind.

"Mr. Tucker. Is there something you would like to say?"

Ray gave me a look, then answered.

"Justice? We're supposed to sneak into Mexico, find these assholes, and bring them to 'justice?' Care to fill in the blanks, special agent-in-charge?"

Zuñiga pursed his lips.

"Let me put it another way. It would be to the benefit of the United States for us to extract these men, but like I said, this will be a dangerous mission. If things go south, there's no telling who may get caught in the crossfire."

Ray chewed on his bottom lip, nodding his head.

"I see. *Kill Hydra* ain't some fancy euphemism. It's a direct order."

Zuñiga did not answer but nodded and pointed a finger at Ray.

"Think you can handle that?" Sharp added from across the table.

Ray glared at Sharp. "Can you?"

I could tell we were still getting nowhere, and we did not have time to build a campfire and thread friendship bracelets.

"Look," I said. "We are wheels up in two days. Recent intel indicates that Mendez is at his compound outside of Camargo. Mata is still off the grid. As much as I want that son of a bitch, our first objective is to neutralize Mendez, and then hunt down El Despiadado. If we are lucky, they'll both be in Camargo and we can take them out at the same time."

"So, we're just going to walk up and knock on his front door?" Sharp said. "He'll have a hundred men around him at the first sign of trouble. He's got *halcónes* all throughout Chihuahua, not to mention on almost every street corner in Camargo, and more firepower than a small army."

My heart rate was rising.

"If anyone wants out of this, now is the time to speak up," I said. I gave each man a look, starting with Ray.

"You know I'm in, Cass," he said.

I continued around the table to Agent Crank. He nodded, then folded his hands in front of him. Agent Sharp was next.

I swallowed what ill feelings I had toward the man and gave him my last professional benefit of the doubt. "Sharp?"

All eyes were glued to him.

"Well, shit. Wouldn't want to miss you taking a bullet in the ass, Callahan. I'll play along."

Zuñiga stood and addressed us all.

"That's good enough for me. Take time to make yourselves familiar with the contents of your folder and get your things in order. We'll meet back here at eleven a.m. on Wednesday. That gives you a little under forty-eight hours."

Zuñiga reached under the table and pressed a button that unfrosted the windows and raised the screen back into the ceiling. The images on the screen clicked off, but the ghostly burn of Mata's face lingered long enough to make my stomach turn.

I'm coming for you, I thought.

Agent Sharp exited the room, and I expected Agent Crank to follow suit. Instead, he approached me and offered a hand.

"Don't like getting off on the wrong foot. Figure if my life is on the line, I'd want you to feel like it was worth saving."

I took his hand and we shook.

"Call me Max," he said.

"All right, Max," I said. "Welcome to the team."

Max turned to Ray. "You're a big SOB, ain't ya?"

This was another test that Ray needed to pass, but he understood the message.

"Better believe it," Ray answered.

"I can live with that," Max said, then stepped out of the room.

Zuñiga turned to leave, then stopped at the doorway and looked at me and Ray.

"I understand that this is personal to you. Let that drive you, but don't lose focus on the main objective."

"I can handle that," I said. "But what am I supposed to do with Sharp? He's a liability."

"You let me worry about him," Zuñiga said as he turned and exited the room.

My mind whirled with scenarios of how things could go south should Agent Sharp fail to acknowledge that I was in charge once we hit the ground. As much as I objected to his inclusion on the team, that was not my call. He, like Ray and Agent Crank, were my responsibility. I knew how to lead, but did Sharp know how to follow?

I reached for my folder and opened it to reveal a stack of carefully stapled intelligence documents. My eyes scanned the briefing at the top of the pile.

Ray's perceptive gaze was on point. "I see that look on your face, Cass. And I know what you're thinkin'."

"What's that?"

His voice dropped to a more serious tone. "You're thinkin' Sharp may get us all killed."

Closing the folder, I rolled it into a tube and locked eyes with Ray.

"I won't let it come to that."

CHAPTER SIX

The smell of hay and fresh manure took flight with the cool October evening breezes that slinked their way into the barn and carried the musty aromas far beyond the wooden walls and the lively stalls to the open air and vast terrain of the CR. The subtle chill caught Raven off guard as she looked in on Luna, the newest foal to grace the ranch, and caused goosebumps to form on her neck and forearms. She crossed her arms and rubbed her palms along her opposing shoulders. Smitten with the tiny horse, Raven smiled and part of her heart melted as she watched Luna's ears prick up, then, as if a firecracker had been set off beneath its hooves, the little foal jumped and bucked around the stall, reacting to the sneaky chill in the barn. Raven's smile fell into laughter.

Flint had been stowing gear on the far side of the barn but stopped and joined Raven at the stall.

"She's so beautiful, Flint. Don't you think so?"

"That she is, Ms. Raven. And growin' strong, too. Won't be long before she's old enough ta begin weanin' away from her mother."

"So soon?"

"Couple a month's is all. But, before then, we'll start showin' her the ropes of what it means ta be ranchin' horse. The two a you should spend more time together. Get her used ta groomin' an' what a halter feels like. We'll take it slow, but the main thing is that she builds trust in us. Do it right, an' you'll have a friend fer life."

"You'll show me what to do?"

"A-yuh. But somethin' tells me yer a natural."

Flint stood next to Raven and watched Luna's frisky explorations of the cool air until she began to tire out. Before too long, she settled down and plopped onto a pile of hay as if she were a dog. The innocent actions of such a young animal fascinated Raven, and she could have stayed all night enjoying the show, but Flint nudged her with his elbow and nodded his head away from the stall.

"Someone's pullin' inta the ranch," he said.

Raven's heart was filled to the brim by the foal, but the prospect of Cass being home caused another level of anticipation to warm her insides. She started for the barn door, then paused.

"Need any help in here, Flint?"

"No, Ms. Raven. I can manage."

"I know that, but if I am going to take on a bigger role here, I should probably..."

"You've done enough fer taday," Flint said. His admiration for Raven grew daily. They had a mutual respect that was developing into an unlikely friendship. There were no hidden emotions between them, which made spending time together, especially when Cass was not around, feel comfortable.

The crackle of stones being crushed by tires became more distinct, then stopped altogether. Raven headed for the barn door but stopped when Flint called out to her.

"Ms. Raven. There is one thing." He walked to the workbench and picked up the rifle she had carried with her on the range. "If ya aim ta carry a weapon, I think you should be the one ta care fer it."

Flint handed her the bolt-action Remington. "Beats

the hell outta that little purple thing ya carry around on yer hip there."

Raven looked down at the leather holster threaded into the loop of her belt, and the color-coated Ruger 9mm resting within she referred to as the Purple Demon.

Raven raised her head and smiled. "Hey, it's fashionable and deadly."

"Just like you, Ms. Raven. I guess it'll do."

"Thanks, Flint."

Raven turned and disappeared through the barn door holding the rifle across her chest as if she were on patrol. Flint shook his head, amused by her quick wit, then went back to work.

CHAPTER SEVEN

I stepped out of the Explorer, its jet-black paint coated with a thin film of fresh dust and looked to the house, hoping to see Raven. Ray exited the vehicle and closed the door.

"Ho-lee shit, Cass." I heard him say.

I thought he might be taken aback by the rustic surroundings, as his comfort zone was more aligned with strip centers, parking lots, and endless fast-food joints mixed in a sea of fragrant exhaust and traffic lights, but I could not have been more wrong.

I walked over to Ray and saw right away what had caught his immediate attention. Walking from the barn, bathed in the late afternoon light, carrying a rifle in a military patrol position and wearing a sidearm that rocked along with each sway of the hip, was a figure I recognized, but a swagger with which I had not yet become accustomed. Work-worn blue jeans, boots, a solid button-up long-sleeve shirt with the arms rolled above the wrist, and a new Resistol 10X Wildfire straw cowboy hat made up the sexiest cowgirl I had ever seen.

"Damn, Cass. You didn't tell me you left Raven and married Rambo?"

I placed my hand on Ray's shoulder. "Isn't she something?"

"Open your eyes, man. Just now figuring that out?"

"Ray, I've known it all my life."

I watched as Raven sauntered over to us. As she approached, a smile spread across her face when our eyes met. Locked in our gaze, she pulled her mouth to one side, a guilty *tell* that let me know she had a secret to share. Her left cheek was stained with a smudge of dirt adding a hint of mystery to the wild, powerful beauty that was my wife. I tracked her every movement, every curve from the crinkles of her jeans to the wisps of crow's feet stretching out from her squinted eyes. She looked both rugged and petite. The icing on the cake was how I watched her handle the rifle with a comfort that suggested she had been born again, but this time was West Texas through and through.

Holding the barrel safely away from me and Ray, Raven stopped close enough so that I would have to lean in for a kiss if I dared.

"Howdy boys."

"Okay!" Ray said, not able to take it anymore. "Who are you and what have you done with Raven?"

Raven cocked her head at Ray and did not miss a beat.

"Didn't ya hear? I shrugged off the schoolteacher and am embracing a rancher's life." She gave me a wink, then added, "Watching a woman handle this hunk of hard steel make ya nervous, Ray?"

Ray turned to me.

"I'm about ta get my ass kicked, ain't I?"

"You said it, not me," I answered, shaking my head while locked in an epic stare with Raven.

Raven stepped closer to me, pressing the butt of the rifle into my midsection. Her scent was tantalizing even after what I could only assume was a day out on the CR. "What about you?"

"How about a last kiss, and then you can give me your best shot?"

I leaned in, but she teased by stepping away and turned to Ray.

"Do you mind?" she said and handed him the rifle.

"No, ma'am, I do not," Ray answered.

Once the weapon was clear of her grasp, Raven flung her arms around my neck and pulled me close, planting one memorable kiss on my lips.

In that moment, my eyes closed and the stars came out, littering the air around us with pulsing light and radiant heat. The soft texture of her lips and the saucy tease of her tongue made me wish two things—one, that all our troubles were solved and life on the CR would continue uninterrupted from this day on, and two, that Ray had stayed at a motel in town.

As gentle as it began, the kiss ended. Raven stepped back and brushed a lock of hair from her face. Damn, she was beautiful! She turned to Ray.

"Hand the rifle to Cass, will ya?" Ray handed me the rifle. Raven opened her arms and gave Ray a squeeze. "It's so good to see you, Ray," she said.

Letting go, Raven took the rifle from me, then grabbed my hand and pulled me toward the house.

"Let's all go in for a beer and a bite. Threw some chili in the crock pot this morning. Should be ready by now."

"Chili and guns. That's what I call West Texas," Ray said.

He slapped me on the back and followed us inside.

Two bowls of chili and three beers later, I led Ray to the porch. We sat and took in the coming evening. The sun's daily routine did not disappoint, flooding the outstretched CR lands with a bevy of color and shadow as it ushered in the dim flecks of distant stars amid the surging darkness. I could tell the atmosphere put Ray at ease.

"Listen," I said. "Thank you for coming out. I feel a whole lot better knowing you'll be on my six once we head south."

"l got yer back, Cass."

"And you always have. You heard the briefing. Zuñiga can say all he wants about how dangerous this mission is, and how important our role will be. Fact is, I don't think he understands how dangerous it is going to be."

"What did Zuñiga say?" Raven asked, coming out the door with three fresh beers in hand.

She handed Ray a bottle of Dos X, then sat down on my lap across from him.

"Well?" she pressed, offering me a fresh beer.

Ray and I shared a glance. I popped the cap off the green bottle and took a long drag, followed in an immediate burp.

"Nothing you haven't heard already."

Raven wrapped an arm around my neck and took a sip of her drink.

"I won't pretend to think that you won't be in danger. Just..." Raven paused, her hand shook as she took another sip of beer. "Just do what you have to do and come home."

Ray lifted his bottle. "That's the plan, Rave."

"Hoo-ah," I answered.

Raven looked at me and smiled, but I could sense a hint of worry in her gaze. She must have realized it too because she blinked and shook her head, then leaned forward and clinked Ray's bottle with hers.

"Hoo-ah," she said.

CHAPTER EIGHT

The onset of evening was meant to be peaceful for Carlos Ruiz-Mata. It was the time of day he looked forward to most because, in his mind, the darkness hid his flaws, his indiscretions, and paved a way to solace in the deepness of night. The gentle rock of the waves beneath *Peniel's Eden* soothed Mata's mind and cradled his boat as he anchored close to shore in the calm embrace of *Ensenada Bacochibampo*. The sun dipped into the waters where the melding of earth and sky became one. Streaks of shimmering yellow and orange skimmed the surface, branching out like a dazzling starburst across the gentle roll of the ocean.

Mata indulged in the fresh salt air as he sat on deck, sipping tequila from a hand-blown copita, and pondered what life might have been like had he not taken a destructive path alongside El Despiadado. Though they were one and the same, Mata knew that his actions were still his own. The scars he bore and the tattooed reminders of lives taken would never allow him to forget his past.

Amid his reflection, a tiny voice resonated deep inside him like a distant plea. It tugged at the edges of his consciousness, like a child pulling at his sleeve, beckoning him to turn inward and listen. Its innocence was undeniable and its familiarity filled him with a warm sensation. Spoken in brief spurts, as if hiding from something greater, more sinister and damning, from El Despiadado, it offered a light that he thought had been snuffed out over a lifetime of terrible deeds.

"*It is not too late.*"

Mata sat up and gazed ahead. He lifted the tequila glass to his lips and swallowed the fiery liquid until the *copita* had emptied. The alcohol sizzled his insides but did nothing to douse the feeling or stifle the voice growing within him. His heart pounded. He forced deep breaths in and out of his nose until the burn subsided.

As he began to settle, he heard the voice again. He rose to his feet, a deep, guttural scream escaped his lips into the night. "What would you have me do?" he cried out.

His hands trembled. Beads of sweat formed along his furrowed brow. He repeated the question, but this time his voice held a different tone—defeated and forlorn. The weight of uncertainty bore down on him, and he was left standing there, caught between the echo of his own question and the elusive voice within.

Alone in the haze of twilight, he wrestled with a possibility that seemed too far to reach. Maybe it was too late for him to change. But then again, maybe it was not.

He stood for what seemed like hours, as the world transitioned into the fullness of night. Stars emerged overhead on what was still a moonless sky. He faced open water but turned back to look upon land when he heard the faint, yet distinctive, churn of an outboard motor. Mata stepped to the railing and scanned the open body of water between *Peniel's Eden* and the shore. Lights from Ciudad Guaymas dotted the crescent-shaped coastline of the inlet. His was the only boat for a hundred yards in any direction. The motor, steady in its rumbling, grew louder.

Mata squinted, then zeroed in on a dark smudge

trolling on the water. As it continued to draw near, he saw a small dinghy and what appeared to be two men onboard.

He stepped back and placed his copita on a small deck table, then made his way to the helm where he opened a small cabinet and removed a SIG Sauer P226 with an SRD9 suppressor. Engaging the slide, he double-checked the chamber for a loaded round, then stepped back to his chair and sat down.

It was possible that the motorboat had other intentions on the water, but the odds of that were slim. This hunch was confirmed when the motor was shut off and a voice called out from below.

"Mata. Mata. *Tenemos un mensaje del Señor de la Droga.*"

Message, Mata thought. He knew that could mean any number of things.

"Do not shoot, we are coming aboard," the voice called out again.

"That is a chance you will have to take," Mata replied. "Come aboard and we will see."

Mata could hear nervous whispers rise from the dinghy as the men argued about who would be the first to climb the ladder, neither wanting to test a known killer's warning. When the chatter ended, Mata heard the unstable thud of slick shoes slipping on the ladder at the stern, and then saw the slow rise of the top of the first man's head appear above the gunwale. Lighting along the edge of the boat reflected in the man's nervous eyes. When his eyes met Mata's, the man forced a smile.

"Señor Mata. It is good to see you are well."

Mata leaned forward in his chair, placed his elbows on his knees, and displayed the gun for the man to see.

"What makes Señor de la Droga think I am not well?"

The man's eyes shifted from Mata to his weapon.

"*Señor, por favor, Señor de la Droga,* he was worried that..."

Mata aimed his pistol at the man.

"Worried? Señor de la Droga does not send men halfway across Mexico because he is worried."

A hushed whisper from below caused the man on the ladder to look down. The whisper turned louder and addressed Mata.

"You have been unreachable, *señor*."

Mata stood and walked toward the edge of the boat. The first man was still on the ladder. His gaze grew larger causing the whites of his eyes to expand in their sockets. It was clear he was not here by choice and knew that this could end in the worst of ways should they be ill received.

"Show me your hands," Mata said.

The man on the ladder raised his hands, showing he was unarmed. With a swipe of his gun, Mata signaled him to climb aboard.

"Stand over there," Mata commanded, then leaned to the side of the railing for a look at the second man.

"Now," Mata began. "I have your man. If you want him returning with you to shore, you will tell me the real reason you are here. Speak the truth or the alternative will not be pleasant for him."

Mata glared at the first man as he spoke. He could not have been older than twenty. His face was smooth save for the soul patch on his chin. His arms were inked with barbed-wire tattoos that wrapped from his biceps to his wrists. One forearm bore a cross in the center of the razor tats, while the other displayed bound, praying hands. He wore the look of a hardened cartel soldier, but his nervous appearance spoke otherwise. The man's eyes darted side to side, then past Mata as if hoping for a quick reply from the man in the boat.

Mata heard an exasperated huff from the man in the boat, followed by a reply that he found amusing but caused the young, tattooed man to flinch with fright.

"Kill him if you wish," he said, then tossed a plastic-wrapped bundle onto the boat. "But the next time Señor de la Droga calls you will answer."

On cue, a buzzing sound came from the bundled plastic. Mata stepped away from the package, then looked at his prisoner.

"What is your name?" Mata asked.

"Hector. Hector Trujillo."

"Well, Hector," Mata said, motioning to the bundle with the end of his gun. "Open it," he said.

Hector hesitated. The buzzing continued.

"I am starting to believe it is I who was meant to open this. I wonder why that is?"

Hector shrugged and shook his head.

"Open the package, or I pull the trigger."

Hearing the final ultimatum spurred Hector into action. With one swift motion, he stepped forward, bent over, and began to tear at the plastic-wrapped package. Mata stepped back, wary of a possible boobytrap, and watched Hector rip it open like he was a kid and this was Christmas morning.

When he reached the center, a small, rectangular-shaped brown paper wrapped with a string was all that was left. He tore the wrapping away to reveal a cell phone. It continued to buzz, seeming to grow more agitated with each unanswered announcement.

Hector held the phone out to Mata.

"Answer it," Mata said.

Confused, but willing to follow directions, Hector pressed the send button and answered the call.

"Hola."

He paused, his face contorting to the words from whatever voice he heard on the other end of the line. He looked at Mata with nervous eyes, then removed the phone from his ear and offered it to him.

"Señor de la Droga," he said.

Mata looked at Hector, then grabbed the phone from his hand and activated the speaker function.

"*El Despiadado!*" the cartel boss bellowed. "You show me disrespect when you ignore me. And after doing such a good thing."

Was it good, Mata thought.

Señor de la Droga continued, "*You will go to Panama first thing tomorrow. A man named Pablo Espinoza is a Customs Officer at Puerto Balboa who is causing me problems and needs to be reminded that his loyalty belongs to the Camargo cartel. He has become greedy and is demanding more money in return for his blind oversight of cargo that we are transporting from our friends in Columbia. All the information you need has been sent as a text to this phone, but there is one change. When you find him, kill only his wife. Take three fingers from his child as a promise to return should he continue to disrespect Señor de la Droga!*"

Mata did not respond. Instead, at that moment, the voice inside him returned.

"It is not too late."

Mata looked at the phone, then at Señor de la Droga's man, Hector.

"*El Despiadado!*" Señor de la Droga seethed with impatience.

Mata walked to the edge of the boat and looked over the gunwale at the man still in the dinghy.

"You tell him that I have other plans."

With a flick of the wrist, Mata tossed the phone into the water.

The man in the boat responded, "I had hoped you would have been more open to Señor de la Droga's request for your continued services." He paused, then called out, "Hector!"

Mata glanced behind him and saw Hector frozen in fear and leaning against the aft railing. He then heard the man below shuffling around in the dinghy. Taking a quick look overboard, he lunged back when he saw the barrel of a gun pointed up at him. A blast erupted as the man pulled the trigger. Mata felt the air burn hot as the bullet tore past him. He rolled to one side and saw that Hector still had not moved.

The man in the dinghy started its engine and throttled up. The small boat rammed the side of *Peniel's Eden*, scraping away at the hull in a frantic escape before turning for shore. The high pitch wail of the motor echoed across the open water.

Mata slid to the railing and peered over at the fleeing boat. He stood, took aim, and emptied his magazine at the man who had tried to kill him. In the darkness it was unclear how he had hit the man, but the way the dinghy veered to one side was clue enough that at least one of his shots had hit its mark.

Mata watched the dinghy circle at high speed in the water, then lurch to a different direction as if the rudder had been yanked to a righted position. Nearing shore, the boat did not slow its approach. Instead, it sliced through the water like a torpedo until it slammed into the patio of Cala Costera Cantina, an oceanside bar. A tiny explosion followed, and Mata could hear screaming from the shore but turned his attention away from the destruction to lock eyes with Hector.

"You have two choices, Hector. Only one, I suppose, if you do not know how to swim."

"I can swim, I can swim," Hector said with desperation in his voice.

Mata motioned to the water with the barrel of his empty gun.

"You're going to let me live?"

Mata nodded.

"Go now. It is not too late."

This time, Hector did not hesitate. He ran across the deck and dove over the rail. Mata stepped to the edge of the boat and watched the young Hector Trujillo splash his way toward shore.

Leaning against the railing, he whispered to himself while he contemplated his next move.

"It is not too late."

CHAPTER NINE

The sounds of morning on the CR could be compared to Craig Johnson's thirty seconds of Zen—tranquil, elusive, peaceful, were it not for the incessant snores rumbling from the guest room. It was the type of breathing that reverberated through the walls and doors so that anyone in the vicinity fell victim to its labor. Alcohol has that effect on some people, but Ray Tucker took it to a whole new level.

"I'm gonna put a bullet in him," I said as I rolled over and draped an arm over Raven.

"Not if I do it first."

Sunlight poured in through their bedroom window with an inescapable brightness that signaled the start of another day.

"You heading out with Flint this morning?"

Raven nuzzled in closer and kissed the side of my neck just below my ear lobe. "Maybe. Unless you have something pressing that needs my attention."

Her voice was smooth, sensual, and I liked where this was going. She kissed my neck again, then pulled away and threw a pillow at the door when the rumbling of our old friend and overnight guest hit a level that could have registered on any seismic measuring device in the region.

If it had not killed the mood, I might have been impressed by its ferocity.

"Damn it, Ray!" I said.

"Okay, soldier. I'm out."

Raven swung her legs over the side of the bed, then leaned back and kissed me square on the mouth. When she pulled away, she looked at me with a longing and a love that only soul mates would understand.

"I love you, Little Bird."

"I love you, too, Big Bird."

"Big Bird?" I said, my voice rising two octaves. "I'll show you Big Bird."

I leaned forward and wrapped my arms around her waist, pulling her across the bed and into my lap, and held her in an embrace that could have stood the test of time. But that was as far as it went. Holding her close was enough for me. Her hands caressed my back. My fingers stroked her thighs. Even with the earth quaking rumbles from down the hall, there was no place I would rather be.

"Come on," she said. "I'll make you and chowderhead some coffee."

"Thanks, Rave."

She slipped into the bathroom and returned again wearing a terry cloth robe and slippers that Spencer had given her for Mother's Day last year. Her hair was frazzled but she could not care less. I loved that about her, too.

I got up, dressed in jeans and my 2022 World Champions Astros T-shirt, and joined Raven in the kitchen after beating on the guest room door. To my delight, I heard Ray thump out of bed, then curse the world for being awake at such an early hour. The smile on my face had yet to subside when a very gruff-looking Ray joined me at the kitchen table.

"Ass," he said, glaring at me through droopy eyes still fresh from the waking.

"Good morning to you too, sunshine."

Coffee steamed on the counter, filling the kitchen

with a tantalizing aroma I had missed having in the house the past few weeks. After surviving the attack by La Sombra Negra, a Camargo cartel sicario, Raven had sworn-off coffee. The smell triggered a visceral memory that made her relive moments during her struggle when she had to fight for her life. It was an easy decision to remove it from our diet, so imagine my surprise when I woke to the smell of fresh, bubbly Jo brewing in the kitchen two mornings ago. When I asked what changed, Raven looked me in the eyes and said, "I won't be ruled by fear." For all the things she had been through—the home invasion, the fire, relocating from Houston, the discovery of bodies on the CR, our son's disappearance, and the attempt on her life—her resolve had grown stronger and her outlook on life moving forward was not held captive to the past. I could not have loved her more.

Raven placed a bag of bagels and three empty cups on the table. Ray grabbed the cup closest to him and examined the writing on the side.

He read aloud, "That's what she said."

He looked confused as if he had missed the joke.

"Look inside," Raven said.

Ray tilted the cup toward his face. After reading the message on its interior, his face blossomed into a wide smile, and he laughed out loud. Raven and I shared a glance, and I could tell right away she had set him up. She stepped over to Ray and placed a palm on his shoulder.

"Fill me up?" Ray said.

"That's my favorite cup."

"I bet it is," Ray said looking up at her.

Raven snickered, then turned for the counter.

"Wait," I said. "I'll get it."

I stood up, pulled a chair out, and motioned for her to sit. Without objection, Raven took a seat while I poured each of us a cup.

Wisps of steam rose from our coffee. Waiting for hers

to cool down, Raven leaned back in her chair and spoke to Ray.

"I want to thank you."

Ray took a sip, though I do not know how he could stand to drink it so hot. The man was hardened to the core.

"For what?"

"You know. For coming out to work with Cass. I'll feel much better knowing the two of you have each other's backs."

Ray pursed his lips and nodded, then looked at me. "Ain't have much choice really. Who else could keep his sorry sack out of a jam?"

Good 'ol Ray—blunt, coarse, and the most loyal man I ever met.

"You're one in a million," Raven said smiling over the brim of her cup.

Ray lifted his glass, took another scalding sip, and smiled at Raven.

"That's what she said."

———

Feeling caffeinated and filled with carbs and cream cheese, Ray and I sat and discussed what preparations we needed to make before heading out tomorrow morning. Raven disappeared from the kitchen, returning a few minutes later dressed for ranch work. Her boots and jeans and hat attested to her rugged side, but the bright yellow shirt with ivory buttons and the blue bandana tied around her neck added a flair that spoke to her immeasurable femininity. Add in the 9mm Purple Demon strapped to her hip and my wife was quite the badass.

"Y'all stay out of trouble today," she said, offering a farewell wink.

Famous last words, I thought.

Spinning on her heels, Raven was out the door and

headed for another adventure. Her recent lifestyle change was unexpected but was just what the doctor ordered. And with Flint teaching her the ropes, I was in complete support of whatever role she wanted to explore on the CR. I could already see the headline of our yearly holiday update to the family:

SCHOOL TEACHER TURNED GUN-WIELDING RANCH HAND, AND HUSBAND CASS, HEAD WEST.

No sooner had the door clanged on its hinges, than my cell phone buzzed to life. I raised it to see who could be calling so early but the caller ID listed the number as PRIVATE. I clicked the red reject button and ended the attempted call. Not a moment later, the phone buzzed again from the same private number.

"What the hell?"

"Ex-girlfriend track you down, Cass?"

"Don't know, don't care."

I clicked the red button again and set the phone down. I glanced at the phone resting on the table, then shared a look with Ray. We both expected it to ring again, but why? Call it a gut instinct. Sure enough, the phone rang a third time. Agitated at the harassment, I picked up the phone, pressed send, and placed it against my ear.

"Listen, asshole. I don't know how you got my number but..."

"*Asshole?*"

I immediately recognized the voice on the other end of the call. I pulled the phone from my ear and saw that the caller ID did not register PRIVATE. It read CHANCE GILBERT! Sheriff of South Brewster County, Chance Gilbert, my good friend, and boss. I returned the phone to my ear.

"Chance, *que paso, amigo?*"

"*Amigo is a whole lot better than asshole, Cass.*"

"About that," I said, feeling sheepish.

"Nevermind. I'm just glad ya answered. Listen, I need ya. We got a fox in the henhouse."

"I'm on the way," I said, then disconnected the call.

I stood and let his words sink in. *"We got a fox in the henhouse."* It was code for trouble. Since the county relocated our base of operations following the destruction of the sheriff's office, this message meant there was a problem at the jail.

"Everything alright?" Ray asked.

"Dunno. There's a situation at the jail." I looked around for my keys. "Wanna go for a ride?"

"Situation, huh. Usually means trouble."

"Maybe."

"This day's gettin' better by the minute," Ray said, stretching his arms above his head. He laced his fingers and cracked his knuckles. The swift popping sounded like firecrackers exploding above him.

"You in, or what?"

Ray dropped his hand and stood up. Reaching behind his back, he produced a small, snub-nosed revolver. He flashed a menacing smile while holding the gun sideways like a gangster preparing for battle and smiled as he spun the cylinder.

"Hell, yes!"

CHAPTER TEN

Chance's sense of urgency got my blood flowing, but it was his reluctance to share details over the phone that piqued my curiosity. We had an ongoing investigation centered around Deputy Warden Mitch James and his possible involvement in the deaths of two inmates at the jail, but up until today all the evidence we had was circumstantial, and most of that was pretty thin at best. I had a hunch about James from the start and was more than ready to see him on the other side of a jail cell to what he was used to, but we were still building a case and had not yet found a direct connection between him and the murders, other than what his lawyers called coincidental.

The cockpit of the Explorer was quiet. My mind raced through scenarios that led Chance to call as Ray and I sped to town. My hands squeezed the steering wheel as I drove along, a telltale sign that I had a lot on my mind. Ray glanced at me and noticed right away.

"Chokin' that chicken won't get her ta squawk."

Ray was a man of few words, but always got his point across. I broke out of my mental fog and released the tension in my fingers. I could feel the skin on the backs of my knuckles relax. Since turning on to RR170, I had slipped into autopilot, a dangerous way to drive while thinking of something without focusing on the road ahead.

"What's on your mind, Cass?"

I let go of the wheel with one hand and pressed a switch on the door that lowered my window. Cool morning air shot into the car, washing my face with a chill that stoked my senses. I took a long, refreshing breath, then closed the window again.

"I told you all about the assault on the sheriff's office and the circumstances around the murders of our deputies and the attack on Raven and her friend at the CR."

Ray grunted.

"Just before all that went down, there was an inmate killed at the jail. The same guy I had put away for murder. Joe Sinclair."

"Yeah, you told me about that turd wad."

"Right, anyway, Joe claimed to have been in bed with the Camargo cartel, so when he was killed, my first thought was it had to have been an inside job. Turns out, the woman who attacked Raven had visited the jail just prior to the attack. We have reason to believe she delivered a kill order to an inmate that could get close to Joe."

"And now he's dead."

"Yeah, but to further add to the cluster fuck, the inmate that killed Joe ended up dead too. Here's where things start to get hinky. His death was ruled a suicide."

"Felt guilty and slit his wrists?"

"Nope. Stabbed himself in the eye about the time he was being locked away in solitary."

"Damn, that'd do it, but who the hell could go through with that?"

"No kidding, but aside from a guard's report, we have nothing to go on."

"Video surveillance?"

"You'd think so, but this is where things get really

sticky and implications start pointing at the deputy warden. An electrical surge occurred at the exact moment Joe's killer was being placed in solitary, causing the power to cut out in that wing. That wing only. It killed the video feed. Complete blackout for seven to ten seconds. When the juice popped on again and after the cameras rebooted, the inmate was dead in his cell with a shiv in his eye."

"What about the guard?"

"He filed a report that the deputy warden signed off on and then tried to bury. At face value, it looked like a suicide, but I just couldn't wrap my head around how the inmate was able to go through with it. At this point, the guard in question went AWOL and the deputy warden was too dismissive to be helpful. About the same time, the assault on the sheriff's office happened and all the attention turned to finding the person or persons responsible, leaving the incident at the jail to sit on the back burner."

"And I thought Houston was a mess." Ray shifted in his seat and looked out the window. "So, what do you think is waiting for us?"

"That's a good question. If Chance felt it necessary for me to drop everything and come in, I'd say we may be in for a long day."

CHAPTER ELEVEN

"Hot damn, Ms. Raven. You learn quicker than a whip cracks!"

Raven pulled the rope tight, wound it around the saddle horn, and held on to Tucker for dear life. The horse did the rest of the work, keeping the line taut between her and the startled cow with small, backward steps. Raven watched from her saddle as Flint approached the cow with a steady hand and a soothing voice. With a veterinarian's touch and a weathered grace, he injected the 5-Way Respiratory Vaccine into its neck. Stepping away, he circled a finger in the air, signaling Raven to ease the tension on the line.

"Now?"

"A-yuh."

Raven coaxed her horse forward causing the rope to slacken. Still within arms reach of the cow, Flint spoke to the animal, giving it a play-by-play rundown of what he was doing. With masterful ease, he removed the rope and backed away from the cow.

"All right, Ms. Raven," Flint said with a rare smile. "Only thirty-five more."

Raven gathered and coiled the rope, then set the lasso.

She gave Flint a gleeful stare and said, "Well, let's get on with it. We're burnin' daylight."

Flint shook his head and retrieved a new syringe from his pack. "The Duke just rolled over in his grave."

Raven's head tilted to one side and her mouth fixed in a questioning curl. "Who?"

"The Duke. John Wayne. Ms. Raven, ya can't be a ranch hand if'n ya don't know who the Duke is."

"Guess I have some homework for this evening."

"Yes ma'am. You most certainly do."

CHAPTER TWELVE

Sleep did not come easy for Carlos Ruiz-Mata which led to his watching the sunrise beyond the stern of *Peniel's Eden*. The long hours of night gave him time to reflect on the events of the previous evening and invited an unwelcome voice to enter his mind.

El Despiadado had a way of drifting into the forefront of Mata's thoughts, bringing with him a shroud of darkness that caused a loss of time and place. On his best days, El Despiadado took over, ruling the day and the night and the deeds that must be done as was the nature of the job and an expectation of a sicario. Though he and Mata were one and the same, it was El Despiadado who enjoyed the killing. He soaked in its majesty as if he were but a witness to a beautiful ballet. Each slice of the knife, each pull of the trigger, each snapping bone, and to mix with all the terror, each victim's screams that accompanied his wrath were all music to his ears. Mata, El Despiadado, began to feel that euphoric urge calling for a quick fix. A single hit would do the trick. Much like a street dwelling heroin addict craving a score, El Despiadado grew hungry for blood.

As night gave way to light cresting over the buildings of Ciudad Guaymas, Mata, for the first time for as long as he could remember, fought back. Should a passing boat have caught a glimpse of what materialized on deck at this early hour, it might have seemed that someone had lost their mind. Mata stomped around, shaking his head. He pounded his palms on the railing and screamed for El Despiadado to go. To die!

"Enough! I am done," he yelled as he leaned overboard and caught his reflection in the wavy salt waters of the Sea of Cortez.

"*You will have to do better than that, my friend.*" El Despiadado's voice rang in Mata's head. "*You cannot live without me. Remember the boy? Remember the rock? Remember when I was born and you were so glad that I was there? And I was there, from the beginning, and I have protected you ever since. You cannot live without me.*"

"Ahhh!" Mata screamed, turning to face the western sky where light had yet to penetrate the receding night.

El Despiadado's words cut at him. He arched his back and screamed as if a knife had been plunged into him from behind. His fists turned white as he grasped the stainless-steel lifeline that wrapped *Peniel's Eden*, each length of metal tubing placed for one purpose, to keep passengers and crew from falling overboard. To keep them safe. He rocked back and forth, pulling at the bars, wanting to rip them from the boat, wanting to rip El Despiadado from his head. He squeezed his eyes shut, tears forming and falling, his breaths shuddering as his chest heaved in and out.

Behind his eyelids, all he saw was red. All he heard was crying. All he thought was why. And then, from out of the darkness, a familiar voice broke through the barriers of turmoil that encapsulated Mata and spoke to him.

"*Hijo, the darkness is not just out there; it is within us, too. Tonight, you've met yours.*"

Mata forced his eyes open. He faced the shore; the east where sunlight shone across the water. Its brilliance embraced his vulnerability. His eyes burned, yet the warmth of the rays felt soothing. Mata bowed his head and gazed into the water. He flinched, eyes bulging larger at the sight of his father's face wavering in the translucence where his own reflection should have been. The voice, now shallow yet still clear, spoke again.

"The darkness is not just out there; it is within us, too." The image of his father seemed to smile. *"But look closer my son, deeper, for good will always overcome. It is not too late."*

In disbelief, Mata wiped his eyes and face, but when he looked again, all he saw was his reflection.

"Papá."

Dropping to his knees, he let go of the rail and turned to lean against the gunwale. He ran his fingers through his hair, then grabbed a fistful and roared.

CHAPTER THIRTEEN

The face of the Brewster County Jail looked different today, like the pale face of a sick animal. Ray noticed as well.

"Place looks like a Tijuana hangover."

The sun shone bright above a crystalline sky which should have brought about a clean, crispness to all its rays touched, which it had for most of the drive to town. The landscape looked like a Thomas Moran painting fresh off the easel, and the cityscape bathed in bright yellow seemed almost cheery. There were not many cars on the road. By chance, I caught the Explorer's reflection in the antiqued windows of a derelict gas station and for a moment felt as if we were driving through 1950s Western Americana.

That perception changed as we pulled into the drive that led to the jail. The building seemed to reject the light. The windows looked dark. Even the shrubbery lining the exterior of the stone walls appeared dejected and old.

The sheriff's office had moved in and was sharing administrative space within the jail as well as parking on the outer rim of the lot. This arrangement was temporary until a new county facility could be constructed to replace the original building that had been destroyed in the bombing.

I parked next to Chance's Ford Interceptor Bronco. It may have been the only positive thing in the vicinity. Its new, muscular tires and black tinted windows gave it a rugged appeal. The fresh paint and pinstriping that wrapped around the driver's door creating a frame around the wording, *Brewster County Sheriff*, made it officially one bad ass 4x4.

Ray stepped out of the Explorer and walked around the front of the new model Ford.

"This county issued?"

"Yep. Chance has had it about a week."

"Perks of the job, or is he a little loose in the pocket with government spending?"

"Chance isn't like that. Turns out a few of these bad boys were rolling off the production line about the time we made national headlines and Ford thought it would be a nice gesture to show their support of law enforcement, so they diverted this one from whatever location it was supposed to go to and gave it to Chance."

"Pretty damn generous."

"Not really. They sent a whole marketing crew along with the delivery and documented the whole thing. Chance hated that. He even refused the vehicle at first. It took a chat with the mayor and a phone call from Governor Abbot himself to sway him into accepting the 'token,' as it was so politically stated."

"There's always someone in it for the money or the fame."

"Or both," I added. "Come on, let's head inside and find out why we are here."

Ray turned and scowled at the building. "We going in voluntarily or do we have to buy tickets to this haunted house?"

"You signed up for this, remember?"

I started for the door. Ray took one last look, grunted, then followed behind me.

We stepped inside and found Chance waiting for us outside the security entrance. A flat, almost annoyed expression took the place of his usual cinematic smile. He greeted us just the same.

"Cass."

We shook hands and I introduced him to Ray.

"Heard a lot about ya, Detective Tucker," Chance said.

"Well, hell," Ray said, looking at me. "This isn't some sort of whacked out intervention on my behalf, is it?"

Chance shot me a sideways glance, then replied. "I wish it were that easy, but yer not too far from the truth. The situation has escalated since we last spoke."

"Bring us up to speed," I said.

"I'll fill you in on the way."

We followed Chance through security, checked our weapons, and continued down the hall past a growing accumulation of deputies and guards. The looks in the eyes of the men and women we passed were one of concern and nervousness. Some glared as we walked by as if placing blame, but for what?

Chance stopped at the end of the hall outside the office door of Deputy Warden Mitch James. Two deputies stood guard on either side of the door. The tension in the air was palpable. It reeked of trouble and growing dissent. It was no secret that the guards saw the Sheriff Office's occupation as an intrusion within the jail. Upon the merger, one overall expectation was communicated to all by both Sheriff Chance and Warden Macias, do your OWN job. Easy to say, but now, with trouble brewing, the air in the crowded hallway felt more like the searing calm before an unavoidable street fight.

Turning around, Chance spoke to us in a whisper. "Mitch James is experiencing a mental episode. He is armed and is threatening to kill himself. So far as we know it, he's alone. His only demand was that he wants to talk to you, Cass."

"Me? What the hell do I have to offer?"

"He won't say, but I feel like we are running out of time."

A loud crash sounded out from behind the office door making most who heard it in the hall jump and look.

"WHERE IS HE?"

Deputy Warden Mitch James's voice echoed through the door. His desperation permeated the walls.

"What am I walking in to?"

"He claims to have a gun," Chance said. "Before we spoke earlier, he called me and demanded I bring you in so he could speak to you. He sounded angry, but under it all, I sensed he was frightened."

"Maybe our investigation has finally struck a chord."

Ray rolled his eyes. "Or maybe he's just a loon."

Chance huffed. He did not know or understand Ray and was not having any of it now. "When I called you, Mitch had not suggested taking his life. The situation escalated just before you arrived."

"Okay," I said. "I'll talk to him."

"Unarmed? Like hell you will," Ray objected.

The three of us stood in a tight huddle.

"Keep yer voice down," Chance insisted. "We're not sure how he got a weapon passed security, but he has made it pretty damn clear that he is armed."

Ray bent down and pulled a Ruger .380 ACP from a concealed ankle holster and handed it to me.

"Got this through with no problem at all." He locked eyes with Chance. "Maybe it's time to revamp the security measures around here?"

I slid the gun into my belt and covered it with my shirt.

"Don't mind him. He's an asshole," I said. "But he's right."

Chance placed his hands on his hips. He gave Ray a

dejected glance, then focused back on me. "Go on. Be careful. Find out what he wants an' get 'em off that ledge!" His voice rose as he spoke. "We'll be out here. If you need immediate backup, yell—"

"Dragon," Ray interrupted. "Old habits die hard."

I nodded at Ray and turned toward the door. Ray and I had served in Dragon Company during our time in the Middle East. It was a familiar term but filled with memories I had filed away and locked in the deepest pits of my mind.

I reached for the doorknob. My heart rate was up and my fingers felt clammy around the smooth metal handle. Before I turned the knob, Chance laid a palm on my shoulder.

"We ain't gonna let no one die today. Let's get this situation deescalated as soon as possible."

"Yeah," Ray added. "If it comes to it, just pop one in his arm. He won't expect it. Might hurt like hell, but it won't kill 'im."

On that note, I twisted the doorknob and called into the office. "Mitch. It's Cass Callahan. I'm coming in."

CHAPTER FOURTEEN

Stale air filled my lungs as I took a deep breath upon entering the office. I closed the door behind me and took a quick inventory of everything I could see in the microsecond before locking eyes with what looked like the fragile shell of an unstable man.

The first time I visited Mitch James, his office looked more like a shrine to the Chihuahuas, a minor league baseball team from El Paso, with baseball paraphernalia covering the walls and littering the shelves. It was a celebration, an unconventional and probable unauthorized attempt at creating a happy space in the middle of incarcerated regret. Now the room appeared as if a disgruntled fan had flipped his lid in expressing their discontent for the team.

Team pennants lay on the floor in a folded mess of broken frames and shattered glass. Shreds of what once was a Chihuahua team poster listing their 2023 season's games covered Mitch's desk in a crinkled mass of ripped paper piles. Staples still held tight the corners of the trashed poster as if in defiance of the brutality. An outline of faded wood, stained from years of incandescent lighting and lingering dust formed a large rectangular spot on the wall where Mitch's coveted Hunter Renfroe jersey had once hung. Now, it clung to the back of his chair like a discarded piece of dirty laundry, its wooden display case smashed and dead on the floor. Official-looking papers and folders lay beneath a window that looked out to the parking lot. The window was shattered. A gaping hole the size of a baseball marked the lower quadrant of the remaining glass while the rest had formed a dangerous spider web of cracks and weakness.

And there, standing behind the tattered desk, amid the disarray, stood Deputy Warden Mitch James. At first glance, he looked sickly. His skin was paler than I had remembered. He had dark rings circling his bloodshot eyes. The top two buttons of his shirt were missing, and his tie dangled loose as if he had started to remove it but had gotten sidetracked. Sweat stains moistened each of his armpits, and his hair looked rough from possible nervous stroking. His fingers twitched at his sides. Where was the purported gun?

He swayed back and forth as we entered into what felt like an old-fashioned high noon showdown. I watched, waiting for a tell or for him to speak first. As long as his hands were empty, I had no reason to feel threatened. Like a drunk staggering around a bar at closing time, Mitch began to pace behind the desk.

I broke the silence. "What's going on, Mitch?"

No answer.

I spoke again, my voice low and as soothing as I could offer without sounding condescending. "You asked for me, and now I am here. What can I do to help you, Mitch?"

He stopped pacing and stared ahead.

"The glass is fragile. See how easily the window was broken? One throw and the ball went right through. But now, it's cracked so bad, no one can see inside. No one can see."

"It's broken for sure," I said, taking one step closer to the desk.

Mitch tilted his head and laughed as if in disbelief. "Don't you get it? No one can see inside. Through the hole, maybe. But it is so tiny. So small."

"It's a window," I said, watching his pupils dance from side to side. "Easy to replace."

"NO!" Mitch flinched, then turned and glared at me like I had just admitted to sleeping with his wife. "It's over. They know. You know. And soon, everyone will know."

I listened to his rant, wondering where his thoughts were headed. He repeated himself over and over as he fiddled with his fingers and rolled his fists around in balls of uncontrollable nervousness.

I took a step closer, now three paces in front of his desk. "Mitch," I said, my voice just above a whisper. "Who knows what?"

Mitch looked back at the window, then yanked his chair from under his desk and sat down. He slammed his elbows on the desktop making an angry wooden thud, then leaned forward and covered his face with his palms.

"Sit." He said through his fingers.

"Let me get you some help," I said.

"Sit. Down!"

In one unexpected motion, Mitch swiped the piles of torn papers from his desk and grasped a small snub-nosed pistol concealed beneath the taters with his left hand. From my peripheral vision, I saw papers flip and twirl in the air like confetti at a ticker-tape parade, but my eyes became locked on the gun now precariously dangling in his hand.

"Whoa, there, Mitch. No need for that." My voice was calm but my heart raced ahead.

"Turn around." He motioned the barrel of the gun at me. "Lock the door and have a seat."

I raised both of my palms out and slowly stepped back toward the door, never breaking eye contact. When I reached the door, I felt for the latch and twisted the dead-bolt until the slide clicked into place.

"Cass." Chance's voice was muffled through the door. "Cass?"

Mitch glanced past me, then recentered his attention as he raised his gun with purposeful intent.

"If I don't answer, they will assume I am in trouble. Am I in trouble, Mitch?"

He cocked his jaw to one side, a thought-provoking mannerism that suggested he was weighing his options. Finally, he spoke.

"No. Tell them everything is all right, then come sit down."

"Okay, Mitch. I'll tell them."

Speaking over my shoulder, I yelled my answer. "I'm good. Just having a chat and wanted a little privacy, that's all. Be out in a bit."

Before removing my hand from the door and while I was answering, I tapped one finger on the wood once, paused, then tapped two times more, followed by a pause and one final tap. Eye contact with Mitch was key which helped mask my message. My hope was that Ray stood close enough to the door to have heard.

I could hear feet shuffling in the hallway, then Chance's voice responded, "Ten-four, Cass."

"There," I said to Mitch. "Now we can talk about whatever you want for however long you want."

I had to make sure he felt in charge. My words were completely "you-sentric." It would calm him; keep him focused on why he had asked for me. Only me. Holding the gun, I would suspect he already felt like he held all the cards, which was fine, but that was not the case. A man on edge would act irrationally, erratically. Houston was full of people just like him, and I had already had my fill over the course of my career with HPD. One day everything is fine, the next, they want to take a dive off the Transco Tower or take a gun into a day care.

"Sit, Callahan."

I moved to a chair across the desk from him and sat down.

"Doors locked. Nobody to bother us. Mind putting the gun aside?"

"What I mind is you. Ever since you arrived, my world has turned to shit."

"Okay," I said with a slow draw. "How can I help you..."

"You can't!" Mitch's voice dropped an octave. "You've already fucked everything up, starting with Joe."

"Joe Sinclair?"

"Yes, Joe Sinclair." Mitch grew more agitated. He dragged the gun back and forth across the desktop, its steel cylinder digging into the wood. "Killing him set things in motion, and now my world is about to collapse around me."

I paused to consider what he had said, then shifted slightly in my seat and crossed my legs. The steel of Ray's .380 pressed against my gut.

"I didn't kill Joe, Mitch."

"The second you arrested him, you signed his death warrant. You saw what happened. You lived it. I tried to intervene, but they sent...her. I knew the moment I saw her at the jail pretending to be a visitor."

"What exactly are you into, Mitch?"

Mitch stood up and stroked his head with both hands, gun and all.

"It doesn't matter. They'll send somebody for me and my family."

"We can protect them. I can protect them. Just tell me something and I'll make sure..."

"NO!" Mitch stopped. A flushed, calming look washed over him. "It's too late for that." His voice was even keel. His fingers stopped twitching. He turned and glanced to the broken window again. Whether it was a crazed look or finally finding peace with what he meant to do, he tilted his head and smiled. He stood for seconds without moving, without speaking, and just stared ahead as if reliving the best moments of his life through memories or visions.

Then, as if planned with perfect timing, the click of his snub nose triggered a final dive into the darkness brewing inside him. Rocking back and forth from heel to toe, he slowly turned to face me. Tears welled up in his eyes but did not fall.

"They know you are coming, Cass. They all know."

A sharp chill stabbed me in the back of the neck. I slowly raised my palms before me like Steve Irwin fending off a wild croc.

"Steady," I said, my voice firm, concerned. "Who knows what?"

A single tear dripped down Mitch's cheek as he raised the gun to his head.

"Señor de la Droga," he said.

With a sudden bang and crack, Mitch spun around and tumbled to the floor. Blood spattered the desktop and the shelf. I jumped to my feet and lunged over the desk. Behind me, voices in the hallway began yelling. The door was kicked open, and Chance bolted inside.

I looked down at Mitch. The snub-nosed revolver cocked and ready to fire but lying beside him. His index finger and thumb were still wrapped around the handle but severed from the rest of his body. The mangled leftovers of his left hand pulsed at his side, spilling streams of blood onto the floor. I grabbed the Renfroe jersey from his chair and wrapped it as tight as I could around the angry wound. He trembled and was going into shock. His face was white.

"Medic!" I yelled. "Get some help in here!"

Everything seemed to move in slow motion, yet all happened within moments. Chance was in the room, as were two guards, followed by a doctor from the jail infirmary. I stepped aside to let them work. Chance joined me.

"Ray?" I asked.

Chance pointed to the window. Through the baseball-sized hole, I could see outside into the parking lot. Ray stood in a tactical stance next to the Explorer, my black Remington 700 in his grip. He was a crack shot. Always was, always would be. I waved my hand in front of me, knowing fair well I was lined up in Ray's crosshairs. He eased his stance and gave me a thumbs up. Chance patted me on the shoulder.

"Come, we have a lot to discuss," Chance said.

Before exiting the office, I stopped and turned to look back on the scene. Mitch's words were still fresh in my mind. "They know you are coming."

"Qué pasó?" Chance asked.

I shook my head, gnawing the inside of my mouth.

"Nothing. Just glad everyone came out of this alive."

Chance's Cheshire smile returned. "Your friend is pretty good shot, but how did he know what to do?"

"Old Dragon Company trick." I knocked a knuckle against the wall—*dah...dit.dit.dah...*—in patterned morse code. Chance raised an eyebrow.

"'X' marks the spot," I said.

CHAPTER FIFTEEN

Well-earned sores formed along Raven's fingers beneath her gloves from the rope work she had been charged with doing. Her hips ached and the insides of her thighs took on a heated rawness that reminded her of the first time she saw Cass come in from the range. His bow-legged strides and slow, methodical movements had been the punchline of many a joke following his ride, but now her humor turned to empathy. It was tempting to ask Flint when they could break from work, but she had not signed on as a city slicker. Raven knew Flint would take it easy on her, but that was not what she wanted. Pain or no pain, she aimed to see the day through.

Peniel's Eden tugged against its anchor line as if wanting to go along with Mata as he sped toward shore in his Zodiac, a motor driven, Rigid Inflatable Boat. The RIB shot across the smooth waters of *Ensendada Bacochibampo*. Mata's hair blew back from his forehead. Black Ray-Ban sunglasses shielded his eyes from the sun and wind and occasional spray that misted him. He held his jaw tight. His gaze was set on the line of boats docked in the marina adjacent to the bar that had seen the impact of his failed killer's dinghy the night before.

The struggles he felt earlier this morning had subsided, but the hangover of it all had yet to pass. All he wanted, what he needed, was to be left alone. There was no respect in calling on him again so soon. The job Señor de la Droga insisted he perform in Panama would not be done, at least not by him, which would end his good standing with the Camargo cartel. No one disobeys an order. No one leaves the cartel. It is a life sentence unless you have the means to survive. Working as long as he had for the cartel, he also knew that if men came for him and did not return, more would certainly be sent. When this happened, there would be no question about their intentions. They would come for one purpose: to kill him.

Mata throttled up and headed for shore. His mind was made up. If the cartel was determined to hunt him down, he would have to allow El Despiadado one final mission—return to Camargo and sever the head of the snake that wanted him dead.

CHAPTER SIXTEEN

A thin line of gray smoke trailed into the air. Fire crackled and a smell mixed of thick coffee and burning wood surrounded Raven and Flint as they sat and sipped, enduring what was sure enough the worst cup of mud there ever was. But, like a seasoned cowhand, Raven slogged back the brew without a word of complaint. Her face, on the other hand, told a different story.

"Don't like it much?" Flint asked.

Raven swallowed the dark liquid. Bits of warm coffee grounds caught in her throat and caused her to cough before answering. Instead of words, she gave him a thumbs up as she fought the convulsive spats. Her eyes watered.

Flint knew the feeling. He smiled and took another swig from his cup.

"Takes some gettin' used to, I reckon."

One final cough cleared Raven's throat. "You don't say." She glared at him, but her bluff gave way to a forgiving smile. She laughed, and before he knew what was happening, Flint found himself doing something he had not done in a long time. He laughed too. Like most people, he chuckled or grunted at jokes or situations he thought amusing, but he had not experienced a heart-felt belly roll of a laugh in ages.

"Well, what do you know? Levi Flint has a funny bone after all."

"Now, don't you go tellin' no one, Ms. Raven," Flint said, collecting himself.

"Your secret is safe with me."

Raven raised her coffee in the air. Flint leaned forward and sealed the promise with a metallic clink of his cup to hers, then together, they suffered through the finality of their drinks before getting back to work.

Midday seemed to arrive earlier than either Raven or Flint had expected. Whether it was the cold front rolling in from the northwest or the day's preparation for the coming time change, or both, the light dimmed across the CR. Before leaving the grove they burned the discarded trash and circled the area together on horseback to look for tracks made by the trespassers.

"Look." Flint pointed. "Just as I thought. The tracks are leadin' northeast straight for the Double SS."

"Should we follow them?"

"Could. Odds are that they're long gone by now."

Raven giggled and spoke with a cinematic flair in her voice. "May the odds be ever in your favor."

Ignoring her, Flint remained focused on the tracks.

"What?" Raven said. "It's from one of my favorite books. They made it into a movie, too."

Without taking his eyes off the ground, Flint responded, "Frankly, my dear, I don't give a damn."

Raven shook her head. "You are full of surprises today."

"Surprises," Flint echoed. He twisted around atop his saddle as if looking for something or someone. "Tell ya what. We've a few more things ta see to before headin' in. Let's get on it, then ride back along the north fence line."

"Something is bothering you."

"Nah. Not really. But since that's where them tracks

are headin', just want ta make sure there ain't no one laggin' behind."

"Okay, Flint."

"Just one thing, Ms. Raven. You do as I tell ya if we run inta anyone. Anyone at all. Understand?" Flint spoke with a firm tone.

Sensing his seriousness, Raven nodded and replied with steadfast understanding. "You're in charge, Flint. I won't do a thing unless you say so."

Flint nodded, then nudged his horse ahead.

Gray clouds moved in overhead, covering the sky. A northern chill overtook the southerly breezes, running them off as if those winds, too, were trespassing. Color faded from the landscape, replaced by a sepia tinge that made the CR look like the antiquated setting from an old western movie.

Raven took a long look at the tracks before following Flint. She slid her hand along her thigh until her fingers ran over the poly coated handle of her gun, the Purple Demon.

"I won't do a thing," she whispered. "But I'll be ready."

CHAPTER SEVENTEEN

The strum of a flamenco guitar and the boisterous voice that accompanied its playing filled the background as I sat with Ray and Chance at a corner table at El Hefe restaurant. Mitch James, former Deputy Warden of the South Brewster County Jail, was tucked away in a guarded hospital room recovering from the injury to his hand while soaring high from a Dilaudid drip. Doctors determined right away that there was no chance to reattach his severed fingers, opting instead to treat and repair what was left of his hand. He would be facing multiple surgeries over time, but that was the least of his problems.

Tensions at the jail were receding, though whispers questioning what may have led to the incident still lingered in the air and in the curious eyes of both deputy sheriffs and jail guards. The breakdown at the jail's front sally port failed to detect the weapons that both the deputy warden and Ray smuggled through, exposing a critical vulnerability in security protocol that had to be acted upon immediately. Once the scene was cleared, the next step would be to start drafting a report while waiting to speak with Mitch again. The report would have to wait as I had a more pressing engagement to attend.

It was nowhere near happy hour, but considering how the morning had gone, I felt I would take sides with Alan Jackson and Jimmy Buffet and call it five o'clock on the nose. Wet rings accumulated on the plastic tablecloth beneath each of our margarita glasses. Salted, homemade tortilla chips spilled out of a red plastic bowl in the center of the table next to servings of salsa and guacamole. The salsa had a noticeable kick, igniting the open passageways between my nose and throat with a burst of authentic taste and raging liquid fire. The guacamole remained untouched, though Ray almost fell victim to its unde-tectable, yet vicious, digestive targeting toxicity that lurked beneath its deceptively fresh appearance.

"Don't go there," Chance warned as Ray reached a chip for the classic green goo. "Tear ya up inside and out. You'll regret it later."

"Yeah, it's not like La Cocina's back home," I said.

Ray popped the empty chip into his mouth. "Fine," he crunched.

We each sipped our melting drinks. The salted rim of my glass tantalized my upper lip and tongue as I enjoyed the mix of tequila and lime.

"So, one of you gonna tell me why the D.W. went batshit crazy?"

Ray popped another empty chip into his mouth.

"According to him, when we stumbled upon the bodies on the CR and linked the murders to Joe Sinclair, we opened up a hornet's nest of trouble with the Camargo cartel. It looks like their outreach spans both sides of the border."

"So, what did he want with you? Why not ask for him?" Ray said, motioning to Chance.

"I wondered the same thing. We were all a part of arresting Joe Sinclair, so it's not like I was the sole one to blame from their perspective." I took a long sip, finishing off my drink. "It was what he said just before he put that gun to his head. He looked at me and told me that they knew we were coming. That Señor de la Droga knew I was coming."

Chance shifted in his seat. "Señor de la Droga. El Jefe himself. Self-proclaimed untouchable El León. He's no lion, but he is as ruthless and savage as they come. If he knows about your mission, he has someone on the inside feeding him information."

"Yeah," I said. "That's concerned me from the get-go. It's why I asked Ray to come out in the first place."

Ray leaned back in his chair. "So, ol' Mitch went off the deep end to warn you?"

"No, he felt that the cartel was going to send people to kill him and his family. He needed someone to blame. Needed a coward's way out. How he knew about our mission or that the cartel knew we were coming is beyond me, but like Chance said, someone on the inside must be tipping them off."

"You should abort," Chance said.

"No, we're just gonna change things up. Run things from my end instead of from behind a desk. When plans change without running them through proper channels, we'll see who starts asking too many questions."

"You thinking your FBI buddy, Zuñiga, has something to do with this?" Ray asked.

"Hard to tell, but I don't see why he would go to all this trouble just to set me up."

"That leaves two people," Ray said. "Thor and Johnny Appleseed."

Chance raised an eyebrow, giving Ray a perplexed look.

"Agent Crank and Agent Sharp he means," I said. "You know Sharp. We only met Agent Crank yesterday. Tough looking SOB. Probably former military. Built like an ox."

I looked around the restaurant. Aside from a lone local rancher sitting with his back to us across the room, and a handful of bored to tears wait staff, the place was empty. Still, I leaned over the table and spoke at a lower register.

"We are supposed to rendezvous tomorrow morning back in El Paso, then head south as one unit."

"Fuck that," Ray interrupted.

"Hold that thought. Mitch won't be much help for a day or two at least. We'll be in and out of Mexico by then. You both knew my intentions following the attack on my family and the sheriff's office. Now, I have unofficial clearance to see it through. This Kill Hydra team, I get it. On the surface it shows the bureaucrats that something is being done to put a stop to the cartels. They don't want to know details. They just want to be able to stand in front of reporters and say that something is being done, then take credit for whatever positive outcome follows. Of course, they'll be the first ones to place blame and demand oversight if things go south. My gut tells me that Zuñiga is expecting results."

"He also said that we'd be on our own," Ray added.

"Right, and that is why I am changing the plan. First thing tomorrow morning, you and I will cross into Ojinaga, Chihuahua, Mexico via the Presidio-Ojinaga International Bridge. We'll take your truck, load up and stash our supplies just as we would have if traveling as originally planned."

"They'll never let you enter with the weapons I suspect you are wanting to bring along," Chance said.

"Right again. That's where you come in."

"Me?"

"Chance, we've known each other only a short time, and I've come to think of you as family. Look me in the eye and tell me you don't have a connection at the border in Presidio."

Chance pursed his lips, then sat back and crossed his arms. I locked eyes with him and knew the answer without him saying it. He wore the same look at the poker table and was why I always cleaned him out.

"Good," I said. "Set it up or come visit me in Ojinaga. I'm sure their jails are top-notch facilities."

Ray glanced at me, then over to Chance.

"So, the two of us are gonna ride in Lone Wolf McQuade style?" Ray asked.

"You have a problem with that?" I said.

Ray paused to allow a sly smile crack through his lips.

"Not one damn bit."

CHAPTER EIGHTEEN

The walk from the Zodiac to his Range Rover should have been its usual, uneventful stroll for Mata had it not been for the rat-at-tat-tat of automatic machine gun fire. A flurry of bullets shot through the air, ripping through the hardened rubber of the Zodiac just as Mata stepped onto the docks. He dove forward, tucked, and rolled to the opposite side of the walkway. Wood splintered where his feet had just been as more bullets missed their target. Keeping on the quick, Mata leaped off the docks onto a neighboring sailboat and crouched behind the gunwale. A pause in the shooting allowed him a glance over the edge of the boat.

Parked parallel to the chain-linked fence that separated the parking lot from the marina was an old El Camino. Its shiny metallic purple paint and ink-black rims did nothing to conceal its presence. The addition of two men standing in the bed of the car wearing black balaclavas, each armed with as AK-47, made this hit an unmistakable display of force. A third armed man ran toward the entrance to the dock. He screamed and waved his weapon like a crazed lunatic.

Mata lowered, satisfied with his quick assessment. He reached into his jacket and pulled a Glock 18 from his shoulder holster. As he pulled the slide back, the distinctive click of metal recoiling into place caused a new sound to catch Mata's ear. It was a quick, high-pitched rush of air mixed with fright. He looked around the deck and discovered that he was not alone, nor the only one in danger of eating a bullet.

Hiding in the companionway was a young, teenage girl. She was alone, trembling; a statue cast with fear and unknowing. Mata could see the terror in her eyes. He twisted and peeked over the gunwale again. The advancing killer charged as if he were invincible, relying on the angry sound in his voice and the show of force with his mean-looking assault rifle to instill fear in anyone who might consider standing up to him. Mata looked back at the girl and gently placed his index finger over his lips.

"Shhh. It will be okay."

In one swift movement, Mata stood, aimed, and fired a burst from his machine pistol. In an instant, the man who charged down the dock was knocked from his feet by a cluster of bullets tearing into his chest. His torso exploded in a spray of red. His rifle clattered onto the dock, and his body went limp, bouncing once on the stiff wooden slats before splashing into the water below.

Mata turned his aim toward the El Camino. The men in the back yelled. One punched the roof of the car while the other jumped out of the bed and reached for the passenger door. Mata was too far to be a dead shot with his machine pistol, but that did not stop him from emptying the magazine at the remaining killers. Each shot, each triggered explosion, vibrated through Mata's arm, rippling through his body until the fuzzy sensation awakened El Despiadado like a snort of cocaine, igniting a fierce intensity in his eyes, a predatory focus that was both terrifying and exhilarating in its sheer ferocity.

Dirt flew, metal groaned, and the man who reached for the door did not make it inside the car. Bullets filled the air like a massive swarm of killer bees attacking the men, covering the El Camino with a relentless volley of stings as bullets pierced metal and glass and flesh. The tires spun, kicking up dirt as the car tried to flee. The sudden jolt of the vehicle knocked the remaining man in the bed of the El Camino off his feet. A flash of flame and thunderous blast escaped the barrel of his gun as his fingers instinctively clenched as he tried to catch himself.

El Despiadado hopped over the gunwale and ran down the dock toward the escaping car. He fired again, exhausting the rest of his ammunition. In a move as skillful as a linebacker scooping up a fumble, he reached down to the dock mid-stride and grabbed the dead killers AK-47 off the wood, flipped it in his arms, and tucked the butt to his shoulder. His skills were natural, perfect. He ran at the ready, aiming the weapon ahead.

By the time he reached the gate, the El Camino was speeding out of the parking lot in a raucous screech of tires and white smoke. He turned, gun still poised for his next kill, and approached the body of the killer his crew had left behind. As El Despiadado approached the man, a smile formed across his face. Seeing a similar AK-47 lying near the body, he kicked it out of reach. The man lay bleeding from wounds to his back, but he was not yet dead.

El Despiadado nudged the man with the barrel of the gun.

"¡Rueda!" he commanded. "Roll over now."

The man groaned and spat. In considerable pain and with minimal effort, he tried once but could not move more than a few inches.

"I do not think you want a bullet in the back of the head, my friend. Look me in the eyes and I will help you."

Sirens in the distance began to wail as emergency vehicles raced toward the marina.

The man tried again, this time pushing with his hands and feet. He growled, fighting with his body as the pain he felt objected to his movements.

"That's it. Just a little farther."

The man collapsed onto the ground. He arched his back as blood seeped into view from beneath him. Mata kneeled next to him.

"What is your name?"

"*Chinga tu madre.*"

Mata clicked his tongue and shook his head, displeased with the man's answer. "That is not a name, but I understand your discontent. You are one of Señor de la Droga's men, are you not?"

The man furrowed his brow and grimaced in pain.

"That is answer enough. I need you to take a message to him. Can you do that?"

The man's eyes widened. His breathing was still vigorous but he gave El Despiadado his full attention.

"I need him to know that I am well. That I will bear no ill will if he stands down." El Despiadado set the AK-47 on the ground. "But, if he continues to pursue me, he will find that I am more relentless than he could ever think to be. Can you deliver the message?"

The man nodded his head in short, furious bursts.

"Good. Now, let me give you the message, but you must promise to deliver. Can I count on you?"

The man coughed. Blood spattered his lips.

"You're...you're going to help me?"

El Despiadado looked at the man the way a parent might look at an ailing child. He put his left hand on the man's forehead and gently rubbed the sweat from his skin. "But, of course."

The man exhaled and closed his eyes. It was what El Despiadado did with his right hand that the man never saw coming.

CHAPTER NINETEEN

Ray and I had less than twenty-four hours to get packed and moving toward the border crossing at Presidio, and Chance had a phone call to make. I needed to leave things as they were at the jail to focus on my mission with team Kill Hydra, especially now that I was scrapping the conditions of our original plan. There were plenty of deputies to do the easy lifting, and Mitch James was alive, under guard, and would have plenty of time to revisit our chummy get-together at a later date.

Ray stared out the window as I drove us back to the CR. He did not share what was on his mind. I wondered how Agent Zuñiga and his FBI buddies were going to take my changing the plans. Since this was already deemed an "off-the-books assignment" they would have little choice in the matter and since Zuñiga had named me team leader, my decisions in the field were final. So, we were not quite yet in the field, but under the circumstances, we were close enough for government work in my book. I would give Agent Zuñiga a heads-up as we rolled into Presidio tomorrow morning. He could relay the message to Agent Sharp and Agent Crank and everything would be hunky-dory, right? I laughed at the thought of Sharp having a conniption about being left out of the loop until the last second. I felt that Crank would go with the flow, but as things stood right now, both of them were on my watch list. My subtle laugh disrupted Ray's focus on the distant terrain.

"Somethin' funny?" Ray gave me a sideways glance and shifted his position in the passenger seat to face straight ahead.

"Just running through things in my head. The second we cross the border we are truly on our own. I trust our FBI pals about as much as a holey parachute on a combat jump."

"But we're lined up and waiting for the green light anyway."

"Yep, something like that." I let my foot off the accelerator as the Explorer approached the turnoff for the CR. "We'll have about a three-hour head start. I don't plan to share our route or where our rendezvous point is until we are settled and have already made a sweep of the area. That should keep us in the driver's seat."

"You think Agent Dickhead and his pet tarantula will step foot across the border without knowing where they are headed?"

"If they want a piece of this mission they will. Sharp seems to get a hard-on for action. He'd drive through a parade of puppies if he thought he could get some glory from it. Not sure if Crank was assigned to Kill Hydra, or volunteered, so I do not have a clear picture as to his motives for joining the team."

"They're gonna shit kittens, you know that, right?"

"Don't care. I told Zuñiga already that I was going after the cartel and the sicario Carlos Ruiz-Mata with or without his team. We agreed that it was in my best interests to join forces, but now that we know there is an informant somewhere between the cartel and the FBI, all bets are off."

Gravel crunched beneath the tires as we left the steady hum of the highway for the rattled vibrations of the undeveloped ranch road that led us to the entrance of the CR.

"The original mission had us headquartering at Hotel Posada El Caminante, the Traveler's Inn located east of Camargo. Looking at a map of the city, the cartel's compound is set near the west edge of town. I've already made alternative arrangements at Hotel Plaza Central. It's on the square in the center of town, has a clear line of sight in all directions from the third-story balconies, and is only two clicks away from our target."

"When did you decide that?"

"About two seconds after Mitch told me they knew I was coming. It had been an alternate location from the start, but Zuñiga made the final decision to go with the hotel on the east side of Camargo. All I had to do was make a quick phone call and we were back on their books. As far as hotel management is concerned, we are a group of university historians on a research trip who thought our funding had been pulled until the last minute."

Ray twisted his head and made a disgusted look.

"University Historians? Do I look like a university historian to you?"

"I suppose I could have told them we were in town to storm the castle. Have 'em leave a welcome mat out for us, maybe a secure locker to store our weapons?"

"This is your picnic, Dr. Jones. Just tell me where I can shit, shower, and shave, and I'll be as happy as a pig in manure."

It was almost four o'clock by the time we rumbled over the cattle guard at the entrance to the CR, each metal pole bending and clanking as the Explorer slowly rolled ahead. The windows of Flint's tiny house were dark, which was not unusual as there was plenty of daylight left to burn, and Flint was the hardest working person I knew. I pulled up and parked and watched the front door to see if Raven had heard us arrive. After a moment, Ray broke the silence with a forced huff.

"We waiting for an invitation?"

I glanced past Ray to look at the barn.

"Nope, just wondering where Raven is."

"Don't tell me that you play out the whole 'cowboy has come home from the cattle drive bit.'" I endured Ray's sarcasm. "Here you are, about to dismount your trusted steed, when the door opens and there she is, eyes all a glaze, face full of smiles, ready to welcome you home to a hot plate of food and a soft bed."

"Ray, you really are an..."

"I know. I know. But you wouldn't have me any other way." Ray's face tightened around a toothy smirk.

On that note, we both exited the vehicle.

I walked to the corral and looked out to the expanse of the CR, wondering where she and Flint were today. Since taking an interest in hard-handed ranch work, Flint had agreed to take Raven on as he would any other, but only if he treated her just like any other. Those were Raven's conditions, not Flint's. She was only a few days in, but I could already tell she had found a new love in the land. It was a feeling that I knew she never even considered prior to moving away from Houston. If ranch work made her happy and Flint was comfortable having her tag along, so be it.

Ray joined me, put a foot on one of the lower cross beams of the corral, then leaned over and spit in the dirt.

"All this," he started to say. He paused as if reconsidering his words, then added, "Never figured you'd actually leave the city. Can't say that I blame you. This is just a big change, but I can see why you like it."

He gazed into the distance, his eyes slowly dancing with the mountains and bluffs lining the riverbanks of the Rio Grande at the farthest edge of the CR, at the border of the US and Mexico.

"Took me by surprise, too. When this is over, stay a while."

Ray turned and leaned against the wooden fence.

"Hell no. I need my smog and congested traffic. And what would the gangbangers do without me hangin' around?"

A lone gunshot echoed across the CR. I dismissed it, but Ray was not yet accustomed to ignoring sounds of which we had trained a lifetime to react. He flinched, then scanned the openness in front of him in search of the source. I saw his hand instinctively reach for his gun.

"Hold up there, cowboy," I said. "Shots like that are more like a jackhammer tearing up the concrete on West-heimer back home."

I had learned the hard way the first time I reacted to gunfire on the ranch, which secured my number one position on Flint's shit list. Thankfully, time, and a good dose of Raven, helped smooth things over. Now, what I did was more of a punchline than anything else.

Ray looked at me and relaxed his body when a flurry of blasts erupted from the distance, one after the other, each time growing closer together. Our eyes locked, and I knew that Ray saw the sudden concern on my face.

"That normal construction noise, too?"

I stepped up on the fencing to get a higher look at the open range beyond the corral. The blasts continued to break the air and prick my ears.

"No, Ray. It's not."

I hopped off the fence, pulled my cell phone from my pocket, and pressed Raven's contact number. Ray stood by. The phone rang once, twice, then an automated message overtook the line. *"The number you have dialed is currently out of service area or cannot receive calls at this time. Please try your call again later."*

"Damn it!"

I glanced at the horizon, at the Explorer, then at the barn.

"Come on, Ray," I said and took off at a sprint toward the barn.

With each racing step, I could not shake the feeling that Raven was in danger. And would I be able to find her in time?

CHAPTER TWENTY

"Keep yer head down!"

Flint took a protective stance in front of Raven, crouching behind a burn pile in the CR's northern quadrant, close to the Double SS Ranch border. They found some shelter, yet their horses towered over the assortment of discarded shack wood, dead scrub, and mesquite limbs—remnants of a once towering tree. Imperfect as it was, this makeshift barrier was their only option. The blasts were loud. A hint of gunpowder lingered in the air as tufts of white smoke wafted away like ghosts disappearing in the night. Raven pressed her palms over her ears. Flint held his rifle by his side and peeked out from behind the woodpile.

Fifty yards due north, just across the fence line, Flint saw people running for cover. Two men stood next to a small brown pickup holding and firing rifles as if taking part in a canned hunt. Bodies lay sprawled on the ground. Men yelled. A woman screamed, her voice sounding desperate as her words choked with terror.

"What are we going to do?" Raven said.

Flint watched the gruesome scene continue to unfold.

"Flint?" Raven tugged at his arm.

"Nothin'. Ain't nothin' we can do 'cept stay out of sight the best we can."

"But those men are..."

Flint snapped his head around. "Those men will kill both of us if we stick our necks out. We're lucky if they haven't seen us."

"Who are they?"

"Dunno. Coyotes. Drug runners. Bad fuckin' people."

Raven was as brave as a barrel full of bears, a humanitarian at heart, but right now she felt as helpless as a sack of kittens sinking in a lake. Helpless and angry. Each blast that rang in her ears, each agonizing wail of another injured soul chewed at her gut. The burn pile they sheltered behind may not have been on fire, but Raven felt a searing heat flash across her body. It came in waves, each crashing over her with growing intensity. She understood the danger they were in. On the surface, she knew if there was something to be done, Flint would do it. It was what lay beneath that came spouting out like lava, uncontrollable. It pushed Raven toward a reckless decision that was as rash as it was desperate.

In one movement, Raven shifted positions, pulled her gun, and lunged for an open view, ready to fire. She was quick, and her movements were strong, but Flint was faster and stronger still. He pulled no punches as he yanked her back to the ground. Like a wrestler, he pinned her in the dirt, dislodged the gun from her hand, and glared at her with surprise and disappointment.

"What in the goddamn hell do you think yer doing?" Flint's eyes bulged and the veins that ran from his temples to the hairline over his ears pulsed.

In an instant, Raven's rush of anger and rugged invincibility faded. Her eyes welled. Her heart pounded. There were so many things she wanted to say, but emotion overruled them all, leaving her vulnerable and riddled with growing regret.

Flint continued to hold her down. Raven did not resist.

Trails of tears carved their way down her face, soaking into the bandana around the back of her neck. She scanned the gray blanket of clouds covering the sky but there was nothing to focus on that would distract her, so she shifted her gaze until she saw the horses.

The two horses stood like seasoned chargers, calm in the presence of gunfire, their bonded nature steadfast and loyal to their riders. For a moment, Tucker seemed to lock onto Raven's gaze. The mare's deep brown eyes looked like pools of dark chocolate. They were inviting, soft, and held a sense of understanding in them that spoke to Raven, reassuring her that everything would be all right. Tucker's nostril flared, and then she looked away, bumping noses with her friend.

What seemed like hours were merely moments. The blasts lessened until all that was left was the fading echo of the last report. Flint relaxed his hold of Raven and repositioned himself for a look. Raven massaged her wrists and felt an ache in her back awaken as she slowly sat up. She glanced at the Purple Demon laying in the dirt near the base of the burn pile. *Useless*, she thought. Turning her attention to Flint, she began to whisper something, then stopped herself. Instead, she remained behind him, unable to see around their protective barrier, and waited.

A wintry chill nipped at Raven's face. Using her bandana, she dried her cheeks and wiped her nose. The cold front had brought a steady decline in temperature throughout the day. The dry conditions made the change bearable, but what felt like a twenty-degree drop still had its effects.

The croaking sound of an engine struggling to turn over filled Raven's ears. Flint eased back from his lookout position and sat next to her. Indistinctive Spanish chatter overlapped the tired truck's attempts to start, until finally, it sputtered to life. Staring straight ahead, Flint spoke.

"When they're gone, I'm going over for a look. You will stay here. Understand? Here." Flint pointed to the ground, then bowed his head. "The unfortunate truth here is shit like this happens all the time. You don't always hear about it on the news or read it in the paper 'less a politician brings it up or happens to be in the area an' they feel like jumping on their soapbox. If you ask me, we need actions, not words. Ain't nothin' gonna improve by just talkin'."

The slam of metal on the truck made Raven flinch. Flint glanced over his shoulder, though he would not have seen anything but scraggily wood and tangled branches.

"They're loadin' up. Won't be long now."

Raven took a deep breath, exhaling with a slow, whispered sigh.

"Flint." Her voice wavered. "I'm sorry."

It was Flint's turn to sigh but his sounded disappointed.

"Ms. Raven, I know yer the type that always wants ta fix things. It's admirable, but out here it's liable ta get the best of ya if ya ain't careful. Last thing I want ta see is you getting' hurt, or worse." Flint gave Raven a look that made her feel small. "If ya want ta continue workin' like ya are, don't ever do somethin' that stupid again. Yer life is more important out here than any other, hear me?"

Raven nodded, then looked away to conceal her trembling bottom lip and second round of tears. It was the first time Flint had spoken to her with a harsh tone, and she knew she deserved it, which made her feel even worse.

From beyond the safety of the burn pile, across the fence line on what was once the Double SS, the truck's engine revved, then diminished as it drove away. Flint peeked around the edge, then stood up, rifle in hand.

"I'm goin' fer a look. Stay here until I get back. I'll call out if I need ya."

Raven looked up at him, eyes bloodshot and watery. Flint cocked his head.

"Ms. Raven. Ain't no ranch hand I know has room fer tears in times like this. Cowboy up."

He was direct. Impactful. Raven swallowed hard as

Flint walked away. She bit her bottom lip to quell the quivers with hopes of replacing her emotional pain with physical discomfort. It did not work, and now she had both an uncomfortable feeling in her gut to accompany a throbbing lip.

As she crouched and followed Flint with her eyes, she felt a sudden gust of warm air on the back of her neck. She turned and came face to nose with Tucker. Her large nostrils and flappy lips looked enormous at such a close range that it causing a well-timed and much-needed smile to emerge out of Raven. Tucker leaned closer and nudged her. Whether she was seeking attention or letting Raven know that she still had a friend close by, it was just what Raven needed to pull herself together.

"You're a good horse, Ms. Tucker."

Tucker huffed, then wriggled her lips, revealing a charming array of sturdy teeth. She bumped Raven with her muzzle again.

"Teeth, nose, teeth." Raven giggled. "It's all I see."

Raven gave Tucker a hearty rub, then glanced back to find Flint. She saw that he was past the fence looking at something on the ground. He stood, continued for a few steps, then knelt again. He repeated the process two more times before he looked back at the burn pile. Raven popped her head further into view and waited. Flint gave a whistle and waved her over.

"Cowboy up," she said to Tucker, giving her a final rub on her cheek.

Reaching down, she picked up the Purple Demon and placed it in the holster on her hip. With a deep breath and a squint of her eyes, Raven jogged ahead to join Flint. A surge of nervous excitement reinvigorated her. Only a fuzzy lingering of remorse remained. It would pass with time but would evaporate quicker through actions worthy of a true ranch hand. Doing the job that was given, doing it right, and working tirelessly until it was complete without complaint; that was a language in which Flint was fluent.

As she drew nearer to him, she slowed to a walk. Her heart began to pound and the thrill of getting back on the proverbial horse disappeared. When she finally reached Flint, she placed a hand on his arm. Raven covered her mouth with her other hand, her breath cut short.

"Oh...my god."

Sprawled across the ground lay seven bodies, each contorted in a bloody, final position. Some looked peaceful, resting as they lay. Others looked frozen in a deadly scream with mouths agape, pleading with what had been a final word. Their eyes were glossy, absent of light and full of fear.

"Sons a bitches." Flint said below his breath. Taking in the murderous scene, he added, "Ms. Raven, grab the sat phone from my pack. See if ya can git ahold'a Cass."

CHAPTER TWENTY-ONE

The feel of soft leather of the Range Rover's steering wheel beneath his palms had a calming effect over El Despiadado as he drove toward a private airstrip at the edge of Guaymas, Mexico. Among his many connections, El Despiadado had acquired relationships of necessity within cartel channels as well as with secret contacts of various skills beyond the knowledge of his employer. His former employer. He often felt he did his best work when he was truly invisible to the world, which included Señor de la Droga, and this time would be no different.

It took only a phone call to set things in motion. By the time he pulled into the hangar, a pilot was waiting for him with the plane pre-checked, fully fueled, and ready to take him wherever he asked. He parked parallel to the interior hangar wall, glancing once in the rearview mirror, more out of habit than with concern, then stepped out of the vehicle.

"*Hola* Señor Mata." The pilot gave a welcoming wave. "We are ready to go at your command."

El Despiadado acknowledged him with a nod. He talked as he approached the plane. "*Gracias*, Capitán

Vazquez. As soon as I can unload and stow the few things I have brought, we can be on our way."

"*Muy bien, señor.* Where would you like to go?"

"If it is not too much trouble, I will tell you once we are in the air. This is a trip for me alone. No need for logbooks or flight plans. I will double your fee for your consideration and discretion."

"*Sí, señor.* It is no trouble at all."

El Despiadado returned to the Range Rover, opened the rear hatch, and began rummaging around for his things. Capitán Vazquez leaned to one side, a failed inconspicuous attempt to see what El Despiadado was unloading, then called out, "Can I help you with your things?" He waited but received no reply.

After a moment, El Despiadado emerged from the SUV with two duffel bags and a backpack. One duffel was long and skinny, the contents of which gave the army green bag a weighted look. The other was no larger than a typical nylon blue gym bag with a small dark stain on one side. The backpack was made of black canvas, had a tactical flair about it sporting metal carabiners and hooks to hold things on its exterior, and had plenty of pockets.

The pilot folded his hands before his waist and waited patiently for his passenger. When El Despiadado walked past, Capitán Vazquez followed him to the front of the plane and stood by and watched him stow his gear behind the passenger seat. When El Despiadado finished, he turned to Capitán Vazquez.

"Let's not waste any time."

The captain gave a dutiful smile. El Despiadado loaded himself into the front passenger seat of the plane and buckled up. Capitán Vazquez secured his door, then hurried around to the pilot's seat and strapped himself in. He adjusted his seat, then methodically began the preflight checks. His hands moved with practiced ease over the array of dials and switches, checking the avionics, the engine controls, and the flight instruments.

El Despiadado inspected the interior of the Cessna while he waited. Behind the pilot's seat were two more rows of seats that were meant to carry four additional passengers. He noticed a small plaque affixed over a rear window with the make and model of the plane, as well as its production year, 1986. The cabin was free of trash and looked to be well-maintained given the age of the aircraft. He saw a first aid kit bungy-strapped to the rear wall panel. A leather satchel stood upright on the floor behind the pilot's seat. El Despiadado's gear was carefully stowed behind him and within an arm's reach.

"All set." Capitán Vazquez put on his headset, then motioned for El Despiadado to do the same. Once in place, he gave a smile and a thumbs up. "Now we will be able to hear each other when we speak."

El Despiadado gave a curt nod. "What are we waiting for?"

Without another word, Capitán Vazquez turned the key to start the engine and the propeller whirred to life. He released the brakes and gently applied power. With ease, the Cessna 206 rolled out of the hangar and taxied toward the open runway. Vibrations from the prop and engine buzzed through the airframe causing soft tingles in the seats and a gentle buzzing to spread about the cabin.

The grass beside the runway swayed as the plane passed, disturbed by the propeller's wash. Reaching the runway threshold, Capitán Vazquez lined up the Cessna with the center of the runway and brought the plane to a complete stop. He donned a pair of aviator sunglasses and gave himself a confident nod.

"Hold on, *señor*. This is the best part."

El Despiadado tightened his seat belt.

Capitán Vazquez advanced the throttle. The engine's roar grew louder, and the plane moved forward, gaining speed as they began to race down the runway.

The landscape outside blurred as the Cessna accelerated, the rumble of the wheels on the runway and the growl of the engine filling the cabin. Capitán Vazquez scanned the horizon and instrument panel in a continuous cross check waiting for the airspeed indicator to reach the takeoff threshold. DrufEl Despiadado felt a rush of adrenaline surge through him and his stomach seemed to drop from his belly when the pilot pulled back on the yoke and the airplane lifted off the ground.

With its nose pointed toward the sky, the plane climbed gracefully into the air. They banked right and climbed higher still. El Despiadado looked out his window and watched as the airfield became but a change of hue in the landscape below. With the ground pulling away, the plane leveled off.

A crackle erupted in El Despiadado's headset, followed by Capitán Vazquez's voice.

"So, *señor*. Where are we flying today? Somewhere nice, I hope. Cabo San Lucas? Mexico City? I have enough fuel to reach Cancún but will need to refuel before we return."

"Take me south of Camargo to Rancho del Halcón. They have a private airstrip. It is rough but will serve our purpose."

"*Sí, señor*. I know the place. I have seen it from the air but have never had reason to land there before. It will not be a problem." Capitán Vazquez paused, then spoke again. "How long do you plan to stay?"

El Despiadado twisted his head and watched his pilot tighten his grip on the steering yoke with growing nervousness.

"You ask a lot of questions for a man who is to be paid double."

Capitán Vazquez did not respond.

"You would like to know the whole plan? Sure. Here it is. You will take me to Rancho del Halcón where a car is parked and waiting for me. Once we have landed, you will remain with the plane until I return from Camargo where I intend to pay a final visit to Señor de la Droga. He is not expecting me, which is why I asked for your discretion. I will be in a hurry to leave and will call you on this phone when I am heading back to you."

El Despiadado reached into his backpack and pulled out a small cell phone and placed it in a cup holder.

"You must be ready to take off as soon as I return. Have the engine running and my door open. Then, we will fly back to Guaymas where your pockets will be heavier and my load will be lighter."

"Oh," Capitán Vazquez said meekly. "A *final* visit?"

El Despiadado shifted his body and rested his head back against the seat.

"Now that you know the plan, you would do well to stay out of sight once we land. Should you be discovered, you may feel compelled to reveal why we have come. Just remember that when you talk, you are the one responsible for transporting the man who planned to kill Señor de la Droga. How safe will you truly feel when sharing what you know? Will you fear the men who are asking, or will you wonder that if I find out, I might be coming to look for you next?"

The headset crackled once, then went silent. Capitán Vazquez licked his lips, then found what El Despiadado considered a good answer in reply.

"I will stay hidden in the plane."

El Despiadado closed his eyes. "I will be gone for at least a day."

Capitán Vazquez swallowed hard.

"It is no problem Señor Mata. Take all the time you need."

Mata, El Despiadado thought. *Mata could never do what I am planning to do.*

CHAPTER TWENTY-TWO

The gray skies and dimming light from a retiring sun made the landscape look bland, a monochromatic encroachment that transformed the colorful familiarity of the CR into a desolate space. Raven was somewhere out there, and the gunshots were not a welcomed sound.

The rumble and grind of the off-road tires on my UTV and the churn of its engine combined to create a low growl as we cut through the dirt and dried shrubbery at high speed in the direction of the blasts. I had purchased the Polaris Ranger 1000 Premium 4x4 side-by-side earlier in the fall following a forgettable first full day's horseback experience. My inner thighs were the most thankful for the change from a hard leather saddle to premium seats. The Ranger had proved itself worthy on more than one occasion already and was now at it again, carving a trail toward potential danger.

My fingers tightened around the steering wheel. My foot pressed the accelerator with an unrelenting firmness. The speedometer displayed a top speed of sixty miles per hour, a feat Spencer and I had topped during an adrenaline-filled father-son off-road expedition prior to his disappearance and the attacks on the CR and in town.

Now, as the needle flirted past the maximum registered capacity of the speedometer, all I could hope for was that we were headed in the right direction.

Through the thuds and vibrations of the UTV, I felt a tingle in my jeans pocket. I reached in and pulled out my cell phone and glanced at the caller ID. My foot let up just enough to slow our speed from Evel Knievel to moderately dangerous.

"Who is it?" Ray yelled as he continued to squeeze the "oh shit!" handle as named by Spencer.

"Sat phone."

I slowed the UTV to half-breakneck speed and answered the call.

"Flint? That you?"

"*Cass! It's Raven. Where are you? We got problems.*"

"Are you all right? Is anybody hurt?"

"*I'm fine. Flint's fine. But...Cass, something terrible has happened.*"

"Ray and I pulled into the drive and heard gunshots. We are already in the Ranger and on the way out. What is your location?"

"*Near the north fence. There's a burn pile and you'll see the horses.*"

"I know the spot." I pulled on the steering wheel and headed straight for the northern CR property line and punched the gas. "Whatever it is, stay back and don't touch anything. We'll be there soon."

"*O...ay, C...ss.*"

"Raven?"

I pulled the phone from my ear and saw that only one bar's worth of signal strength remained.

"*...ass?... lov...*"

Raven's voice cut short, and the call disconnected. I slipped the useless piece of tech into my pocket and choked the steering wheel.

"Trouble still brewing?"

"Don't think so, but by the sounds of it, our shit ta do pile just got bigger."

"Great," Ray said. "Nothin' like no sleep before a mission. You'd think we were back in Dragon Company."

"Then you're used to it," I said, slapping him on the leg.

I found the floor with my foot once more and accelerated to ridiculous. My mind raced. Raven's voice was clear, concise, but there was definite concern mixed in. It made my heart stop jackhammering inside my chest to know she was safe, but the mystery of what she was facing toyed with my imagination.

The wind blew cold against my face. Even beneath my thin woven, cotton Astros t-shirt, my skin was riddled with goosebumps. Every Texan knows that the weather can change in an instant. One minute it's warm and dry, the next it's high winds and pouring rain with drastic temperature drops. It is a constant joke back in Houston that we could experience summer and winter on the same day. The same goes for West Texas, and I had made the mistake of not being properly prepared. Learning the hard way out here is becoming all too familiar, but that was not going to stop me.

I continued to drive like a bat out of hell until I spotted the fence line and what looked like two grazing horses on the horizon. Before long, two horses, the burn pile, and the images of two people milling about came into focus. I pulled next to the barbwire that separated the CR from the Double SS and eased my foot off the accelerator as we drew near.

"That Raven?" Ray said, pointing to a person waving their hands high above their head.

"Looks like."

Upon approach, nothing seemed too out of the ordinary. I pulled up short of the burn pile and cut the engine. Raven met us, her eyes deep, her face wearing an unmis-

takable veil of concern. Before I could fully exit the
Ranger, she wrapped herself around me.

"Oh, god. Cass. It was terrible."

"What was, Raven? Where is Flint?" I could feel her
heart thump as I pulled her close to me.

Before she could answer, I heard Ray's voice. He had
wandered away from the Ranger and was looking at Flint
across the fence. "He's walking among the dead."

CHAPTER TWENTY-THREE

I t took Chance close to thirty minutes to arrive on scene. Deputy Marie Bostwick and Deputy Diego Leo followed at a slower pace, leading what looked like a small fleet of refrigerated coroner's vans across the rugged Double SS terrain. It was getting close to the golden hour, but with the overcast skies, darkness seemed to storm in ahead of schedule. Raven, Flint, Ray, and I stood huddled together as Chance took everything in.

"What a travesty," he said, his voice wavering in disbelief. "How did y'all get wrapped up in all this?"

"Bad timing is all, Chance," Raven answered.

He looked her up and down. "Cass told me yer ranch handin' it these days."

"I am. Doing what I can to help out. Flint's been guiding me along, telling me what to do."

Chance turned his attention to Flint. "You tell her ta follow ya here? A might dangerous don't ya think?"

"Ranchin' can be dangerous work, Sheriff, especially out here. Don't act like you don't know that."

"I know it all too well. I just wonder if yer decision to..."

Raven stepped forward, interrupting Chance. "The only condition I placed on Flint when he agreed to take me on was to treat me like any other ranch hand, no matter the conditions. We found a load of trash near the grove. After we burned it, we found and followed the tracks of whoever left it behind, which led us here. We were hiding behind the burn pile and saw seven people on foot. That's when a truck arrived. Two men got out and started shouting. A few of the walkers loaded some things in the bed of the pickup, then stepped aside as if waiting for something. That's when the men with the truck started shooting."

Tears formed at the corners of Raven's eyes.

"It was a game to them. They shot once in the air and the group of seven started to run. That's when they opened fire and didn't stop until everyone was dead."

We all listened intently. Chance nodded, then said, "Y'all hunkered down, didn't try ta stop 'em?"

Flint and Raven shared a glance. Chance noticed.

"What were we supposed ta do, Sheriff?" Flint said, his voice rising in defense. "I'll tell ya...nothin', 'cept stay out of sight and call you when it was all over."

I spoke up. "What's done is done. The most important thing here is you're both safe." I turned to Chance. "Raven's right though, this is bad timing. Come first light, Ray and I, we be in the field, unreachable for at least forty-eight hours. Hate to say it, but this looks pretty cut and dried. Drug runners paying off their mules with a bullet instead of a new life. The best we can hope for tonight is to find something on one of the bodies that can identify them, where they came from, or who they were working for. We can follow the tire marks and see where they lead, but my guess is that they'll find pavement soon enough and disappear."

"You make this sound like an unsolvable situation, Cass," Chance said, sounding a bit surprised.

"Not unsolvable. Let's get to work and see what we come up with. It's going to be dark soon enough." I turned to Raven. "You can stay or head back to the house. You and

Flint have seen enough today, but I'm not about to make any demands of you." I glanced at Flint. "Either of you."

Flint nodded. Raven nodded as well. To my surprise, they both turned and walked back toward the burn pile and the horses.

"She's tougher'n you, Cass," Ray said, watching her go.

"That she is."

The next few hours we had the undesirable task of working with the bodies of seven illegals shot dead in their tracks. Ray joined Deputy Bostwick and followed the tire treads. Deputy Leo and I worked with the coroners and began preliminary procedures to document and iden-tify the victims while collecting any forensic evidence in the process. Chance coordinated with DPS in Lajitas via radio. He gave descriptions of the truck and conveyed the urgency of the situation with an estimated time frame for the suspect's escape, all in an effort to secure assistance in locating the fleeing vehicle.

The grayness of the world faded as I guessed life would escape a dying man—a slow drift into darkness. Ray and Deputy Bostwick returned empty-handed, and our documenting efforts were beginning to wind down. I stood with Chance and leaned back on his Bronco. The metal was cool to the touch.

"This is not how I expected today to go," I said.

"Most days are like that for guys like us, aren't they, amigo?"

I nodded. Ray joined us. Chance offered him a hand.

"I appreciate your assistance today, Detective Tucker. A man who is off duty should not be drawn into problems that are not his own."

I started to speak, but Ray beat me to the punch.

"Off duty?" He laughed as if someone had missed the punchline of a bad joke. "Guys like us are never off duty."

"Sheriff Gilbert," Deputy Leo called out from the side of one of the bodies. "Better come have a look."

The three of us walked in step and circled around Deputy Leo and the corpse he was kneeling beside. It was a man who looked to be in his early twenties. He had dark hair, a dark mustache, and long sideburns. His cheeks showed day-old stubble. He wore a blue flannel shirt stained with blood from wounds to his chest and stomach, faded blue jeans, and tattered boots.

"Here," he said, lifting the flap of the victim's flannel. "Check out the tat."

Inked over his chest was a blackened skull with the words *Sombras y Sangre* wrapped around the bottom like a smile.

"*Sombras y Sangre*," I said. "What does that mean?"

"Shadows and Blood," Deputy Leo said.

"Mean anything to you, Cass?" Ray asked.

"It should," Chance said.

"Yeah. Shadows and Blood. It's the Camargo cartel's calling card," I replied, my voice heavy with realization. "This guy was one of theirs, no doubt about it. The tattoo is a badge, signifying his allegiance to the cartel. But it also makes him a target for rival gangs. Being marked like that, it's a constant reminder of the dangerous world he lived in. Operating from the shadows, they're not afraid to spill blood to maintain their power."

"Probably a NarcoEscolta," Chance added.

"A what?" Ray asked.

"They are like a shepherd watching over their flock. The cartel will sometimes send someone to make sure their drug couriers complete their task without interference or complications."

Ray shook his head. "So, he was killed by his own men?"

"Maybe. Hopefully," Chance replied.

"Hopefully? Where are you going with this?"

"If he was killed by the men in the truck and they were also Camargo cartel, that would be unfortunate for them, but—"

I interrupted. "But if the men in the truck were not with the Camargo cartel, we may have a bigger problem on our hands."

"Exactly," Chance agreed.

Ray clapped his hands together, then motioned as if he were washing them. "Well, it's a good thing we're gonna lop the head of this de la Droga mother fucker. Could be that we kill two birds with one stone."

Chance pursed his lips. "You two head out. We'll wrap things up here. When you get to the Presidio-Ojinaga International Bridge, there'll be only one lane until yer in Mexico, then it splits into separate red and green lanes. Stay left."

"You make the call?" I asked.

"*Sí, mi amigo.* I made the call."

Ray and I turned to walk away when Chance called out.

"One more thing...give my regards to Señor de la Droga."

"Will do," I said.

"And, Cass..." Chance gave me a look more solemn or devoted than I had ever received from him before. "Don't miss."

CHAPTER TWENTY-FOUR

Sunset kissed the horizon, sending beams of brilliance across the earth below. The mountains to the north and west caught the light full faced. The gliding shadow of the Cessna 206 rippled over the ground, hurdling buildings and mixing with patches of trees, growing ever larger as the plane made its slow descent.

El Despiadado's headset crackled, then Capitán Vazquez's voice rang in his ears.

"Señor Mata, we are nearly there. We should be on the ground in just a few minutes."

"Very good. I see we have made excellent time. Good job."

"*Sí, señor*. The best." Capitán Vazquez looked ahead, a proud smile reaching from ear to ear.

The plane circled the airfield once before making its landing approach. The ranch looked deserted. With the exception of a single orange windsock blowing in the breeze, there was no movement to be seen, no curious or wandering bodies wondering who might be landing. The fields were empty as was the runway. A corrugated metal hangar large enough to house two small planes side by side stood at the far end of the tarmac. In the last light of day, it looked more like a gaping mouth or the entrance to a cave.

Upon final approach, the engine altered its pitch from a high-volume constant hum to a lower churn as the pilot reduced speed in preparation for landing. As the runway neared, the pilot expertly performed a flare, gently raising the nose of the aircraft to ensure a smooth and graceful touchdown.

El Despiadado sat patiently, his nerves calm, his mind focused on what was to come next, and did not notice when the wheels met the runway. Capitán Vazquez applied the brakes and throttled down the engine.

"Yeah. Now that was a greaser if I ever saw one!"

El Despiadado pointed to the hangar. "Park inside there."

Capitán Vazquez steered the plane to the end of the runway, then headed for the hangar. The whir of the propeller became amplified as they entered the large metal shelter. Once inside, he turned the nose of the plane to face outward, then cut the engine.

Without a word, El Despiadado unlatched his belt and opened his door. He exited the aircraft, stretching once his feet hit the ground. Looking around, he saw the car he was counting on waiting for him as expected. A black GMC Trailblazer was parked along the far, curved wall of the hangar. Its tinted windows and black rims made it look like a shadow at first glance.

"Good," he said. "You are right where you were meant to be."

El Despiadado turned and reached into the plane and began removing his things. Capitán Vazquez remained in the pilot's seat and watched.

"Remember the plan." El Despiadado's voice was direct, firm. "One day. Keep the cell phone charged and be ready when I need you."

"*Sí, señor.* I will be right here."

With a glare bordering on threatening and a nod to

Capitán Vazquez, El Despiadado whirled around with his gear and walked away from the plane.

The SUV was unlocked. He opened the rear hatch and stowed his bags, then walked around to the driver's side door and got in. He found the keys in the center console, fired up the engine, and drove out of the hangar. Camargo was a short drive from Rancho del Halcón and El Despiadado had things to do.

His first stop would be Hotel San Luis. The meager hotel was off the beaten path and offered a degree of anonymity to its occupants. It was not high class by any means, mostly catering to hourly customers and those who wished to simply disappear for a while. He had a standing room, paid each year in advance which afforded him the opportunity to come and go as he pleased with minimal interactions between him and hotel staff. The maids were made aware of the room's occupancy following each stay, so no one knew exactly when he was coming, only when he had already left.

The glow of the navigation screen in the dash illuminated the interior of the Trailblazer like candles on a cake. El Despiadado's face absorbed the light, but his eyes, his steely eyes remained black pits. He drove in silence, listening to the hum of his tires and the rise and fall of music fading in and out of range from passing vehicles. One such vehicle, however, did not pull away like the others. It hovered in the lane next to him, surging forward, then falling back a bit, but for at least a mile, did not leave his side. El Despiadado smiled, his teeth gleaming like a jackal.

Fifty feet ahead, a traffic light turned from green to yellow, then to a glaring red. El Despiadado slowed to a stop, as did the car next to him. Music blared from inside the vehicle. The car bounced as if its occupants were in full-on party mode. El Despiadado removed his right hand from the steering wheel. With one quick motion, the passenger doors of the adjacent car flew open. Smoke and music spilled out as two men jumped from their seats, each holding handguns pointed at the black SUV.

The front-seated man lunged at El Despiadado's door, yanking at the handle and screamed.

"Abre la puerta, puta. Open the door, or I will kill you!"

The red light beamed overhead. El Despiadado unlatched his seat belt, then pressed a button on the door panel and unlocked the door. The carjacker ripped the door open and shoved his gun in El Despiadado's face. Before he knew what was happening, the man found himself being pulled into the vehicle. El Despiadado had grabbed the man's wrist, twisted the gun away from him and heaved him off balance. With his right hand, he thrust the blade of his combat knife forward, a true friend and extension of his arm, into the neck of his assailant.

El Despiadado then rose from the car, shielding himself with the first attacker's body while manhandling him like a master puppeteer. The second man advanced but was met with a flurry of bullets shot from his dying friend's gun. He twitched as each bullet pierced his torso until a final shot found a lethal spot beneath the bridge of the man's nose. His face split in two just before he crumpled to the street.

El Despiadado fired into the vehicle. The windows shattered, and the music died, as did the remainder of the occupants inside. Feeling the weight of the man in his arms, El Despiadado fired one final bullet into the back of his head then let him fall away. He looked at the bloody remains of the botched attack and shook his head as if disappointed in the men's lack of skill.

In a matter of moments, that which had started was now over. Two thugs lay dead in the street, their car and driver's fate just as grim. Above the intersection, the red light blinked out and turned green. El Despiadado tossed the handgun onto the body of its former owner, got back into his SUV, and closed the door. He took a moment to wipe blood from his hands, then slowly pulled away.

Night fell over central Mexico. Speckles of light from the city broke through the blackness, but still, the darkness loomed. El Despiadado was used to the dark. It was when monsters lurked about. When he was a child, he had been afraid of what he could not see. His imagination ran rampant, materializing beasts and killers around every corner. Now, he was the beast. He was the killer. He was the king of monsters and tonight he was hungry for blood.

CHAPTER TWENTY-FIVE

Takeout barbecue from the Lone Star Smokery, Brewster's newest restaurant optimally located south of town and already growing a reputation for their delicious meats, a few cold beers, and a roaring fire pit did nothing to ease any of our minds following the tumultuous day we each had experienced. I sat with Raven draped across my lap. Ray stretched out in his chair, propping his feet close to the fire. Even Flint stuck around, which was a rare but welcomed occasion. None of us spoke. Not at first anyway. The flames flickered off each of our faces, telling a story of its own, though I do not think any of us paid close attention. We looked like zombies frozen in a hypnotic trance, waiting for something to stimulate us beyond our little group.

Finally, Raven broke the monotony. "You think more will come?"

"They always do," Flint said. "It's a cycle. Sometimes comes in waves. Ain't nothin' that can stop it."

Ray sat up in his chair and leaned forward inspecting the beer bottle in his hand.

"We'll see what me and Cass can do about that."

Flint tilted his head and spoke to Ray. "Look, I ain't sayin' what yer plannin' ta do ain't gonna work. But it ain't gonna solve the bigger problem. So, you arrest a few, maybe kill a few. Hell, takin' out the cartel leader might make a pretty good dent, but them Mexican drug cartels flow like water. When one hole opens up in the dam, they each fight ta try an' be the next one through."

"One at a time," I said, taking the attention. "We don't have to stop them all at once. That would never happen, but one by one?"

"You aim ta take 'em all down, Cass?" Flint said.

"If it comes to that, but the Camargo cartel and their dog, Mata, are the first ones on my list. That's what matters most to me right now. Seeing them crumble means keeping this place safe." I raised my beer and circled it above my head. "Keeping my family safe."

I lowered my hand and polished off the remaining drink in the bottle. I could feel Raven's arms tighten around me. I knew she was afraid, but she was in my corner one hundred percent.

"I need you to keep a watchful eye around here until we get back, Flint."

"Always do," he replied with a smirk, then drained the last swigs of his beer.

I huffed softly and nodded my head. Raven slid off my lap and stood up.

"There's more in the fridge. Anyone want another?" she offered.

"Till they're gone, Raven," Ray said.

Flint tipped his empty bottle, signaling he could use another.

"Thanks, Rave," I said.

We watched her walk to the house. When the door swung closed, I turned and faced Flint.

"You need to know this. Only you, so I'll be quick. We learned earlier today that there is an informant for the cartel, most likely within the FBI field office in El Paso. They know about our operation. They know we are coming."

Flint tossed his bottle into the fire pit, then gave me a stern look.

"An' yer goin' anyway? You hopin ta get killed, Cass?"

I ignored Flint's comment and continued. "Ray and I altered the plan, but yes, we're going first thing tomorrow. If all goes well, we'll be back within twenty-four hours." I glanced over my shoulder at the house; no sign of Raven returning, yet. "You know we killed the sicario who attacked Raven and her friend here at the ranch and that the other bastard got away scot-free. I'm telling you this because if the cartel knows we're coming, they might send somebody back to finish what they started. I don't have any intel suggesting that, but it's something we must consider."

"They're some proud sons a bitches," Ray said. "Wouldn't put anything past 'em."

The front door clanged shut, drawing our secret conversation to a close. Raven returned with beers all around.

"I didn't miss anything, did I?"

An unfortunate pause in reply caused Raven to lock eyes with me. Flint swooped in for the save.

"No, Ms. Raven. We were just talkin' about the CR's newest ranch hand. A little green around the ears, but tougher'n nails."

Raven brushed her hair back with her fingers. "Green, huh?"

She moved opposite the fire as if taking center stage, twisted the cap off her beer, and chugged. Ray cheered her on. Flint smiled and shook his head, laughing under his breath. A surge of pride welled up inside of me as I watched my badass wife step up to the plate once again to prove her worth among the rugged. When the bottle was empty, she tossed it in the fire and belched louder than a bullfrog in heat. She wiped her mouth, flipped each of us the bird, smiling all the while, then finally bowed to a round of applause and whistles before returning to her spot on my lap.

She kissed me. The taste of cold beer hung on her lips. When we parted, she gazed into my eyes, taking what was left of my breath in one lasting stare. A quiet filled the space where laughter and braggery had just been.

The crackle of burning wood overtook the silence around us. A swirl of rising embers caught in a fiery dance hovered like distant stars beneath the overcast sky. Ray slunk back in his chair and crossed his feet at the edge of the fire pit. Flint looked out toward the CR. I wondered what thoughts, or memories perhaps, had entered his mind. Raven lay her head on my shoulder, nuzzling close.

This was how the world was meant to be—peaceful, full of friends and family, a kind of Christmas morning hangover feeling. I closed my eyes and let it all soak in.

As was my life, distractions or interruptions seemed to know exactly when I was least ready for them, so the rumble of frustration that erupted in my gut mirrored the buzzing of my cell phone tucked in my pocket. Raven felt it too, which caused her to shift positions, then get off me altogether.

"Back to work," she whispered.

The phone continued to buzz as I watched her gather a handful of empty bottles, and head for the house.

I dug into my pocket, silently cursing whoever was on the other end of the line. I glanced at the caller ID. PRIVATE.

"You again?"

Ray shot me a glance.

"Girlfriend?"

"Nope. Private number again."

"You gonna answer it?"

I looked at the phone. The dark bold letters P-R-I-V-A-T-E dared me to engage.

"Nope. If it's important, they'll leave a message."

"Probably some red dot offering their overseas tech support expertise," Ray said.

I pressed the red *decline* button and set the phone on my lap. Ray was one of a kind in many ways. One of which was that he really did not like people. Not just one group or another, Ray despised everyone. His comments were always so colorful, regardless of who he spoke about, but I knew a different side to Ray. Deep down, he was a humanitarian at heart. He had served his country. Now, he worked to serve and protect as a detective back home in Houston. Why else would he put his life on the line for those same people he so despised? As calloused and crude as he was, Ray was a good man, and he was my friend. There was no one else on earth I would want standing by my side when the shit hit the fan.

The remaining logs in the fire pit were charred. A bed of orange glowing coals lay beneath them. A thin line of smoke drifted up from the center of the ashen pile like the tendril stream of a dangling cigarette. A chill moved in where the flames had been, cooling the air around us.

"Fellas, I'm callin' it a night." Flint stood up and brushed his thighs. He stepped over to me and offered a hand. "You be careful. Don't you worry one bit about us back here. Ain't nothin or nobody gonna git close to Ms. Raven while I'm around."

"Thank you, Flint." I stood and took his hand. We shook once, then he turned to Ray. "An' you, too. Keep this guy in the saddle." He thumbed a hand at me, then turned without another word and walked away.

"Where'd you find him?" Ray asked, his voice teetering on sarcastic.

"Oh, he was born from the earth and rocks right here on the CR. I imagine he'll die here too, one day."

"Kinda salty if you ask me. I like him." Ray slapped me on the back. "Come on, princess. We both know you need your beauty sleep."

As we walked to the house, I felt a soft, pulsing vibra-

tion in my pocket. This time, the notification was different. Someone had just sent me a text. Once we were inside
the house and Ray had headed to the guest room, I walked
through the kitchen and laundry room to my uncle's old
office. I turned on a lamp at the edge of the large, walnut
desk that commanded the center of the room and sat
down in the wingback chair behind it. Pulling my cell
phone out, I pressed the texting icon and read the
message.

¿Listo para jugar con fuego?

I reached below the desk into the kneehole and
removed my chrome cast-reinforced aluminum tactical
case. I dialed the code on its combination lock, opened it,
and removed my Heckler and Koch G36. With ease and
experience, I assembled the rifle and tucked the butt into
my shoulder, taking aim at the darkness through the
office window.

"Am I ready to play with fire?" I whispered. "Hell yes."

CHAPTER TWENTY-SIX

E l Despiadado sat in the dark. The blinds covering the window in his small room were cinched closed. Muffled voices spoke somewhere outside, but he paid them no mind. Situated across his lap was a Savage Arms 110 BA Stealth sniper rifle that he had just finished reassembling. He reached into his army green duffel, retrieving a ten-round magazine, and began loading it with Federal Gold Medal .308 Winchester Hollow Point Boat Tail rounds. One by one, he slid each round in place, repeating the same phrase for each deadly bullet, "*Portador del destino, mensajero de la muerte*, bearer of fate, messenger of death."

A Sig Sauer P320-M17 boasting a SureFire Ryder 9M Ti suppressor, and two seventeen-round steel magazines loaded to capacity with Sig V-Crown 9mm rounds lay on the bed behind him. His duffel lay empty at his feet.

When he finished loading the final round, he set the magazine and the rifle to one side and stood. Activating his cell phone, he opened the camera app and walked to the bathroom. He turned the light on and stepped over to the bathtub. The smaller nylon bag sat on the acrylic surface beneath the water faucet. El Despiadado leaned over and unzipped the bag.

The first thing he pulled out was a pair of latex gloves. Like an experienced surgeon, El Despiadado donned the pair and removed the next item from the heavy-duty, black lawn bag. The contents made a dull thud as he placed it in the tub. He removed the empty duffel and tossed it out of the bathroom door, then proceeded to untie the knot holding the lawn bag closed. His eyes squinted as he worked, his mind and thoughts steadfast. When the knot had been undone, El Despiadado reached into the bag with one hand and readied the camera on his phone with the other.

"Time to deliver a message as promised, my friend."

El Despiadado lifted his arm and removed the severed head of the man from Guaymas, one of the men that had tried to kill him but was left for dead by the marina. His eyes had crusted over. The skin on his face was gray. Trails of dried fluid streaked from his nose and the corners of his mouth.

"If only I could send the smell along with your picture." El Despiadado crinkled his nose at the stench. "Now, be a good man and smile for El Jefe."

One picture was all he needed. For a moment he contemplated as to why he had waited so long to snap the photo and questioned his reasoning for bringing the head along in the first place. When it came down to it, it was not a question of why, but a question of necessity. Had he left it to roll away from its body, or to bob around in the marina as fish food, he might have regretted not having it along for the job. Besides posing for pictures, it may come in handy, and El Despiadado prided himself on always being prepared.

He attached the photo to a text message, assigned the number, and sent the text.

"Come, my friend. Back in the bag. I may need you again." El Despiadado paused and looked at the decomposing head in his hand. "What was that? You're afraid of the dark?" He smiled. "Do not worry. Soon, I imagine, you will have some company to call your own. Then you will not be so afraid."

He set the head back in the bag, then twisted and knotted the opening. The plastic stretched as if recoiling from its grisly contents when El Despiadado lifted the bag out of the tub. He placed it in the sink before walking to the window. He held his cell phone in view, waiting for his message to be received.

CHAPTER TWENTY-SEVEN

The clock on my bedside table read 4:14 and I was wide awake. It was dark, save for the glow from a hallway nightlight flirting with the base of the bedroom door. I lay under the covers with my arms supporting the back of my head. I had tossed my pillow across the room hours earlier when sleep seemed to be too far out of reach. Instead, I stared at the ceiling and visualized the moment when I would stand face to face with the man who bought me coffee, then killed my friends.

Raven slept by my side making chirping noises as she breathed. I rolled over and watched her sleep for a time. Even in the dim light, her beauty was striking. Pure and natural. I wondered something I had always wondered— how could I be so lucky?

My thoughts shifted from how I would end things with Carlos Ruiz-Mata, El Despi-fucking-adado, to memories further back in time when Raven and I first met. I replayed my first attempt to kiss her. It was a life fail, but a story that would outlast us all. I laid my hand on her hip as I fell deeper into that moment so long ago. God, how I wish life were that simple today.

———

"UM, what do you think you are doing?" Raven said, dodging her head back from mine.

"I...uh...thought maybe?"

"Maybe what?" She stepped back one step while producing the craftiest of smiles. "You used to girls that just...go for it?"

I cocked my head to one side feeling somewhat confused. All the signals I had picked up, all the tells I knew were giving me the green light, it was textbook kiss me now material. My mouth dried up, but I forced a swallow as I searched for a reply, the right reply that might get me out of the hole I was in and back in the driver's seat.

"Yeah...I mean. No. I'm not like that."

"Says who?"

I looked around as if someone behind me had the answer to her question. It was a trick, for sure. That, I was smart enough to know, but for the life of me, I had no answer that did not paint me as any other horn-dog college boy. I tried to change the subject. Mistake number two.

"I like your eyes."

Raven balled her fists and punched them on her hips.

"My eyes?"

"And your name is cool, too."

Her mouth fell open as if she had just heard some shocking news. She followed that up with a laugh, only covering her mouth after shooting a drop of spit in my face. Her look went from teasing and amused to mortified in an instant.

"I guess I deserved that," I said, wiping my lips and cheek.

"Oh, Cass. I didn't mean to."

It was my turn to laugh, which I did without showering her with the likes of me.

"Well, sorry if I made you uncomfortable. It wasn't what I planned."

She raised an eyebrow, the "hairy eyebrow" as it is now called but did not say anything.

I put my hands in my pockets and turned to one side. "Crash and burn. Way to go, Maverick," I whispered to myself.

"What was that?" she asked, her voice sounding softer than before.

"Nothing." At that moment, I knew I had blown any chance with her. "Listen. I've seen you around campus. I know we've bumped into each other a couple of times. Wish I could say it was by accident."

"So, you're stalking me?"

"No. I mean." *Shit*, I thought. *Nothing is coming out the way it was meant to sound.* I turned my head to look at her feet "I like you. I just..."

Raven surprised me and stepped closer.

"Why would you say that? We don't even know each other."

"I say it because it's true. I like the way you walk. I like how you smile at everybody. I like that you want to become a teacher. I like that you agreed to walk with me to Ice Cream Joe's tonight."

"You a detective, Cass?"

"One day, maybe." I paused to lift my head and look directly at her. "And, I do like your name. Raven." I felt a tingle surge from my neck to my fingers. "It's like you're a beautiful bird. You're just flying too high for me to catch, I guess."

Without warning, Raven stepped into me, pressing her lips to mine with a gentle passion that I was not expecting. It was not the kind of kiss that led anywhere except for her to melt into my arms. The touch of her fingers across my back, the feel of her warmth radiating all over me, and the tender pulse of her lips upon mine were the most magical thing I had ever experienced in my entire life.

When our lips parted, she stayed in my embrace. It

was comfortable. It was natural. It was something that I hoped would last forever. Our eyes met, and I was immediately overwhelmed, lost within her to the point that life, on the outside, did indeed stand still.

With a breath as soft as the flapping of wings, she gazed at me and whispered, "You caught me."

———

A SOFT SNORT followed by the most delicate of sighs pulled me back into the room, back onto the bed, right next to Raven. My wife.

I rolled over, glancing at the red analog numbers of the clock. It was nearing five a.m. which meant go time.

In keeping with our tradition, there was no pre-deployment fooling around or last-minute hurrah before I left. We saved all that for when I returned. Before cutting the lights, Raven kissed me just as she had the night we first started dating. Gentle. Natural. Loving.

I slid my feet off the bed, moving with slow, deliberate movements so I did not disturb her sleep and stood up. I walked to the window and peeked between the blinds. The clouds had vanished leaving a sprinkling of brilliant stars to light the early morning sky.

Twenty-four hours never felt so long, never seemed so far away, but that was the time frame, and the clock was ticking.

CHAPTER TWENTY-EIGHT

R ay before six a.m. is about as pleasant as a
wolverine with a hernia.

"Remind me why I give a fuck about this
Droga character again?" Ray groaned as we pulled off the
CR and headed for town.

"Oh, I don't know. Something to do with almost
having your godson killed, for starters?"

"Yeah, I know, I know. And I gotta make sure his goons
don't put a bullet in your sorry ass."

"Thanks. I'd appreciate that."

Ray slunk over and rested his head against the
passenger window and began to mumble. "Gonna stick
out...like a pimple on a cheerleader."

"What?"

"This thing...your car. Looks like a DPS rig a mile
away."

"Already considered that." I glanced at my cell phone
and saw a new text from Chance. "We're making a pitstop
at impound on the way through Brewster."

"You couldn't have gone car shopping without me?"

"Where's the fun in that? Figured you'd want to have
first refusal."

"Sounds like you already have something in mind."

"That I do."

RR170 gave us a smooth ride, having been recently repaved. The fresh white stripes dividing the northbound and southbound lanes flashed by like tracer rounds on a nighttime combat mission. It set the mood. That, and Ray's snorts as he dozed off reminded me of when we were aboard a C-130 headed for our first tour in Iraq. It was a long and bouncy flight, but somehow Ray slept, even through the worst of it.

The green city limits sign welcoming travelers to Brewster reflected the Explorer's headlights as we passed by. Streetlights were sparse in Brewster, but the illumination of business signs lined the road with their bright, sometimes neon glow. We passed a Sinclair gas station and its animated dinosaur that lifted and lowered its head with alternating passes through three separate neon tubes. A series of construction barricades topped with orange flashing lights looked like cattle waiting to be set to pasture as they stood grouped together ready to block the next stretch of RR170 for a long overdue facelift. The red ellipse of Dairy Queen came into view. I glanced at the parking lot as we drove past and imagined seeing Spencer's car there just like it had been the night he went missing.

Places fall victim to ruin just like people sometimes do, I thought.

A few minutes later, I pulled into the South Brewster County impound yard. As early as it was, I saw Chance's Bronco parked near the sliding chain link gate. I reached over and nudged Ray's shoulder.

"Wake up. We're here."

Ray groaned in protest. As we approached, Chance stepped out of his vehicle and the gate to the yard began sliding open. He waved us through and followed us on foot until I found a spot to park. I watched in the rearview mirror as the gate slid closed.

"Time for some different wheels."

I opened the car door, activating the Explorer's interior dome light.

"Coffee," Ray said. "I need coffee."

"Come on," I said.

I got out and closed the door. Ray followed suit. We met at the rear hatch, waiting for the door to rise when Chance caught up to us.

"*Buenos días, amigos.*"

"Nothin' *bueno* about it."

"Detective Tucker, good to see ya again." The two shook hands, then Chance reached into his pocket and handed me a keychain. "Are ya sure this is what ya want?"

I took the keys from him and nodded.

"I had the yard manager fill 'er up last night. Should get ya ta Camargo and back without a problem."

"And your guy at the border?" I asked.

"Tells me he's on duty 'til noon. He'll be on the lookout. Just remember to stay to the left once yer past the bridge."

I reached into the back of the Explorer and removed two bags and a backpack. I handed one bag to Ray. I kept the rest to myself, then pressed the button on the frame to close the door. I handed the keys to Chance.

"I'll get these from you tomorrow."

"Damn right ya will, Cass."

I glanced at Ray. "You ready?"

He stretched and let out a voracious yawn. "As I'll ever be."

"I'll be standing by the gate to let you out," Chance said.

He headed for the entrance while Ray and I walked to our new ride.

"You've got to be kidding me," he said as we walked up to a small, two-door Toyota Hilux pickup truck. Its white color gave it a ghostly appearance as it sat in the back corner of the yard.

"Yep. This is it."

Ray looked around the impound lot. "We could have had any number of these cars, and this is the one you pick?"

"True, but the owner of this won't be coming to look for it. Ever."

"Pretty sure of yourself."

"Pretty sure of the bullet I put in its owner. This is La Sombra Negra's truck. Unless she's gonna rise from the dead, it's all ours. Plus, I could give a crap what happens to it while we are south of the border."

I placed my bag into the bed of the truck, placed my backpack on the floorboard behind my seat, and got in. Ray walked around to the passenger side and set his bag next to mine beneath the rear window.

"We going to cover the bags in the back?"

"No. If all goes as planned, we should be waved right on through."

"And if things *don't* go as planned?"

I looked at Ray and shrugged. "Won't matter if we cover 'em or not."

"You're putting a lot of faith in your sheriff friend's connections."

"Have to."

"I get it," Ray said with a huff. "Just remember this if things don't go our way."

"What's that," I asked as I turned the key to start the truck.

"Don't drink the water, and for god's sake, don't drop the soap."

I revved the engine, drowning out Ray's comments in a flurry of sick-sounding sputters of the aged truck.

"We'll be fine. Trust me."

Ray gave me the side-eye. "Famous last words, Private."

I pulled the truck out of its parking space and aimed for the gate.

"Going there, huh."

"Just get me some coffee."

"The magical elixir that transforms Lieutenant Tucker from an insatiable drag to a tolerable prick. One coffee, coming up."

I could see Chance standing and waiting for the gate to finish opening as we rolled through the impound yard. By the time we got to the exit, we pulled straight through. I rolled down my window and spoke to Chance.

"Any last words?"

Chance put his hands on the open window ledge and bent over to look inside the truck. "*Sí, mis amigos.* Don't screw up." He smiled his Cheshire smile, then stepped back and tapped the roof of the truck.

He raised a hand, then called out, "*Buena suerte.*"

"Luck," Ray said as we pulled away. "I'll take all we can get."

CHAPTER TWENTY-NINE

E l Despiadado heard the buzz of his cell phone announcing an incoming message and smiled.

"I wonder who that could be?" he said to the empty hotel room. He swung his legs over the edge of the bed and sat up. "Let us see who sends a text at such an early hour."

Standing, he stretched his muscles. The tattoos inked across his body contorted as he twisted one way and then another. The scorpion on his wrist seemed to scuttle up his arm, engaging in a ceremonial dance with the woman and sword etched high above his elbow. The skulls on his right shoulder cackled, each eye socket waving the daggers that were lodged in blackened bone. The Virgin Mary's tears flowed across his chest with each twist, each bend, each crooked motion. He leaned forward to touch his toes, stood straight, then rotated his arms in small circles, working his way to large revolutions. His blood was pumping now, as was his eagerness to verify the sender of the message.

Warmth flowed through him as he crossed the room. He picked up the phone from the dresser and pressed the text icon, opening his thread of messages. Written beneath the photo of the severed head were three words.

He walked to the center of the room, his smile growing wider with each step and read the message aloud.

"You will pay."

He read the words over and over as he walked to the bathroom where he gazed at himself in the mirror. Pasted in the amber glow of the wall socket light, El Despiadado looked more sinister, more evil than he had the pleasure of remembering. It thrilled him. His teeth gnashed onto each other. His eyes seemed to sink into his sockets like tiny black holes hovering above his cheeks. The manner in which he stared at himself helped rage to grow, helped desolation to brew, helped conviction to strengthen, all for one purpose—hunt down and kill Señor de la Droga.

He read the message one more time, now speaking directly to his monstrous reflection. "You will pay." He paused, then answered with slow, deliberate words of his own. "But, of course."

CHAPTER THIRTY

The drive to Presidio took about an hour and a half, which included a quick pit stop at Lucia's Taco Truck at the north edge of town parked just beyond the city limits sign. It was Lucia's usual spot. She claimed it helped her avoid the higher city tax rate versus what she would owe the county once the year was up, but I doubted Lucia ever wrote that check at all. With a grateful smile, she bagged two bacon, egg, and cheese tacos with a small side of red and green salsa for each of us and poured the most scalding cup of coffee possible for Ray.

"Gracias," Ray said to Lucia, raising his cup to her.

Lucia giggled.

We loaded back up in the tiny pickup with food and drinks that should hold our appetites for most of the day. I packed a few protein bars for backup knowing Ray would not partake unless he was starving.

"You can live on 'em, but they taste like shit," was his standard reply whenever I had offered in the past.

I fired up the engine. Lucia gave us a wave from the service window of her converted U-Haul moving truck turned mobile taqueria.

"I think she likes you," I teased.

Ray took a bit of his taco, then spoke as he chewed. "What's...not to...like?"

Now, we sat in the weathered parking lot of the Presidio Payless Shoe Source trading looks at the border crossing through a pair of Swarovski binoculars.

"Doesn't look that bad," Ray said. "More people trying to get into the US than heading to Old Mexico. Typical, but at least they're going about it the right way."

I took another look. "Yeah. Maybe take us ten, maybe fifteen minutes once we roll past the first checkpoint." I lowered the binoculars and noted the time. "It's getting close to nine o'clock. We've got two hours before Special Agent Zuñiga and the rest of the Kill Hydra team misses us. By then, we should be more than halfway to Camargo."

"You gonna give special agent-in-charge a heads up?"

"Let's get safely across the border and out of Ojinaga first. Then, we'll see about letting the cat out of the bag."

"It's your party, Cass. I'm just here for the entertainment."

I opened the door and stepped out of the pickup. The morning air was cool. Moving to the bed of the truck, I leaned in and pulled my duffel to the side, unzipped the zipper, and slid the binoculars inside. The bag's matte gray interior caught my eye. Before zipping it closed, I took a moment to thank the tech gods for creating SpectraVeil, a revolutionary technology hidden within the linings of each of the bags.

On the outside, each duffel looked like an ordinary, oversized sports bag complete with nylon straps, but on the inside, it was a composite marvel, interwoven with rare earth elements and advanced polymers. The key to its effectiveness lay in its ability to scatter X-ray photons, rendering the contents virtually invisible to standard security scanners. It was like looking at a blurred shadow in a fog, impossible to discern. Adding to its versatility, its phase-change microcapsules absorbed and normalized heat signatures, masking them against thermal detection. Having these specific bags was essential for the mission, especially since we were transporting a small cache of weapons across the Mexico border.

A dull tapping sound brought my attention to the rear window of the pickup. Ray's knuckles dangled in the air and the look on his face told me everything he was thinking. *What the hell is taking so long?* I got back into the truck and turned the key.

"Ready?"

Ray rolled down his window and rested his arm on the ledge. "The bad guys aren't waiting around to kill themselves."

"Remember, if anyone asks our business, we are university historians heading south for research."

"Ha! Still think that's a load of horse shit, but I'll play along. Let's hit the road, professor."

I shifted into drive and turned left out of the parking lot. The Presidio-Ojinaga International Bridge loomed ahead with Mexico looking over its shoulder. I was mission focused, but a small semblance of revenge mustered in the center of my chest. I was a soldier. I was an officer of the law. First and foremost, I was a father and a husband, determined to keep my family safe at all costs and by any means necessary. The three internal parts of me had never once come together for something as big or as dangerous as what I was doing, but I felt comfortable knowing they would all work seamlessly together to see the job done.

The road narrowed. Orange cones divided the outgoing and incoming lanes. Cement barricades lined the shoulder preventing anyone from pulling over or trying to cut the line. We approached a large steel canopy marking the first checkpoint. Cameras stood mounted like marksmen waiting to fire as vehicles were instructed to stop at a designated point in the road and wait for a signal from ahead to proceed. Traffic remained sparse in the outgoing lanes, so our turn to wait and wonder if the cameras were detecting anything suspicious on our faces or in our vehicle lasted only a few moments. A green light flashed on a signal stand next to the driver's window allowing us to move ahead.

My stomach tightened as we approached the guards waiting under the canopy. As we pulled closer, my angst turned to disgust when I saw that they were more interested in what was on their cell phones than who was leaving the US. One gave us a glance and waved us past. The other never lifted his head.

"Guess it's adios amigos as far as they are concerned," Ray said once they were behind us.

We continued over the Presidio-Ojinaga International Bridge, crossing the border next to an honorary bronze plaque marker displaying the line between the US and Mexico. The Great Seal of the United States and a Mexican flag were etched on their respective sides of the border. There was no significant inscription. Just the words UNITED STATES OF AMERICA | ESTADOS UNIDOS MEXICANOS.

We passed what looked like an exodus of cars and people waiting for their chance to gain entrance to the US. Looking ahead, the line was just as thick for as far as I could see.

"I bet these folks have been waiting for hours," I said.

"At least they're dry," Ray replied.

"And then there's that." I shook my head, then gripped the wheel tighter. "Round two up ahead. Take a look."

A more formative checkpoint stood at the far end of the bridge. The approach looked similar with the cameras and signage, but there was a distinctive two-lane option beyond the initial stopping point. I applied the brakes, stopping the pickup at the designated spot for incoming vehicles. Looking ahead, the lane to the left, the lane we were supposed to aim for, moved rather quickly. Following what looked like armed border agents asking questions through the driver's side of the cars in front of us, they performed a minimal inspection, walking around each side and looking them over. Of the two cars in front of us, the first was allowed to pass into Ojinaga, Mexico. A red light flashed over the second car as the inspection was being held. The border agents stopped what they were doing and directed the car toward the right lane.

"That's what we don't want," I whispered.

"Hope our guy is there."

"He will be." Then I thought to myself, *he better be*.

Once the vehicle was clear of the lane, we were signaled to pull forward. A young-looking border agent approached the pickup. I rolled down the window and waited for him to greet us.

"Bienvenidos. What is the purpose of your visit to Mexico?"

"We are on a research trip to Mexico City," I said.

"How long do you plan to stay in Mexico?" The agent wore dark sunglasses that prevented us from seeing his eyes.

"Couple of days, four to be exact. Have to get back to the university for class next week."

"University?" The agent stepped closer to the window. He spoke with an air of curiosity. "Which university?"

Ray leaned over and spoke directly to the border agent. "Por favor, disculpe a mi colega. Somos de la Universidad del Verbo Encarnado en San Antonio. Es la primera vez que él viene a México."

The border agent glanced at me, then back at Ray. "His first time coming to Mexico, huh?" He stepped back away from the window and adjusted his glasses. "Good luck with your research. Pull forward."

I smiled and nodded, then released the brake. The pickup rolled forward.

"That wasn't so bad," Ray said under his breath.

"Since when do you speak Spanish?" I asked.

Ray gave me the side-eye and smirked. The lanes ahead were clear. The green light pulsed in front of us.

"I think you may owe me a margarita for that one," Ray said, leaning back as far as he could in the tiny cab.

As we approached the checkpoint, my heart went from rest mode to full-on sprint when the green light before us changed to red. Two guards stepped onto the road and motioned for us to enter the right lane.

"Shit," Ray said, sitting up in his seat. "This can't be good."

"No kidding."

I turned on the right blinker and followed the marked lines to a stopping point where a sign with dark, bold letters read, *Estación de Inspección. Apague su motor— Inspection Station. Turn off your engine.*

I pulled to a stop and cut the engine. An older border agent walked to the front of the truck, pulled a notepad from his pocket, and flipped through the pages before he stopped to read his notes. He looked up at us, then back at his notepad before returning it to his pocket. He appeared cautious as he approached the driver's side window.

"This our guy?" Ray whispered through his teeth.

"No idea," I said, smiling as I turned to meet the border agent's gaze.

"¿Este es su vehículo?" The man repeated the question in English. "Is this your vehicle?"

I looked the agent square in the eyes and lied. "Yes, sir. Bought it at auction just last month. Fun little truck."

The man looked at a second agent observing from behind cradling a Heckler & Koch G3 rifle. The inspecting agent turned back to me and spoke with a low, subdued tone.

"This is not your vehicle, and you did not purchase it at any auction. I know this truck. It is the truck of the cartel killer, La Sombra Negra."

He squinted his eyes, searching the depth of mine for information. He parted his lips, revealing yellowed teeth in desperate need of dental care. His mouth was close enough to me that I could hear his breathing and smell his breath. He leaned closer still.

"I also know that you are the man who killed that savage beast of a woman."

Without another word, he retreated from the window and stood straight. With a simple glide of his hand before him, he signaled us to go.

Our eyes remained locked as I started the engine, and though I broke free to drive away, I could see in the rearview mirror that he followed us with his gaze until we had driven out of sight.

The cab of the pickup remained quiet for some time. As the distance from the border crossing grew, I began to rediscover the feeling in my legs when my heart allowed what blood had stopped pumping through my veins to flow free once again.

"That was not what I expected," I said.

"Yup. My butt was puckerin' pretty tight there for a minute." Ray shifted back and forth in his seat.

After a series of right and left turns, we found ourselves heading south on CHIH67. Camargo was 160 miles to the south, which meant we had a three-hour drive ahead of us. With the road becoming more desolate with each passing mile, I felt it was time to let Agent Zuñiga in on my change of plans. I reached into the cup holder on the center console and picked up my cell phone. I opened my list of contacts and scrolled until I found Agent Thomas Zuñiga's number, then hit send.

"Time to let the cat out of the bag?" Ray asked.

"Something like that," I said as I waited for my call to be answered.

CHAPTER THIRTY-ONE

El Despiadado did his best to let only the parts of Carlos Ruiz-Mata he wished to use run free as he interacted with a barista in Café del Zócalo.

"The smells inside are so invigorating. How do you get anything done?"

The young barista smiled. "It is what it is because we have mastered the art of our one true passion."

El Despiadado took a deep breath, more for show than true interest in what the girl had said. From the looks he received, his attempt at flattery was successful.

"Have you decided on which coffee you would like, *señor*?"

He looked around the café noting that he was the only one in line and that many of the tables were empty. An older couple sat at the back, engrossed in conversation. A lone, younger man wearing a beanie and an absurd number of earrings absentmindedly sipped his drink while his eyes were glued to a computer screen. There was one additional barista behind the counter, but she was focused on what looked to El Despiadado as a finger war with her phone as she read and answered text after text.

"*Señor*?"

"My apologies. There is just so much to choose from, I

don't know where to start." He leaned his elbows onto the counter. "Would you be kind enough to choose your favorite for me..." His eyes drifted to the barista's nametag. "...Maria?"

Maria tried her best to keep from blushing but lost the battle in rather poor fashion based on the deep pink color in which her cheeks had flushed. She pulled her lips to one side, smiling only with half of her mouth, then said, "You should try Café de Olla. It is my favorite and a specialty of Café del Zócalo. It consists of traditional Oaxaca coffee brewed with cinnamon and piloncillo."

"Sounds delicious."

"If you would like to find a seat, I will bring it to you," Maria said.

"Very well."

El Despiadado found a table next to the window that looked out to the street, then glanced back at the counter. He caught Maria in a dreamy gaze, which she immediately snapped out of when she realized he was looking back at her.

He folded his hands on the table and turned his attention to the street. It was Wednesday, just past mid-morning, and the foot traffic on the sidewalk matched that of the road. Sparse at best, which gave him a clear view in both directions. It also allowed an unobstructed view straight across the road at the guard house that stood at the entrance to the Casa de los Fuertes, Señor de la Droga's compound.

He pulled his cell phone from his pocket and set it on the table. He had a series of missed calls, of which he was aware but had chosen not to answer. Since he had received the text from Señor de la Droga and not responded, his phone had been blowing up with incoming calls, all from the same number. All from the same man. El Despiadado's silence was doing more to antagonize his former employer than any exchange of words ever could. And that was what he wanted—anger, frustration, a sense of felt disrespect that would cause Señor de la Droga to act in an irrational, vengeful manner. El Despiadado did, however, have one thing to say once he was face to face with him.

The clinking of glass on the table pulled his attention to what now sat in front of him. Steam wafted from the brim of a customized Café del Zócalo mug of aromatically infused coffee. Maria stood next to the table with her hands tucked behind her back. El Despiadado called upon Mata once again.

He leaned forward, using his hand to capture the smell, and brushed the steam toward his face. Its smell was tantalizing. He closed his eyes for marked effect, then groaned as he opened them again to look at Maria.

"The smell is so good I could kill myself."

A surprised look fell over the barista. El Despiadado noticed.

"What I mean to say is that if every cup of coffee I had smelled this good, I'm not sure how I would be able to focus on more important matters of my day."

"Oh." Maria giggled. "I didn't think you would actually...you know." She placed a hand next to her temple and pretended to shoot herself with her thumb and index finger.

El Despiadado smiled. "No, my dear. That would for men far worse than I."

Maria placed her hand on El Despiadado's arm. "I don't think you're that bad, but then again, I don't even know you." She paused, eyes locked on his. "Still, I can read people pretty good. I bet there isn't a mean bone in your body."

"No, not one," El Despiadado replied. He glanced at her hand still lingering on his arm.

"Oh. Sorry." Maria's face flushed pink again as she withdrew her hand. "I'll be right over there if you need anything else, okay?"

"Thank you, Maria. I will call on you if a need arises."

Maria backed away two steps before twirling around and walking on light feet to her station behind the counter. El Despiadado reached for his coffee and took a sip. He had to admit that it was an exceptional brew. Using the mug as cover, he eyed the coffee shop once again. The same customers sat in the same spots, none of them giving any indication that they had noticed him. Blending into public places was an acquired skill. While Mata was a professional, El Despiadado had not the time nor the interest in becoming somewhat of a chameleon.

Mata, you did well, my friend, he thought. *I'll take it from here*.

A second sip of coffee pleasured his tongue. He swished the liquid around, swallowed, and returned to looking out the street-side window at the fortified walls, guard shack, and main entrance to *Casa de los Fuertes*.

I know you are in there, Señor de la Droga. Soon, I will be as well.

CHAPTER THIRTY-TWO

The house felt emptier this morning than it had since Raven and Cass had first arrived on the CR. The familiar smells of breakfast and citrus candles and the undertone of ranch dust beneath it all did nothing to ease the worry in Raven's heart. She had not said goodbye to Cass but wished him good luck and a safe return before going to bed. Now, sitting alone on the couch with half the morning gone by the wayside, she wished she had gotten up to see him off. The silence in the house was by far the most troubling. It was a mind game played in her head, and the devil on her shoulder was winning.

Drifting in and out of worrisome scenarios, she heard a faint knock at the door. When she did not get up to answer, the knock came again, this time with greater intention.

"Ms. Raven. Ms. Raven?" It was Flint. Good ole hard-ass turned softy but don't tell anyone or suffer the consequences of a foul mouth and right hook, Levi Flint. "I'd like to show you something, if ya'd come on out ta the barn."

Raven mustered the energy to get off the couch and

walk to the door. By the time she opened it and looked out, Flint was halfway to the barn.

"Hey," she said, her voice carrying on with a half-hearted attempt to reach him.

Flint heard. Hell, he would hear a cow fart from half an acre away under the right conditions. He stopped and turned his head to connect with Raven.

"Whatcha got?" she asked.

"Have ta get dressed, an' come find out." Flint motioned for her to come on, then continued to the barn without another word.

Raven shook her head, then realized she was still in her sleepwear and in full view of the entirety of the CR as she stood in the doorway. Her undersized, pink shorts hugged the tops of her thighs while a soft cotton Astros shirt of Cass's hung loose on her shoulders. A warm surge of self-consciousness washed over her. She ducked inside, but the damage, if one could call it that, was already done.

She walked to the laundry room and changed into fresh jeans and a more suitable work shirt. She grabbed socks from a pile of unfolded laundry, donning what ended up being a mismatched pair, then slipped on her work boots. She elected to forgo a belt and let her shirt hang loose over her waist. Feeling sluggish but curious, she headed for the barn leaving the house unlocked and her cell phone on the kitchen charger.

"Where you at, Flint?" Her voice disappeared into the rafters.

"Over here. Hope yer a little more work ready than before."

"Very funny," she said as she walked along the row of empty stalls.

Raven stopped at what was her favorite spot in the barn and looked over the rail. There, standing on strong legs with a flowing brown mane and the deepest eyes was Luna, their newest foal.

"Time we start trainin' the youngin'. Figured you'd be the right one fer the job."

Raven entered the stall and slowly approached the horse. She held her hand out to its muzzle, then with gentle hands, stroked her between the eyes and behind her ears.

"I don't know anything about training a horse."

"Not much to it. We'll start with a halter. She may not like it, but she's got ta learn ta wear it. When she's comfortable with that, you can lead her around the corral with it. Takes time an' patience, but also a tender heart. I think you outrank me there by a mile."

"All right, Flint. When do we start?"

"Ya already have, Ms. Raven. Ya already have."

CHAPTER THIRTY-THREE

"Let me see if I understand what you are saying," Agent Zuñiga spoke in a sharp, accusatory tone. "You have already crossed into Mexico, altered mission parameters, and are openly asserting that someone in Kill Hydra, your team, has compromised classified information vital to our operation, is feeding it to the Camargo cartel and you waited until now to tell me?"

The cab of the pickup fell silent. I knew more was coming, and I was correct.

"Cass. I cannot say I approve, I..."

I stopped him right there.

"I don't need your approval. I told you what I was planning to do following the incident in Brewster. You were on board. I agreed to join and lead your team. You were on board. I sat in your office and watched Agent Sharp do what he does best, annoy the crap out of me, and cause trouble when things don't go his way. Now, there *is* someone in *your* office that has shared information with our target. That means the element of surprise has vanished. Unless." I paused long enough to catch my breath. Agent Zuñiga was quick to fill in the blank.

"Unless you proceed with an alternate plan that is shared on a need-to-know basis."

"Right."

"How can you be so sure? Where did you get your information? Who told you that our plan had been burned? How can you be sure it was someone under my command?"

"One, I know because the source who spilled the beans had a gun on me and was hoping for a cop-assisted suicide. He told me they knew we were coming. He named Señor de la Droga. When he realized I was not going to send him over the rainbow bridge, he turned the gun on himself."

"So he is dead then."

"Nope. The dumb bastard wasn't quick enough. We had a sniper put a safety round into him which ended things right there. He'll be doing one-handed push-ups for the foreseeable future."

Ray backhanded me on the chest, then pointed to himself and mouthed, "Sniper? That was me!"

"I'm pulling the plug." I could hear the exasperation in his voice.

"No," I said. "Tell Sharp and Crank to proceed with the established protocol. We'll rendezvous with them in Camargo. Effective immediately, all OTA communications will be conducted using only call signs."

"What is your ETA?"

I glanced at Ray. We both nodded, silently agreeing that there was no way we would divulge any information with regard to our current mission situation.

"I'll contact you once we reach Camargo. Until then, I suggest you not share anything with anyone. If Sharp questions you, and you know he will, put him in his place for once."

The line went quiet.

"Zuñiga," I said, my voice sounding more even-keeled. "I'm not leaving Mexico until we find and stop de la Droga *and* Mata. Let's not forget about him."

"I know you won't, Cass. You're driven by factors none of us could even begin to fathom. Be careful."

With a single click, the line went dead.

"Well? What did Pancho Villa have to say."

"Nothing we didn't expect."

"You know what I think?" Ray said, twisting his body to face me.

"I have a feeling you're going to tell me anyway."

"Damn right. And here it is. Fuck 'em, Cass. Let's get this guy Droga and his man bitch. Nothing gets in our way."

I nodded.

"Say it," Ray said.

"Nothing gets in our way."

"You can do better than that, Cass."

I spoke louder. "Nothing gets in our way."

"Sound off, Private!"

I let loose the soldier and the war cry that he knew so well. "NOTHING GETS IN OUR WAY!"

CHAPTER THIRTY-FOUR

Morning turned to afternoon and the midday sun blazed overhead. El Despiadado remained in his seat at Café del Zócalo taking mental notes of who and what cars arrived and departed Casa de los Fuertes. His skills as a killer were exceptional, earned over time, but he felt his mind was a gift. Deep down, he knew he was undeserving of such an invisible weapon, but since it was his, why waste what has been given.

Maria went about her duties while keeping tabs on her new favorite customer. From behind the counter, she noticed he had finished what was his third serving of Café de Olla. Baristas routinely encounter all types of coffee enthusiasts, yet she could not help but be concerned. Such intense caffeine consumption hinted at a deeper restlessness. She had been drawn to him from the start, but her initial infatuation, fueled by a mix of youthful exuberance and a penchant for danger, succumbed to empathy. He had the rugged charm of a Latin Pierce Brosnan, but beneath that handsome exterior, there was an unmistakable air of loneliness. Something, or someone, was on his mind. Letting her curiosity get the best of her, she went over to speak with him.

"*Disculpe*. Would you like something different to drink, or maybe a desert?"

El Despiadado turned to Maria.

"I have had my fill, *gracias*." He tilted his head and gazed at her smile when a thought came into his mind. "Do you know who lives across the road? The architecture along the roofline is magnificent. It must be someone of great importance to have such high stone walls and security stationed at the entrance."

Maria's smile faded.

"Oh," she said. "I wouldn't know." She took a deep breath and composed herself.

"Too bad." *You know exactly who lives there*. "I was hoping to get a look on the inside." El Despiadado shrugged. "Such is life. It is always a mystery."

Maria cocked her head. "What is?"

He squinted, allowing a glimpse of the real El Despiadado to come forward when he spoke.

"That which we cannot see, my dear."

They shared—what was to Maria—an uncomfortable moment. Her heart fluttered as if she had been cornered by something inescapable. El Despiadado's eyes weighed upon her before shifting to the abrupt buzzing of his cell phone. Retrieving the device, he noted the caller ID.

Still hoping that I will answer. He glanced back at Maria, his eyes softening to what they had been before.

"I am sorry, Maria. Would you excuse me for a moment?"

Maria turned and walked to the counter with the feeling of eyes watching her every step from behind.

El Despiadado lifted the phone in front of him. As it buzzed for a fourth time, he relented. *No le busques la cola al diablo*—Don't look for the devil's tail.

"No," he whispered, raising the phone to his ear. "It is the devil who is searching for me."

CHAPTER THIRTY-FIVE

The small pickup's tires rumbled over the cobblestone streets as we approached the heart of Camargo and the Hotel Plaza Central. I parked across the street from the hotel entrance and stepped out of the truck. Ray got out as well, stretched, and stared up at the building.

"Damn," he said, walking around to me. "Now that's something you don't see every day."

The hotel looked like an ancient masterpiece mixed with a modern-day blend of architecture and artistry. Long, narrow windows lined the building like soldiers standing in formation. A third-story balcony with ornate ironwork wrapped around the exterior of the building. Its elaborate railings and window grilles, integrated with geometric patterns, made it look both formidable and captivating, a testament to strength and beauty. A grand, domed cupola with stone columns encircling its base loomed over everything.

Looking ahead, a pair of large wooden doors, both majestic and imposing, welcomed guests with open arms. Ornamental clay pots filled with flowers that boasted both a pungent yet delectable aroma and a colorful palette of hues lined the sidewalk leading inside. A large, circular stained glass window depicting the Virgin of Guadalupe in vibrant colors, embraced guests with the rich cultural and spiritual heritage of Mexico.

"How 'bout we stop standing here gawking like a couple of tourists and head inside?"

"Just playing the part, Ray. But it is quite a sight."

"Think those balconies are strong enough to hold a man?"

I grabbed my backpack from the cab and started walking toward the mighty wooden doors. "Let's hope we don't have to find out."

The lobby of Hotel Plaza Central was just as elaborate as its exterior. The open layout boasted a large fountain that greeted visitors coming into the hotel and guests descending a grand staircase from the second and third-story rooms. Talavera tiles lay in exquisite patterns along the floor. Murals of all sizes were hung in fancy frames, while some had even been painted directly on the walls. The lobby was adorned with an abundance of ironwork, including candelabras and chandeliers, alongside minimalist art pieces used for decoration. These were strategically placed throughout the space, ensuring that no matter where a guest looked, something intriguing would catch their eye.

I walked over to the front desk and was greeted by a young man dressed in a pressed suit. He was clean-shaven, and his hair was slicked back from his forehead with what seemed to me with an excessive amount of gel.

"Bienvenido al Hotel Plaza Central. I am Miguel Castroviejo." The young man bowed slightly upon greeting me. "Are you checking in, Mr...."

"Bregman. Professor Alexander Bregman. This is my colleague, Professor Ryan Nolan. I believe we have acquired a room on the top floor?" I turned to Ray and crafted an excited smile. "I am told the room I requested has an unobstructed view of Saint Anne's Church."

"Parroquia de Nuestra Señora de Santa Ana? Let me

double-check." The clerk flipped through a series of papers attached to a clipboard, then entered something into his computer. His eyes scanned the screen before him. "*Sí*, Señor Bregman. Your room is one of the best."

"Excellent."

"May I have your credit card and passports *por favor*?"

I heard a muffled grunt from Ray behind me. "Absolutely," I said. I unzipped my backpack and reached inside, producing two passports and a wallet. I pulled a credit card out of the wallet and handed everything to the clerk.

"*Gracias, señor.*"

I watched as clerk Miguel inspected our passports and swiped the credit card. When he was finished, he slid everything back to me and produced two keys for the room.

"You are all checked in, Señor Bregman. Your room is on the third floor, as requested. You may take the stairs or there is an elevator in the back. Do you need assistance with your baggage?"

"No. I think we can manage it on our own."

Miguel nodded and bowed again. "If I can be of any further service, please do not hesitate to ask.

"*Gracias*, Miguel."

Miguel leaned to one side and looked past me. "And you, as well, Señor Nolan. *Los dos son bienvenidos.*"

I glanced back at Ray. He answered the pleasantry with a smile, but I saw caution in his eyes. I returned the credit card to the wallet and placed it, along with the passports, back inside my backpack, slipped one set of keys into my pocket, and handed the other to Ray.

"Come on," I said. "Let's take a quick look around. Then we can grab a bite and head to the church."

"Sounds good," Ray said as we walked out of the hotel.

We did not speak until we were back in the pickup.

"Ryan Nolan?" Ray looked amused. "And when were you going to tell me about the passports?"

"Those were something I worked out in El Paso before

you arrived. Pulled your picture from an online Dragon Company directory. You're younger, but still look like an ass."

"I bet yours isn't much better."

"Nope. I look like an ass, too."

"Great. We're a couple of asses on an illegal mission in Mexico. What in god's name could go wrong?"

I turned the key and started the engine.

"Let's take a drive; buzz the tower, then we'll reach out to the rest of our team."

"Good. I'd like to see firsthand where Ol' poppie Droga and his band of little javeinas hole up."

"Yeah?"

"Yeah. This big bad wolf can't wait to blow their house down."

I pulled away from the curb and headed in the direction of Casa de los Fuertes.

"I know how you feel, Ray. And you'll get your chance. We both will."

CHAPTER THIRTY-SIX

"Your tenacity precedes you, *señor*, but your understanding of the situation is elementary, at best."

Standing up from his table, El Despiadado held his phone to his ear. He left a one-hundred-dollar bill for Maria under his coffee mug and walked out of Café del Zócalo. He could hear the rush of air being sucked into the nose of his caller on the other end of the line. It was an angry sound, most times followed by a barrage of words spoken so tightly together that all there was to do was sit and wait it out. Sure enough, he was right again.

"Who do you think you are dealing with, Mata! You are a dead man. You have always been a dead man, but now your time to pay up has come. *Vete a la chingada*! You kill my men. You send me this picture. You forget that I know you. I will send a hundred men to bring me your head. They will find you, kill you, and leave your body to sink with your boat, then return your head to me where I will place it on a spike in my garden so that the birds have something to peck."

He paused to snort a fresh gob of air and continued.

"There is no place you can go where I will not find you. Pray to whoever you think will listen because by the time the sun sets over Mar de Cortés, your blood will stain the water, and your body will feed the fish below."

Señor de la Droga paused. El Despiadado offered a few words of his own.

"In a manner of speaking, you are correct. You have a way of knowing...things. But you forget that I have a way of knowing, too. It will not be my body that feeds the fish tonight, and it will not be my head that graces the birds in your garden. Send your men. I welcome the challenge. Just make sure that they know how to fight and know how to swim."

Before Señor de la Droga could reply, El Despiadado ended the call. He turned the cell phone off and slipped it into his pants pocket. He looked up and down the sidewalk in front of Café del Zócalo. Two homeless men crouched on the ground near the corner of the block. They looked dirty. Their clothes were tattered. Each wore one shoe, but on opposing feet. For an inkling, Carlos Ruiz-Mata surfaced, aware of where he was and of the compassion that seemed to be shared between the two poorest of men. A few tourists roamed about, posing for pictures, unaware that their American noise and behavior made them stick out like cockroaches on the kitchen floor. They walked past the two homeless men in their designer clothes, expensive camera phones, and bulging fanny packs without giving them a second glance. The sight of the wealthy ignoring the weak sickened Mata. It was his empathy that caused El Despiadado to regain control.

His gaze followed the tourists, stabbing at them with his eyes until one of them noticed. Their loud display turned quiet in an instant. Whispers were shared, and caution took the place of wonder and adventure. One glanced at their phone, then gestured to the sidewalk behind them. The group turned on a dime like a flock of birds changing direction, walked at a brisk pace back past the two homeless men, and rounded the corner out of sight.

El Despiadado turned his attention to the entrance of Casa de los Fuertes across Calle Quinta. A large window on the face of the guard shack allowed him a clear view of the guards inside. Its design was to deter those who might want to get too close, like the tourists El Despiadado had just scared off, but it was also its biggest flaw. Everything the guards did was in plain sight.

He pulled a pair of dark aviators from inside his jacket and slid them into place. Traffic was light in both directions. A small, green Chevrolet Matiz passed by on the opposite side of the road. A silver Dodge Attitude, followed by an old, white Toyota Hilux two-door pickup, passed within feet of where El Despiadado stood at the curb.

He noticed each vehicle, but his focus was on the sudden activity in the guard shack. One guard was on the phone, while another walked out as the front gates slowly slid open. The temptation to cross the road, walk up to the guard shack, and announce his arrival with two rounds to the guards' heads, then proceed inside unannounced tugged at him. He felt the weight of his concealed Sig Sauer grow heavier, coaxing him, almost speaking to him. "Turn me loose."

A silver Mercedes AMG G-Wagon drove through the gate and stopped next to the guard shack. A rear window rolled down and the guard who had been on the phone approached the vehicle. El Despiadado could not hear what was said, but the way the guard stood at attention and the manner with which he seemed to only listen made it very clear who was in the back seat.

The conversation ended with the guard nodding once as the G-Wagon pulled away and made a left turn onto Calle Quinta. Before the rear window rolled up completely, El Despiadado got a glimpse of black and silver hair and the eagle-like profile of the man himself, Señor de la Droga.

"The fox has left its lair," El Despiadado said to himself.

He patted his chest, consoling his weapon, then walked away from Café del Zócalo. He turned at the corner to head down the block to his car but stopped to look upon the two homeless men first. He knelt next to them.

"*Mis amigos*," he started to say.

He reached into his jacket. The man wearing the right shoe watched with hope in his eyes. The man with the left shoe displayed more caution than El Despiadado liked. Finding his wallet with his fingers, he spoke to the men.

"*El que cuida las gallinas nunca llega a comer*—he who watches the chickens never gets to eat."

The man with the right shoe laughed, then placed an empty palm in front of him. The man with the left shoe appeared confused. El Despiadado removed his hand from his jacket, pointed the suppressed barrel of his Sig Sauer, and fired once at the man wearing the left shoe, hitting him in the chest. He buckled once, then slumped over. The man with the right shoe looked on but did not flinch.

El Despiadado reached over and untied the left shoe of the dead man and pulled it off. He reached into his pants pocket and removed some change then dropped the coins inside the shoe and handed it to the truly homeless man.

"*Gracias, señor*," the man said. His face beamed as if he was the grand prize winner of some mysterious contest.

"Now you have the pair and some money to spend. Go. Go and find something to eat, my friend."

The man slipped on the shoe, leaving the money to clink about between his toes. He stood up and walked away from the corner as if nothing had happened.

El Despiadado rose and walked the rest of the way to his car. He got in and pulled away from the curb, turning right at the corner where the shoeless man lay slumped over on himself.

"You will have to do better than that Señor de la

Droga. You may have eyes and ears everywhere, but none of them will see me coming."

He pulled onto Calle Quinta and drove past Café del Zócalo. In the distance, El Despiadado saw the silver G-Wagon. *Let the hunt begin*, he thought. He pressed the accelerator and sped to catch up. His focus on pursuit was relentless, but it prevented him from seeing one thing—Maria standing at the entrance of the coffee shop holding a cell phone to her ear, watching as he drove away.

CHAPTER THIRTY-SEVEN

"That's it," I said. "One security hut, cameras on both the main gate and mounted on a post near the entrance. What did you see?"

"Some place called Café del Zócalo across the street. Let's stop. All this time in the car is wearing me out. I could use some more coffee."

Damn it, Ray, I thought as I pulled the pickup to the side of the road. I stopped and looked in the side mirror to watch for oncoming traffic.

"We are going to make another pass. The target will be on *your* side of the truck. How about you give it a good look as we drive by and see if you can find a way to contribute on this little excursion."

"Panties in wad, Cass?"

I twisted to look at Ray dead on. "I need your full attention. We can't afford to miss anything. The smallest of details might mean the difference between success and being strung up on the overpass with our dick in our hands."

Ray pursed his lips. I glanced in the mirror again waiting for a clear spot in the traffic to pull a U-turn. A beat-up Ford Focus lumbered past, followed by a ritzy G-Wagon. Moments later, a black GMC Trailblazer and a motorcycle sped by. The road was clear behind them. We did an about face and headed back for another look.

"Sorry, Cass. Afternoon funk. I am all eyes from here on out."

"Good."

"Just one thing, though."

My patience was teetering. "What?"

"If we do get caught, make sure you're holding your own dick."

I squeezed the steering wheel, but it was not enough to keep an unwanted chuckle from rising.

"There he is," Ray said.

"Fine. Just stay frosty. The compound is coming up."

I kept our speed steady, relying on Ray's oh-so-keen observation. At forty miles per hour, he had just under four seconds to take mental notes on what he saw. I kept my eyes on the road, counting to myself, *one-one thousand...two-one thousand...three-one thousand...four-one thousand.*

With the compound shrinking in the rearview mirror, I asked Ray what he had seen.

"Well, not that much. Saw the cameras you mentioned, but..."

"Shit! We're going around again." I took my foot off the gas and coasted, looking for a safe place to pull over.

"Why?" Ray asked. He held up and wiggled his cell phone in front of me. "Got it all recorded right here." He gave me that, *you still have a lump of coal up your ass*, look. "How's about we head back to the hotel, contact Agent Shithead and Deputy Dog, grab some coffee and have a little watch party, eh?"

"You win, Ray."

I shook my head, realizing that maybe I was operating too tight in the saddle. Ray knew it, could see, and was the only one who could call me on it. Having him agree to be a part of this mission may be the one ingredient that gets us all out alive.

We arrived back at Hotel Plaza Central and opted to ride the elevator in the back of the lobby to the third floor. It shined both inside and out, a polished tribute to an ancient lift system, but the creaks and groans of its antiqued motor and steel cables made me grateful that stairs were still an option. We each carried a duffel, and I had my backpack slung over one shoulder. As the elevator doors opened, I fished the room key out of my pocket and noted the number—301.

"End of the hall," I said, motioning to the left. "Past the stairs."

Our room was as promised. We had an unobstructed view of Saint Anne's Church, as well as the plaza that opened up to a bevy of shops and restaurants adjacent to the hotel via a window, but we could also step out to a balcony through a solid, sliding glass pane door.

"Too bad Raven can't see this. She'd love the view."

"Bring her back." Ray's tone bled with sarcasm. "You know, after we topple one of the most powerful drug lords in Mexico." He joined me at the window. "It is something, if you're into that kind of thing."

We were deep into fall, but most of the trees still had a full bloom of green. The sky overhead was pale blue. Tiny wisps of clouds strung along the upper atmosphere like scratches on a new paint job. The buildings below were a mix of old and new, modern and baroque architecture, and looked like a field of wildflowers proudly displaying colors from across the spectrum.

I reached for my phone to contact the rest of the team when there was a knock at the door. Ray froze, then pivoted to look at me.

"You order room service and didn't tell me?"

"No."

"Then who the hell is knocking?"

I walked to the door and peeked through the spy hole. The clerk, Miguel, stood in the hall. I opened the door a crack.

"What can I do for you, Miguel?"

"Señor Bregman. I am sorry to intrude, but you have visitors waiting on you in the lobby."

"Visitors?"

"Sí, men from your university, I think."

Hearing the click of a slide being engaged, I glanced over my shoulder and saw Ray armed and ready. I lifted a palm to my waist, then turned back to Miguel.

"Thank you, Miguel. We've been expecting them."

"Should I tell them to come up?"

"No, no. I'll come down."

"Bueno."

Miguel bowed slightly. As he stood upright, I caught a glimpse of black ink trailing below his collar. It was hard to say what the tattoo was, but I could not help but think that what I saw were fingertips.

"I'll be back," I called to Ray.

"Want me to come along?"

"No need. I'm sure it's our Murphy friends."

Ray nodded. Murphy, or Sergeant Murphy from Dragon Company, was a crude-minded, fully capable soldier whose main role on our team was overwatch. I knew that Ray would understand that I wanted him to cover me from the third-floor balcony while I went down to the lobby.

I stepped into the hall and followed Miguel down the staircase to the first floor.

Son of a bitch, I thought.

Standing next to the fountain was Special Agent Sharp and Agent Crank.

"Professor!" Agent Sharp cracked a wide grin and waved as I approached with Miguel at my side. "It is so good to see you. Guess we missed your message, or we would have been here sooner." He handed Miguel a five-dollar bill. "Thank you for helping us out, Mr. Castroviejo."

"It is no trouble. *Gracias, señor*."

"And where is your partner?" Sharp placed a hand on my shoulder. "It's okay to call him that, right? Or are the two of you still, you know...is it not yet common knowledge?"

I remained calm, but my eyes stung from his insolence.

"He's in the room. We were just about to call you."

"Sure, you were," Sharp replied through his teeth.

Agent Crank stepped forward and offered a hand. "Glad to be here."

At least I would not have to kill both of them. Crank, I could deal with.

"Come on, follow me, and we can get started. The church closes to the public at eight, so we will have a little time, even after the sun goes down."

"Ohhh. Walking around Mexico after the dark," Sharp rubbed his hands together. "How exciting."

I turned away and headed for the stairs. Miguel was back at his post helping new arrivals. A glance to the third floor saw Ray retreating from the top of the stairs toward the room. As we climbed the steps, I asked Agent Sharp the one question whose answer I was dying to know.

"How did you find us so quickly?"

We rounded the second floor and climbed to the third.

"You think we're only keeping tabs on the other guys?" Sharp answered. "And we have a plane."

"Big Brother isn't very trusting," I said.

Sharp lowered his voice. "You are a loose cannon wired to explode. Did you really think the FBI would just bring you on without knowing your every move, even before you made it?"

When we reached the third-floor balcony, I stopped and prevented Sharp from climbing the final steps.

"Listen, Sharp. This is my mission, with or without you. Get on board or go home. Maybe if you kept your eyes focused ahead and not on me, you might have noticed who was leaking mission information to the cartel."

I looked down on him. My voice was low, but to anyone watching, it was clear that Sharp and I were at odds.

"Come on," Agent Crank said. "Let's finish this in the room."

My eyes were locked on Sharp, but I heard, and agreed, with Crank. I turned around and walked down the hall to the room where Ray waited at the door with gun in hand but tucked out of sight. He greeted us as we walked in.

"Afternoon, ass clowns. Ready to kill some bad guys?"

Sharp ignored the remark, but Crank cracked a smile.

"Hell yes, Nancy. Let's get to work."

Ray closed the door, then joined me at my side as the four of us stood facing each other. Ray leaned over and whispered into my ear.

"Let's toss the little one off the balcony, but the big guy is growing on me."

I silently agreed, then addressed the team.

"We have a lot to do. Grab a chair, and I'll bring you up to speed."

CHAPTER THIRTY-EIGHT

The morning was filled with gentle whinnies and playful snorts as Raven worked with Luna in the CR corral. The bond between them had already begun to blossom in the days following the tiny foal's birth, which made transitioning from pats and rubs of the hand to wearing a halter rather seamless. Luna already followed Raven like a lost puppy. Flint explained the first few steps they would take to train Luna to Raven but left her to do all the work. It took patience and love, and she was full of both, plus it kept her mind on what was in front of her and not with Cass on the battlefield. Before lunchtime, the foal had taken to being led around the corral by a lead rope as if it were second nature.

"Lookin' good," Flint called out from the fence. "Time ta give 'er a rest. We've got other chores ahead."

Raven turned and approached Luna with outstretched hands. She cupped her muzzle, stroking up and down with long draws. Luna pressed in closer to her as if she wanted to cuddle up, which made Raven laugh.

"Oh, you are a sweetheart. But, the big, mean man says playtime is over."

Raven shot Flint a playful look, then led Luna to the

edge of the corral. Flint opened the gate and gave the foal a pat on the neck.

"You'll be ridin' her before ya know it."

"Really? Isn't she too small?"

"Hell yeah, but time out here flies faster than a jackrabbit runnin' from a ki-yote. You'll see." Flint closed the gate behind them. "Let's get her into the pasture with her mother, then we're gonna take a ride."

"Where we going?"

"Fishin'."

CHAPTER THIRTY-NINE

El Despiadado followed Señor de la Droga's G-Wagon at a distance. He remained undetected yet never lost sight of the vehicle. Camargo was not a big city by modern standards, so there were only a limited number of places the drug lord might go should he choose to leave Casa de los Fuertes. Having been in the service of the Camargo cartel for several years, El Despiadado was familiar with the tendencies of Señor de la Droga. Traveling along this route meant one of two things—he was either headed to the airport or to the police station.

If Señor de la Droga was indeed heading for the airport, that would bring about complications for El Despidado; however, if his intended destination was the police station, the hunt would be far from over.

The Camargo city police were deep in the pockets of Señor de la Droga. The Camargo cartel was growing more powerful by the day, and ranking authorities within the Camargo city police department found it in their best interests to support and protect Señor de la Droga and follow whatever orders were handed down. Arrangements between what were the two governing powers in the city were made following a few graphic displays of what might happen should a police officer or city official choose to be a problem for the cartel. Securing the backing of the police was yet another example of how much control Señor de la Droga had gained over the region.

The state police were another matter, more expensive and unreliable, but Camargo was a geographic hotspot. With its close proximity and direct routes to the US border along Texas, New Mexico, and Arizona, it was the perfect place to build an empire. Drug smuggling and human trafficking were multi-million-dollar enterprises, and with the Zetas and Gulf cartels at each other's throats, Señor de la Droga was poised to take full advantage with the Camargo cartel. And now, with his own private security force, what, or who was going to stop him?

Señor de la Droga was a cruel, dangerous man, but he had taken measures within the community to establish a positive connection with its people. He funneled monies through the city council to build parks, improve conditions within local schools, and made considerable donations to Parroquia de Nuestra Señora de Santa Ana, Saint Anne's Church. To most of the population, those who chose to turn a blind eye to the despicable acts for which he was responsible, he was a man of the people.

The G-Wagon continued on Calle Quinta until the road stopped at the intersection of Calle Guillermo Prieto. El Despiadado slowed down and watched.

"Let us see which direction you will go."

The G-Wagon's right turn signal flashed. El Despiadado nodded, and a small fizzle of air escaped from his cracked lips.

"It is good of you to stay in town, *señor*. It would have been a shame to travel all this way only to be made to sit and wait for your return."

The G-Wagon turned right. El Despiadado approached the intersection. Calle Guillermo Prieto was a main thoroughfare that ran through Camargo's northern districts and was far busier than Calle Quinta. Cars passed by in waves. He tapped his fingers on the steering wheel while he waited for the two cars in front of him to go. He was in no hurry now that he knew where Señor de la Droga was headed.

When it was his turn, El Despiadado continued to the right and drove ahead until he saw the gray-painted cement exterior of Comisaría de Policía de Camargo. The G-Wagon idled in a secondary driveway at a security gate. Pulling the Trailblazer over to the curb, El Despiadado watched a security officer approach Señor de la Droga's car. After a brief interaction, the officer promptly returned to the security hut and raised the barricade so they could pass.

"To the patient hunter, the rewards of a kill will be tremendous," El Despiadado whispered to himself.

He pulled back into traffic and drove north two more blocks before turning around. The parking lot at Bodega Aurrera overlooked Calle Guillermo Prieto and offered a clear line of sight of the front entrance to Comisaría de Policía de Camargo as well as the secondary security entrance where the G-Wagon had taken Señor de la Droga.

"Now," he said, looking at himself in the rearview mirror. "Now, we wait."

CHAPTER FORTY

The wide expanse of West Texas was full of mystery, the likes of which some never surface unless it wants to be seen. The rocky crags and deadly cliffs, the towering bluffs and wide-open range, all of it has a story of its own. The folktales and tall tales passed down from generation to generation were born from danger or misunderstanding, or a combination of both, and over time have been twisted by storytellers so that time itself has rewritten each tale in some way or another. As Flint and Raven sauntered over the CR, Flint offered a bit of history, iced with a touch of flavor as only he could.

"Where we headed, Flint?"

"Not so much where we're headed, but for what reason, Ms. Raven."

"Will I need to..."

"Pardon my sayin' so but stop yammerin' with all the questions. Set back in the saddle an' I'll tell ya everything ya need ta know..." He paused to spit. "And maybe a bit that ya shouldn't."

The horses clomped on, their hooves pounding silent prints in the earth with each quiet step.

"Up until 1958, the Callahans had near 'bout one-hundred thousand acres of land that stretched south and east along the Rio Grande, across the highway, and far as ya could see on a clear day. Pat Callahan, Cass's grandfather, and Lane Callahan, his great uncle, worked the land fer cattle and horses, among other things, alongside Timothy Callahan, their father. Life was kind to the family. It was almost like this place..." Flint encircled a hand above his head, regarding the land and everything within. "...had a magic about it."

"Magic, Flint?"

"Not like pullin' a damn rabbit out of a hat, but a feelin' that when it hits ya, is unexplainable."

Flint paused and gazed upon the ranch as if drawn into a daze.

"Flint?"

"Yeah." He shook his head. "Well, Pat an' Lane knew every inch of this land an' they 'bout swam an' fished every inch of the river. It was said they could ride blindfolded, horse an' all, an' still get ta where they were goin'."

Tucker's well-timed snort and head bob made Raven laugh.

"I think she's calling bullshit."

"Ain't bullshit. Those boys were the real deal, an' it's on account of them that there weren't more trouble at the river than there already was. Back before the fancy GPS and moderntinizing of things, landmarks were how people found their way. If ya wanted ta send a message or make a path in plain sight, ya might arrange a cluster of rocks ta mark the way or tie a piece of cloth to a tree limb, which ain't so subtle, so the next time ya come 'round, it'll be easier, an' faster ta get wherever yer goin'. Pat an' Lane could spot those signs like they were flaming torches er bright neon signs er somethin'. They'd topple the rock piles and remove the pieces of cloth, but they'd always seem ta get replaced. Maybe not in the same spot, but near enough. It got ta the point that they searched the Mexican side of the river, near to a mile back fer anything that might help smugglers find their way."

"Smugglers? You're talking drugs then."

"Not so much back then. Drugs weren't the main issue like it is today. Back then it was people. Seems like the flood never ends. As long as there's money ta be made, it never will. An' that's money on both sides of the border, Ms. Raven."

"Yeah," Raven said. "Is that what we're going to do? Look for rock piles, Flint? I thought we were going fishing?" Raven said.

"We are, sort of. Fishin' fer signs left by the last band of wetbacks that came through."

"Don't you mean *illegal immigrants*, Flint?"

"One and the same."

"They're still people, most of whom are searching for a better life."

Flint stopped his horse. Raven pulled up next to him.

"You think those Mexicans that were killed yesterday found a better life? It's people like them that make this part of the US some of the most dangerous territory there is."

"Flint, but if..."

"Ms. Raven, let me say this. I ain't got nothin' against someone wantin' a better life fer themselves as long as it don't interfere with the people I care about or me."

A slip of the tongue with his last statement caused his eyes to shift away from Raven.

"Illegal. Wetback. Brownie. All them words ain't so nice, but over the years I've had my fill of 'em, an' it's wore me plumb out at times. Show me a group of people who get here right an' proper an' I won't be callin' them any names. As fer the rest, accept my apologies if I've wounded yer humane sensitivity."

Flint cocked his head and faced Raven once again.

"My heart goes out to those people, Flint. They didn't deserve to die the way they did."

"Shouldn't have put themselves in that position in the first place when they agreed ta carry whatever it was they were carrying. We saw 'em load the truck."

"Can I finish? I know we are new here, Cass and I, and we haven't seen or experienced even a fraction of what you have, but let me tell you something that you have probably forgotten over the years—people aren't inherently bad. Seems to me you're throwing out the bushel when you find one bad apple. The rest only get bruised when they are cast aside."

"So," Flint huffed. "Let 'em all in. That what ya want?"

"No, Flint. That's not what I am saying. What I'm saying is that if we keep our eyes open wide enough, we can spot the bad hiding within the good. If we can do that, most of our problems will fix themselves."

Flint squinted his eyes at Raven. She stared back, riding his gaze like a bareback bronc rider. Weathered emotions and new perspectives do not often mix well, but Raven and Flint were the yin and yang of the CR. She was the first person that Flint had known that could challenge him in a way that broke through his callous nature. Finally, Flint broke the silence of their showdown.

"Ms. Raven, I'm not so sure this old dog has it in him to sift through what I know smells like shit. I know what I know, and I feel what I feel."

Raven's face softened.

"All I'm asking, Levi, is that when the time comes, look for the horses even if the shit starts to pile too high."

Raven clicked her tongue and nudged her horse ahead. Calling over her shoulder, she said, "Come on, ya old dog."

Flint kicked his heels and caught up to Raven.

"You're still taking me fishin', aren't ya?"

CHAPTER FORTY-ONE

A palpable tension hung in the air as remnants of my contentious exchange with Agent Sharp lingered. The soldier in me forced those feelings aside to focus on the mission ahead. What was a historical and artistic corner room in the beautiful hotel had been transformed into our makeshift base of operations. Maps and satellite images covered the walls. Detailed floor plans and schematics, each marked with precise entry and exit points of Casa de los Fuertes, were spread out across the queen-size bed. We huddled together as I led the mission briefing.

"As you all know, this operation requires absolute precision. Our objective is clear: infiltrate the Camargo cartel's stronghold, neutralize the target known as Señor de la Droga, and exfil without a trace. We go in under the cover of darkness. Keep comm channels open. Callsigns only. Tucker is Dragon. Crank...Hulk. Sharp...Blade. I'm Rowdy. We'll use the security entrance on the east side of the compound for our primary entry point. Intel shows it's the most vulnerable point, being only guarded by one guard, but it houses the main server that oversees surveillance of the property. Blade and Hulk, you'll take out the guard and disable the external security systems.

Blade, you'll be eyes and ears from there. Make sure we have a clear extract point. Dragon, Hulk, and I will proceed to the main building for target neutralization."

Crank, built like the brute force his callsign *Hulk* suggested, cracked his knuckles and nodded with a hint of eagerness in his stance.

"Wait!" Sharp looked pissed. "This is bullshit. You're leaving me behind to do nothing?"

"Could leave you here," Ray said.

"Fuck you! You shouldn't be here in the first place," Sharp said, pointing a finger in Ray's face.

"Both of you! Knock it off." The tension in the room went from truce-bearing to critical in moments.

"Sharp, we need continual surveillance. If what Agent Zuñiga says about you is true, you're the man for the job. You'll have access to all internal camera feeds and will be our best shot of leading us out if something goes wrong. Plus, you'll be our first line of defense if reinforcements of any kind arrive." I continued addressing the group. "Timing is critical. We have a small window before they realize they're under attack. Once the target is down, we exfiltrate back through the east entrance. If that is cut off, we head to the west corridor. It's a tight squeeze, but it will lead us straight out of the compound. From there, we're on foot until we can double back to the truck. As a last resort, we ditch the weapons and quick change into civies: T-shirts, ball caps, something non-military and easy to carry. It's not ideal, but staying alive will be more important if we find ourselves staring at the last option."

I picked up a curious glance from Ray as I brought the meeting to a close.

"Once the target has been neutralized, Blade will set charges in the security hut as a diversion and will rendezvous with us at the west end of the courtyard. We all leave together." I gave Agent Sharp a clear, unmitigated look. "All of us."

"Check your gear, double-check your comms. We

move at zero hundred hours. Remember, we're ghosts in there—swift, silent, and invisible. This ends tonight, one way or another."

Everyone nodded in agreement. Despite the danger, there was an adrenaline-fueled clarity that came with knowing we were working to dismantle a dangerous cartel. There was also a personal satisfaction brewing in me, filled with a vengeful determination which I was ready to unleash.

Crank and Sharp left the room to retrieve things from their vehicle parked outside. As soon as the door closed, Ray approached me.

"I want you to know upfront, I ain't ditching my weapon."

I respected Ray more than anyone and understood what he meant by saying that.

"I hear you. Let's just make sure we get out of Dodge alive."

I opened the glass door to the balcony and was stepping outside when my cell phone chimed, announcing an incoming text message. I glanced at the screen, then slipped the phone into my pocket. Looking out into the blackness beyond the safety of our hotel room, I heard the faint rhythm of music echoing in the distance.

"Anything you care to share there, pard?"

With eyes watching the night, I answered.

"Not yet."

CHAPTER FORTY-TWO

The patience of a killer, one who is seasoned in the art of taking lives, is immeasurable to those who have not savored the final moments when a victim's light is snuffed out. It is an internal clock that slowly *tick tick ticks* until that one perfect moment when the timing is just right and the rush of darkened adrenaline mixes with passion and fury, all exploding in one violent surge that coaxes a killer into action. El Despidado was a master. He knew the feelings, but this time would trump them all.

He waited and watched for the G-Wagon to reappear until the sun began to sink overhead and shadows grew longer behind that which they had been hiding. When the SUV did appear, it exited past the security gate, then turned right onto Calle Guillermo Prieto and drove past the parking lot where El Despiadado lurked and headed deeper into town.

With a twist of the key, the Trailblazer fired to life. El Despiadado pulled into traffic and followed behind. After only a few blocks, the G-Wagon turned into a long drive that led to Camargo's most exclusive nightclub, Salón Pata Negra.

"It is early for food and music, but I think I can

manage a meal and maybe a little excitement." El Despiadado spoke aloud as if talking to someone else in the car.
"I have just the thing to get things started."

The G-Wagon pulled up to the entrance where Señor
de la Droga and his driver got out and walked inside. A
valet drove the vehicle to a parking spot marked VIP, then
jogged back to his post at the front of the nightclub.

"I think you are growing too comfortable these days to
be walking around with only one man to accompany you.
There was a time when you would demand an entourage,
complete with women and guns, to follow your every
move. Why are you acting so different today?"

El Despiadado bypassed the main entrance and
instead pulled around to the backside of the club and
parked with the workers' vehicles, where he waited for a
time before getting out.

Evening was fast approaching. When the sun was low
enough for its rays to cut across the tops of buildings
instead of showering down on them, he got out, grabbed
his small duffle, and headed for the service entrance.

Glancing around the property, he saw two cameras
mounted on the top corners of the nightclub, but they
were directed toward the guest lot, which meant there
was a good chance he had not been seen walking from the
Trailblazer to the service entrance.

He opened the door and stepped into a hallway that
ran along the backside of the building. Walking down the
hall, he noted an offshoot passage that led to the rear of
the kitchen. Further ahead was the entrance to a main
stage used for live music and Bailarinas de Cabaret, but it
was early and he did not see any showgirls preparing for
an evening of entertainment.

"*Perdón, señor?*"

El Despiadado turned around to see a young man
wearing a formal, white button-down shirt and bowtie
standing in the hallway near the kitchen entrance.

"Guests should not be back here, *señor.*"

El Despiadado's face softened around a warming smile.

"*Mis disculpas*. My apologies." He stepped over to the young worker. "My boss is here tonight for..." He stumbled over his wording. "...dinner. A meeting. Honestly, I am at a loss. I keep all Señor de la Droga's appointments in my cell phone, but I am just getting back into town and left it on the airplane."

El Despiadado spoke with his best blend of worry and agitation.

"You work for Señor de la Droga?"

"Yes, for many years." El Despiadado cocked his head. "What is your name?"

"Diego."

"Ah, I had a friend with that same name when I was a boy." El Despiadado looked away as if swept into a memory.

"Señor de la Droga is here for an early dinner. He is meeting with Isabella Constantine Salazar when she arrives."

"The actress? Now I remember."

"*Sí, señor*." Diego's cheeks lifted next to an excited smile. "He is so lucky."

"Why would you say that?"

"Because she is beautiful and talented, and..."

"Single? I think a young man like you would be more to her liking than an old man like my boss."

Diego's smile curled further as the mere thought of her caused him to become starstruck.

"Tell you what, I have a surprise for Señor de la Droga, but I will need your help to deliver it. If you do, I will make sure to introduce you to Isabella before the night is over."

"Really?"

"Yes. But it must remain a secret."

"*Sí, señor*. What do you need me to do?"

El Despiadado felt the weight of the bag in his hand

pull at him as if reminding him of the role in which it would play.

"First, I need a rolling cart with a large silver tray and a cloche."

Diego listened, following the instructions with nods of the head.

"Make sure it looks exquisite. Nothing but the best for Señor de la Droga. Bring it to me here, and I will arrange the surprise, then you can deliver it to the table."

"Oh, this is exciting, *señor*. What are we hiding?"

El Despiadado placed a hand on Diego's shoulder.

"It is something special." He paused and raised a hand to his chin in thought. "Something, how can I say this... one of a kind."

"Is it in there?" Diego pointed at the duffle.

"Yes, my new friend. It is a dessert to die for."

CHAPTER FORTY-THREE

S hadows of the neighboring Mexican mountains reached across the CR like long bulbous giants slowly crawling over the ground. Flint and Raven rode along the river looking for anything that seemed out of the ordinary. So far, the search had come up empty.

"The way technology has become so advanced these days all anyone has to do is drop a pin to save a location on a device. From there, they have precise coordinates which they can then share to anyone with a comparable piece of tech. Cell phone, laptop, tablet, they all have the capabilities to be used even in the most remote places depending upon its method of data connection."

Raven spoke like she was a true techie, although most of her education in that department had been from her watchlist of favorites on Prime.

"You really think we're going to find something, Flint?"

"We look hard enough, maybe."

They made a second sweep of the immediate area from the north fence at the Double SS to the south fence bordering the Flyin' H. Both passes had nothing to show for themselves but wildlife prints on the riverbanks and some leftover garbage that had blown from who-knows-where.

"Let's call it a night, Ms. Raven. Figured it was worth a look. Good thing is, we didn't find a thing. Bad thing is..."

Raven finished his statement, "We didn't find a thing."

"Yep." Flint reined his horse around. "Let's ride back past the grove, then we'll head fer the house."

Raven did not reply. Instead, she sat in the saddle and looked at the landscape that made up Old Mexico. A feeling from out of nowhere caused her to gaze beyond what she could see and yet was left to only wonder if Cass was safe and possibly, at that moment, on his way home to her. It was too early to tell. Deep down, she knew that, but she could not help but drum up a worry that had been pressing on her gut for most of the day. Flint had done all he could to keep her mind elsewhere, but no matter the distraction, there was no way she was going to put Cass and his dangerous mission out of her mind completely.

Flint looked over his shoulder and noticed she had not begun to follow.

"Ms. Raven?"

She sat still, her silhouette seeming to glow in the waning light.

"Ms. Raven?"

"I know, Flint."

She looked at him, her face a shadow of itself. Reining her horse toward him, she stopped and cocked her head to one side.

"You hear that?"

"Hear what?"

Raven swiveled in her saddle and looked back toward the river. A few trees clung to the bank, all hunched over like a group of old men hovering over a chessboard. Limbs dangled and swayed causing thin shadows to ripple back and forth across the ground.

Straining to listen, she craned her neck as if the extra

focus might help produce the sound that she had thought she had heard.

"The land talkin' to ya?"

Flint brought his horse next to hers.

"I thought I..."

A whine, like the sad call of an abandoned puppy, wailed once, then abruptly stopped.

"I know you heard that," Raven said.

Flint scanned the immediate area. The stillness following the noise was unsettling; natural, yet with an air of caution only a human would know. He removed an 1873 model Winchester short barrel from its saddle sheath. In one smooth motion, he dismounted while seamlessly drawing and cocking the rifle. Raven followed suit, unclipping the safety strap from her hip holster and laying a hand along the grip of the Purple Demon.

Daylight was escaping. The dull haze of twilight seeped in around them. Shadows grew longer. Darker. The usual chime of crickets and cicadas were tamped out by the cooler weather, forcing them to find warmer places to hole up for the night. The ripple of the river offered a background serenade, but that went unnoticed by Flint and Raven.

With her voice softened, Raven whispered, "What do you think?"

Flint, still focused ahead, raised a palm to his side. Raven understood the signal. She kept quiet, holding back any further questions that were popping into her mind. When Flint moved, she moved. They were three paces away from their horses when they heard a soft whimper coming from the trees near the water's edge.

Raven quickened her steps, but Flint grabbed her forearm to stop her.

"Don't go jumpin' inta the water when ya don't know what's beneath."

"It sounds like..."

"I know what it sounds like. Could be what yer thinkin' but it could also be a whole mess a trouble."

The whimper continued to grow. Raven reached Flint without saying a word. Her eyes spoke of her need to see. Flint was a hard man, solid and unwavering. At least he used to be.

"Ms. Raven, you follow right behind me."

Raven nodded. Step over cautious step, the two advanced on the whimper. The closer they came to the craggily trees, the louder and more distinct the sound became. Flint paused when he heard a soft thump, but Raven had already laid eyes on the cause.

Defying Flint's instructions to stay behind him, she moved forward ignoring his grumbles. She removed her hand from her pistol to place it with the other in front of her, showing that they were both empty as she approached the base of the nearest tree. When she was close enough to fully see, her heart sank as her eyes widened.

"Dear god," she whispered.

The timid, brown eyes of a young boy looked up at her. To Raven, he looked no more than four years old. His face was streaked with tears and mucus. He leaned against the tree, shaking. His clothing looked damp. He wore a short-sleeved shirt with a picture of Elmo holding his arms out for a hug with the words, ¡Elmo te quiere mucho! He had dark blue cotton sweatpants on, but both legs were torn revealing gashes on his shins. His shoes were covered in mud and looked to have been hand-me-downs ten times over.

"Flint," Raven said as she kept her eyes on the child. "Put down your gun and come here."

Flint lowered his weapon and stepped forward next to Raven.

"Damn."

Raven sank to her knees and smiled at the boy. He looked back, eyes full of fear, and to Raven, seemed to have given up hope. He was so exhausted and in pain that when Raven approached, he hardly even flinched.

"Oh, little man. You're hurt."

The boy's body twitched in rhythm with each convulsed whimper.

"And you look so cold," she continued. "Flint, do we have anything to cover him up?"

Without hesitation, Flint removed the light jacket he was wearing and handed it over.

"There's a rag in the pocket. I'll grab some first aid supplies from my saddlebag..." He paused. "...but Ms. Raven."

"Not now, Flint."

Her voice remained gentle, but the words were sharp and full of intent.

Slowly, she worked her way closer to the boy. When she was an arm's length from him, she reached forward and placed her palm on his head and gently stroked his hair with her thumb.

"You're okay now."

The boy stared straight ahead.

She repeated herself, "Ahora estás bien. Mi nombre es Raven."

The boy broke the rhythm of his whimpers to look Raven square in the eyes.

"Mamá?"

Raven could feel her heart tremble with each thump that followed. She mustered a smile to keep her own tears at bay, then showed the boy Flint's jacket."

"*Vamos a calentarte*," she said. "Let's get you warmed up, and I'll take a look at the cuts on your legs."

Raven opened the jacket up to him. In a move that surprised her, the boy leaned forward and crawled into her lap. She embraced the child, wrapping him up, swaying side to side, consoling him with soft shushes and gentle squeezes.

Flint returned with a pouch and handed it to Raven.

"There's salve and gauze in there. It's kinda old but should do the trick."

"Like the stuff you gave me for the burn on my leg?"

"Something like that." Flint smiled at the tiny jab. He looked at the child, then looked away, speaking more to the river than to Raven. "I don't have ta tell ya how he got here."

"No, Flint. You don't."

"What 'er..." He stopped midsentence and turned to face her.

"We're going to help him. Get on the sat phone and give Chance a call. Tell him to meet us at the house. Tell him why."

Flint kneeled and looked at the child. He had stopped whimpering but still looked frightened.

"Don't worry, little man. Ain't nothing Ms. Raven can't do when she puts her foot down."

He stood again, towering over the two. "And Sheriff Gilbert, he'll set things straight."

It was clear by his blank gaze that the boy did not understand. Flint smiled, catching a glimpse of Raven as he turned and walked away.

Raven used the rag from Flint's jacket to wipe the boy's face and spoke to him with a soft voice as she explained that she was going to clean his wounds. With delicate hands, she went to work as only a mother knows how. The boy winced at Raven's first touch to his cuts with the gauze but settled as she applied the oozing salve. With each wrap of his tiny legs, he became more comfortable under her care.

Night was all but settled in. Only a thin line of golden light outlined the peaks and valleys of rock that lined the Mexican side of the border. Flint returned with the sat phone.

"You reach Chance?"

"A-yuh. Says he'll be out within the hour."

"Good. We need to get this guy back and in some warmer, dry clothes."

"Ms. Raven, pardon my sayin' so, but how do you plan on ridin' back with him in yer arms? I know ya can handle yerself, but ridin' fer two ain't the same."

Raven looked down at the child. He had calmed down. His tears had stopped and was teetering on falling asleep. Gazing into his brown eyes, Raven answered, "I have an idea about that, Flint."

CHAPTER FORTY-FOUR

The sounds of clanks and bangs accompanied a rise in voices from the kitchen as more help arrived and preparations were made for the evening at Salón Pata Negra. Theatrical lights blinked on and off while the stage crews tested the equipment for what was sure to be a special show. Word spread quickly throughout the staff about Isabella Constantine Salazar's arrival and that she was expected to sing for Señor de la Droga following their meal. While the buzz in the building continued to grow, El Despiadado waited patiently for Diego to return with the items he had requested.

Anticipation grew inside of him like a young child might experience when waiting to blow out the candles on a birthday cake or spring a surprise on a friend. He stood at a point in the hall where the corridor split into two separate passages. One led backstage while the other opened into the dining room. Staff dressed like Diego passed by El Despiadado in the hall, but none gave him the same attention as did the young man.

It is good to go unnoticed, he thought. *It will be so much easier to disappear once dessert has been served.*

While he waited, El Despiadado discovered that he

could see into the dining room at an angle when he stood in the doorway that led backstage. It was not the best view, but it was all he needed to see that Señor de la Droga had been seated at a table in the center of the room. His driver stood against the wall to the side like a servant waiting to be called upon. That was what he was. A servant. It was what Carlos Ruiz-Mata had been as well. If not for El Despiadado, his servitude would not have been as glamorous or as fulfilling as it was.

El Despiadado cringed at the thought of returning to be the lackey of such a man as Señor de la Droga. His ill thoughts continued when he considered that Mata would undoubtedly expect to regain control once these final deeds were done.

Maybe it is time to say farewell to Mata as well?

He continued to consider this as he spied on Señor de la Droga. Lost in thought, his vulnerability nearly cost him his cover.

"*Señor?*"

El Despiadado whirled around coming face to face with an older man wearing a suit coat and a very suspicious, unwelcoming look.

"What is your business here?"

"I am waiting."

"For whom are you waiting, *señor*, that it requires you to be in the service hallway?"

"I am waiting for Diego, the kitchen boy."

"Diego is a waiter and is doing his job preparing for an elaborate night. If you please, follow me and I will lead you out the back entrance. There is no need to disrupt our special guests."

"Special guests?"

"*Señor.*" The man grew agitated. "Time is precious and I cannot afford to waste any more of it on you. Now, are you going to follow me out, or should I call security?"

A simmering heat began pulsing through El Despiadado. His eyes shifted, turning from a harmless gaze to a ravenous glare as he looked back at the man.

Stepping against the wall, the man in the suit waved an arm before him, pointing toward the exit door on the far side of the building. "*En silencio, por favor.*"

El Despiadado breathed through his nose. His nostrils flared, but he raised his hands as if surrendering. With a nod of his head, he gave the man a savage smile and whispered, "But, of course."

El Despiadado took one step then, with the speed and force of a cage fighter, rammed his elbow into the man's throat. He pressed harder on impact, using the wall behind the man for leverage. Through the gargles of a crushed windpipe, the man struggled to breathe, to scream, but such things are impossible when your neck has been ruined. The man's eyes bulged from their sockets. His face turned beet red. Veins over his eyes swelled from the pressure causing his face to look like a pulsing crown of agony.

El Despiadado leaned close and whispered into the man's ear.

"Remember, *señor. En silencio, por favor.*"

With one final thrust of his arm, the man's neck snapped leaving his body to dangle before El Despiadado like a marionette.

"Now, that's a good man. Let's find you a suitable place to put up your feet. It seems that you have worked very hard and are most deserving of a break."

El Despiadado released enough pressure from the man that his body started to slump forward. He grabbed one limp arm and slung it over his shoulder, then hoisted the dead body off the ground. Turning around, he walked backstage, descended into the orchestra pit, and placed the man behind a set of timpani at the rear of the orchestra pit. The set of three large drums were large enough to conceal the dead body no matter in which position El Despiadado left him.

Feeling a tinge of sweat begin to build on his forehead, El Despiadado wiped his brow, then bid farewell to his latest victim with a wave of his hand and a bend of the knee.

"*Adiós, señor.*"

The man's eyes still bulged from their sockets. Burst vessels stained what little white there was left to surround his glassy, eternal stare. The color of his face had drained and was now looking more pallid above a neck so crushed that his head cocked back in a mangled position against the metal drum. His mouth hung open, and yet he would never speak to anyone again.

El Despiadado made his way out of the pit and back to the spot where he watched Señor de la Droga and waited for Diego to return. As he stood alone in the hall, he hummed a tune, but could not recall where he had heard it before. He shook his head, but the song would not stop playing in his mind. He beat his chest once, cursing himself under his breath.

"Mata, *cabrón*! This noise is all your doing. Let me be to finish the job. Then we will discuss the conditions of your return."

Not a moment later, Diego poked his head out of the rear kitchen entrance, wearing a cheeky smile while pulling a service cart behind him, and headed straight for El Despiadado. A large, silver cloche sat on a platter, all of which took up the entirety of the cart's top surface area.

"Is this large enough for you, *señor*?"

El Despiadado patted Diego's shoulder with his palm, speaking as a proud father might address his son.

"You have truly come through in my time of need. Well done, Diego."

"Now will you tell me what it is we are serving?"

"And reveal the surprise? Where is the fun in that?"

The main room of the nightclub erupted in applause. El Despiadado looked from his hidden spot but could not see the cause of the attention.

"It is Isabella. She just arrived, *señor*." Diego looked over his shoulder. "I should go back to the kitchen before I am missed. I will be back soon and will make the delivery for you."

El Despiadado reached into his pocket and pulled out a money clip. He removed a one-hundred-dollar bill and handed it to Diego.

"For your trouble..." Diego reached for the tip, but El Despiadado pulled it back just enough to draw the young man's attention to his face. "...and your discretion."

"*Sí, señor*. I will not tell a soul."

"Good man." El Despiadado said, handing the bill to Diego. "Run along. I will prepare the cart and be ready when you return."

Diego turned and silently jogged back to the kitchen entrance, slipping inside and out of sight. The applause from the nightclub floor had died down. El Despiadado saw Señor de la Droga sitting across from a beautiful woman wearing what looked like a very revealing red dress.

Ah, the actress, Isabella Constantine Salazar. You are a lucky man, indeed Señor de la Droga. Enjoy your time while you still can. Soon enough you will be running, and I will be closer than you ever expected me to be.

CHAPTER FORTY-FIVE

Clomp for clomp, Raven rode next to Flint. A warm smile, unaffected by the cool northern breeze that swept in small bursts across the flattened CR terrain, filled her face as she watched the small child bobble back and forth, bundled up in Flint's jacket and resting securely in his arms. Her concerns for Cass were solid, impermeable, but the child was here and needed help more than anyone else in the world.

As the horses ambled on, Raven caught Flint looking down on the child. She could not make out his whispers, but she was sure what he said was comforting in some way because the child snuggled closer to him as Flint lifted his head. They shared a glance, to which Flint shook his head and rolled his eyes.

"Don't look now, but I think you have a soft side after all."

He showed teeth behind a forced smile, then whispered in a gentle, soothing tone, "Don't you tell a fucking soul."

Raven laughed aloud, causing her horse to prick its ears back to stand at attention. "Language?" she said playfully with a scolding stare.

Flint chuckled. "Even if he could understand, he's

asleep, Ms. Raven. I may be a foul-mouthed SOB at times, but never in front of children or a lady."

Raven placed a hand on her hip and raised an eyebrow. "Excuse me? And what am I?"

"Greenhorn ranch hand," he fired back with a straight face, though his chin began to wobble with uncontrollable tremors.

"What?"

Flint couldn't hold it in any longer. He laughed with his mouth closed, muffling the sound and jolt of his body the best he could, then added, "It's how ya asked me ta see ya out here, right?"

Raven shook her head, lips pursed and eyes squinted. Flint's abrupt movement caused the child to stir in his arms.

He lowered his voice and settled his tone. "But I'll say this, yer the most ladylike ranch hand I've ever worked with. Graceful in the saddle, hard workin' with the land, an' learnin' like ki-yote in the rain."

"Okay, that's a little better, but I learn like wet coyote?"

"A-yuh. Ya sop up all ya can an' still go on about the day."

"Wouldn't a better way to say it be 'I learned like a sponge soaks up water?'"

"Maybe, but we ain't got sponges out here."

"You are hopeless, Flint."

"That's what they all say."

Raven looked upon the child, now resting comfortably again. The warm look of a concerned mother returned. She lifted her eyes to Flint. "If others could only see what I see."

"Nah. I wouldn't have it any other way."

The horses walked on under what was becoming a brilliant display of stars sprinkled across a blackened sky. The Big Dipper began collecting its fill of night as it appeared just over the horizon to the north of the three riders. The moon, staged in a waxing crescent, looked like the Cheshire cat's smile hovering just above the mountain peaks. In the distance before them, lights from the ranch house looked like tiny blurs of yellowed cotton hanging over the ground.

"You're a good man, Levi Flint," Raven said. "You're a good man."

CHAPTER FORTY-SIX

I stood on the balcony outside our room staring at Parroquia de Nuestra Señora de Santa Ana as the last light cascaded through the bell tower. The carillons had chimed at six o'clock, and again at six-thirty, and I found that the time between the clanging had been lost on me.

A purple haze filtered behind the church like a royal sash had been laid along its stony ridges. It had a fuzzy appearance that slowly turned darker and darker, its edges filling in until they looked inky smooth. Lights turning on all over had begun to bring about a new feeling to the city. To some, it may have been exotic or mysterious, but to me it was sinister. For every light, shadows loomed around the edges. Maybe I was feeling stark. Maybe my mind was settling in for the job ahead. It did not matter the reason; I knew darkness and what hides behind its blackened shield.

"You believe in monsters?"

Ray walked up behind me.

"The big, ugly kind with sharp teeth and claws, or the kind that kill women and children without a second thought?"

Ray leaned forward on the concrete ledge and looked over.

"Either. Both. Hell, if you ask me, there are some mean motherfuckers roaming around, some of which you'll never see until it's too late."

"I'd have to say both, Ray, but not how you might imagine."

"Enlighten me."

I turned around and rested my hip against the parapet and crossed my arms over my chest.

"If I can look at someone knowing the terrible things they have done, see the evil in their eyes and put a bullet through their head, then that is something I can easily believe in. It's real. It's tangible. It's something I can act on." I shifted my weight, feeling the rough edges of the wall against the small of my back. "What scares me. What truly scares me are the flashes of imagination, the heat of emotion, the ragged thumping of my heart that beats so hard at times it makes my soul ache; those are real enough, but the worst thing is they are all a part of me. I felt it when Spencer was missing. I felt it when Raven was attacked at our home and I wasn't there to protect her. I'm scarred that way, which makes me worry that even after this mission is over, will I be able to step back into the light, or will I find that the darkness around me is more comforting?"

Ray spit over the edge and watched it fall, then turned and crossed his arms next to me.

"Cass, I've known you for a long time. You're a hunter. Always have been. Always will be. It's in your blood. But you're also a fixer, which means you want to find the good in people or the positive in a situation." He turned to look at me. "Take the ranch, for instance. You packed up your life and moved out to the most barren place in the whole goddamn world. And why? To start new so that your wife could heal. You had no idea what you were getting into, but you did it because you felt it was the best thing to do. And you know what? You were right. Fast forward to now. Here, on this very balcony, you're hours away from storming the castle and taking out one of the most powerful turds in all of Mexico, and you never batted an eye. Why? Not because of those monsters nagging at your insides, but because it is the right goddamn thing to do. That's you, Cass. You're a hunter. You're a fixer. You'll be that way until you've taken your last breath."

Ray slapped me on the shoulder and gave me a solid look in the eye.

"Thanks, Ray."

"No problem." He meandered back toward the room. "Now, if you'll excuse me, I have to take a shit."

I turned around and laughed. It felt good, which was the point of it. Ray's words hit home, and in his own special way, made me feel better.

Glancing at my watch, I regarded the time and decided to take a final look over things before prepping my gear and grabbing a quick bite. I stepped back into the room and slid the glass door shut behind me. As I sat in a corner chair, my cell phone buzzed, alerting me to another incoming text. I fished it out of my pocket and read the screen.

CALLER ID: PRIVATE / WEDNESDAY 6:47 P.M.: *Dylan Sharp is not who you think he is.*

I held the phone in front of me and reread the short nine-word firebomb over and over. This was the third time I had received a private message, and the only time the sender was able to get through to me.

"Hey, Ray," I called out. "You need to see this."

The whir of the vent fan sang out as Ray appeared from the bathroom, then dissipated to a muffled hum when he closed the door behind him.

"What?"

He walked over and I handed him the phone. His lips

moved as he read to himself. He made a curious grunt that rumbled from the back of his throat, then handed the phone back to me.

"Timing couldn't be worse. Think it's legit?"

"Dunno," I said, staring at the display.

"Text 'em back. See if they'll offer up anything solid."

With a quick tap of my fingers, I texted back.

WEDNESDAY 6:50 P.M.: *Message received. Please identify yourself. Request further details.*

"There." I hit send, then set the phone on the desk next to me.

"Think they'll respond?" Ray asked.

"Probably not."

I started to stand when my cell phone buzzed again.

"Then again," Ray said. "See what it says."

I grabbed the phone and stood so we could both see the screen.

WEDNESDAY 6:51 P.M.: *Anonymity is the only thing that will keep me alive. Watch your back.*

I dropped my hand and slid the phone into my pocket.

"Well, that's a dead end."

"Can't ignore the warning though."

"No. We can't"

"What are you going to do about it?"

I reached behind me and pulled my battlefield green Glock 17 from my belt, removed the magazine revealing a full load, then slid it back into place with a commanding click.

"I'm gonna watch my back."

CHAPTER FORTY-SEVEN

The silver platter and polished cloche was the perfect size to conceal the thought-provoking message El Despiadado was planning to deliver. His only disappointment was that his plan did not involve him getting to see the look in Señor de la Droga's eyes firsthand. He usually had a front-row seat to such things, but if he was going to make a statement that all of Mexico could hear, he would have to do it somewhere else. Somewhere more meaningful. Then he would quench that satisfaction ten times over.

Peering at the two unsuspecting dinner guests, El Despiadado imagined what it must be like to feel untouchable, though by the flirtatious smiles from Isabella, and the gentle caress of his hand on hers, Señor de la Droga was posturing to be well touched before the evening was over.

"Too bad for you, but I believe dessert may change your mood." He turned his attention back to the service cart. His duffel lay on the floor beside it, crumpled and nearly flat on the floor. In that same moment, Diego poked his head into the hall from the rear of the kitchen. El Despiadado gave him a thumbs up, which caused an excited smile to form across Diego's face.

Turning to look at Señor de la Droga one final time before exiting the building, El Despiadado said with a voice that sounded hungry, "In fact, I think now is as good a time as any to be served."

Diego, more ready than ever to spring the surprise, glided down the hallway until he was standing at the front of the service cart.

"You look ready, my friend. Have you ever met a movie star before?"

"No, *señor*. Not really. But even if I had, none would compare to Isabella."

El Despiadado smiled. "I could not agree with you more." He stepped closer to Diego. "When you arrive at the table, make sure that the cart is placed between both Señor de la Droga and Isabella. He will be wondering what you are doing."

"Should I tell him it is from you?"

"No, that is not necessary. Simply say, 'With compliments from a dear friend.' That should be sufficient. Then remove the cloche and reveal the surprise."

"And then you will introduce me to Isabella?"

"Yes, yes. But not until after they have finished for the evening. I will remain back here until then. Do you understand what to do?"

Diego nodded.

"*Bueno*. Now, go be a good man and make the delivery."

Diego pulled the cart down the hall and turned into the kitchen. El Despiadado collected his duffle, the remaining contents shifting and rattling together, then walked to the exit at the end of the hall. He took a final look back, imagining all the fun he was going to miss, but anticipating all that he was about to have.

He pushed the door open and stepped outside. The clanking of pots and rolling chatter from the kitchen fell trapped behind the door. Lights in the staff lot encircled sections of the blacktop where workers' cars were parked waiting for their owner's shift to end.

Sconces imitating burning torches were mounted along the exterior wall, their bulbs flickering in random twitches of yellow light. El Despiadado moved beneath them on his way to the front of the building. He kept the time in his mind, a visual estimation of each step Diego was taking as he made his way through the kitchen and into the dining room. He suppressed the smile that intended to accompany the thoughts in exchange for a deeper focus, a savoring of the moment to come.

Rounding to the side of the building, he walked along the wall built with stone and concrete meant to give the nightclub an air of the past, disappearing and reappearing each time he passed under a flaming sconce. When he reached the front, he paused and peered around the corner. The guest lot was beginning to fill with patron vehicles. Like cattle waiting their turn to enter a slaughter chute, people stood in line at the door of Salón Pata Negra. It was still early, but the crowd was already growing anxious to gain entrance.

Señor de la Droga has no timetable, he thought as he looked at them. *He would make the Pope himself wait if that was his wish.*

With bag in hand, he walked past the growing line, heading for the valet stand. It was unmanned while drivers hustled to park the growing number of vehicles, but he could see a board half full of dangling keys mounted on an easel behind the chest-high counter. Acting as if he belonged, he walked around the edge of the stand and spied the key fob to a Mercedes hanging on a hook near the top of the board. There were no others like it, which meant Señor de la Droga's vehicle was his for the taking.

Too easy.

He leaned over and removed the key fob, then turned to face the parking lot. He found the G-Wagon and pressed a button on the key fob to unlock the vehicle. Its lights flashed and the horn chirped once. He replaced the key fob on the board and stepped around the valet stand when he noticed a group of three women had been watching him. His trap was nearly complete, but he was drawn to the gazes of the beautiful onlookers. He summoned a Carlos Ruiz-Mata smile and tilted his head just enough to signal his interest.

His mental clock was aware that his surprise would be revealed at any minute, but he was compelled to blend into the crowd. Slowly, his swaggered steps brought him over to the women.

"Buenas *noches, señoras*. Why is it that I find you all on your own?"

The women answered with their eyes, scanning him from his designer shoes to his perfect hair.

"If this were my place, you would not have to wait in such lines."

Two of the women smiled. The third raised an eyebrow, then motioned to the valet stand.

"It's not? Then why were you helping yourself to the keys over there?"

Her friends' smiles disappeared as if they knew where this was going and had most likely been in a similar situation before.

"Julia," one whispered, her face a mix of embarrassment and irritation. "Yeah, c'mon. He was just."

Julia turned to her friends, cutting them with a glare that made it clear to El Despiadado that she was the alpha, or queen bitch, of the group.

"Ladies, I simply do not like to wait. As you can see, the valet is very busy and I need to place my bag in my car." He locked eyes with Julia. "We don't have a problem, do we. Julia, is it?"

Julia shifted her hips and smacked her lips, then took a step closer to El Despiadado. Her friends bounced their looks between them.

The scent of Julia's perfume filled his nose. A crafty twinkle in her eyes sparked a curiosity in El Despiadado, but he did not have any more time for distraction.

"Are you a bad man?" Julia whispered.

The front doors to Salón Pata Negra opened.

"Do you like bad men?" he asked.

She lifted her eyebrow again, then opened her mouth a slit and bit down on her lower lip.

"I like..."

An ear piercing, high-pitched scream tore through the doors from the heart of Salón Pata Negra. The crowd jumped, unsure of how to react. Voices began yelling. A single gunshot erupted, causing the waiting crowd to turn and stampede away from the entrance.

El Despiadado slipped to the side as a wave of people engulfed the girls, pulling them along as if caught in a rip tide. Shouts and screams filled the air. El Despiadado avoided the raging current, maneuvering to the edge of the building, then alongside it until he came to the G-Wagon. He opened the rear driver's side door, climbed in, and shut it behind him. He placed the bag at his feet and unzipped the zipper. Reaching in, he removed two small devices that looked like the faces of a smartwatch, then peeled a protective coating back on one of them halfway and stuck it to the seat in front of him. He placed the other in his lap. He then removed his Sig Sauer from the bag and held it up to his face. The suppressed barrel added length, discretion, and an additional visual edge of hostility to his weapon. He regarded it as one might an old, familiar friend.

Flashes of bodies running past the grille of the G-Wagon caught his attention, but before pulling his eyes completely away from his weapon, he consoled it with a raspy breath.

"It is almost time."

Moments later, two men ran toward the vehicle. One aimed for the front driver's door while the other ran to the rear door on the opposite side. Both men jumped into the G-Wagon, the man in the rear yelling as he entered. His voice cut off the instant his eyes met El Despiadado and the threatening barrel of a gun pointed at his face.

"Good evening, Señor de la Droga. Please, sit down and buckle up. I would not want any harm to come to you while we are driving."

The driver whirled around, but El Despiadado stopped him with one calm phrase.

"Move, and I shoot."

Señor de la Droga's throat buckled as he swallowed nervous gulps of spit. The driver looked at him.

"Do as he says."

"Yes. I suggest you do as you are told," El Despiadado added with a gentleman's tone. "We are but old friends anyway who have been missing each other as of late. Turn around and drive us to Casa de los Fuertes."

The driver looked at Señor de la Droga, who gave a reluctant, yet furious nod. Twisting to the front, he started the engine and pulled out of the parking spot.

"We are in no hurry, so drive like you are giving your grandmother the grand tour around town. Understand?"

The driver did not answer, but the manner with which the G-Wagon drove through the crowds of people in the parking lot proved that El Despiadado's message was received.

As they turned onto Calle Guillermo Prieto a score of flashing red and blue lights raced closer. Sirens screeched, but the G-Wagon paid no attention. The emergency lights swept across Señor de la Droga's sullen face as they passed by, each rotation painting a darker anger on his brow.

"Do not be troubled," El Despiadado said. "You are out of harm's way and will soon be safe at home."

"Safe?" Señor de la Droga said with a laugh. "You are a dead man, Mata. Do you hear me? A dead man."

El Despiadado kept the gun pointed at Señor de la

Droga and removed the small, black device from the rear of the driver's seat with the other. Using his teeth, he pulled the remaining film from the adhesive base of the device and spit it onto the seat next to him. With a smile, he reached forward and pressed the sticky base to the driver's neck. The driver flinched.

"Keep your hands on the wheel, my friend." Glancing out of the front window, El Despiadado continued, "Pull over, *señor*. Anywhere will do."

Señor de la Droga shifted uncomfortably in his seat.

"Ah, ah, ah." El Despiadado glared at him.

The driver stopped the G-Wagon as instructed. Streetlights lined the road in both directions. Buildings looked on like timid animals hoping to make it through another dark night. The G-Wagon's idle was smooth, quiet, a luxurious perk of such an expensive Mercedes.

"Now, please *señor*. Get out and walk to the front of the vehicle. There is something on the hood I would like *El Jefe* to see. Please go and point it out."

"There is nothing..." the driver started to say.

"There is something you are not seeing. Get out and have a closer look." El Despiadado commanded. "Now. And leave your weapon behind."

The driver huffed and exited the vehicle, placing his weapon on the seat before slamming the door. Señor de la Droga dropped his eyes and gave an exasperated sigh.

"By all means, please. I want to show you something."

"There is nothing on the hood. There is nothing to see at all, *cabrón*."

The driver stepped into the headlights, looked at the hood, then through the front window. He raised his hands to the side in question.

"You say I am a dead man?"

El Despiadado reached into his pocket and revealed a small device the size of a credit card. There were two indentations on the card. A tiny red bulb blinked between them.

"What are you doing?" Señor de la Droga said.

El Despiadado smiled. He slid his index finger over one indent then placed his middle finger over the other. The blinking red light turned amber.

"Showing you what it means to be a dead man."

CHAPTER FORTY-EIGHT

Chance leaned against the grille of his red-and-white two-toned 1985 Ford F-150 pickup, its shiny paint gleaming under the warm glow of the gooseneck barn light that overlooked the southwest corner of the barn and the main entrance to the corral. Darkness swallowed the CR beyond the light, but still, he waited for Raven and Flint to arrive. His stomach rumbled, a sign of a long, work-filled day, and it had not yet come to an end. A chirp sounded out from a handheld radio resting on the passenger side of the bench seat inside the truck. Chance tilted his head to listen.

"*Control, this is Unit eight. It's a ten-ninety out here, over.*"

"*Copy that, Castillo. It's quiet across the board.*"

"*Ten-four, Dispatch. It's been a long one. All quiet on the western front, over.*"

"*Maintain ten-two. Enjoy the quiet but stay alert. Dispatch out.*"

The radio chirped once, then fell silent. Chance stepped away from the truck and repositioned himself at the corral fence. Placing a foot on the lowest cross beam, he leaned forward and continued to scan the dark for his friends. In the white-speckled ink above him, a barn owl glided past. It swooped just over his head and let out a sharp, eerie shriek that pierced the night and caused him to jerk in surprise, his foot slipping as a wave of startled tension gripped him.

"¡Órale!" Chance looked up and shook his fist in the air. "¿Qué haces, pájaro? You think I am dinner? Ve a buscar comida en otro lado!"

He rolled both of his shoulders, working the chill from his spine, and repositioned himself on the fence. From the dark, he heard a new sound. This time, it caused him to bashfully shake his head and smile. Like a fresh breeze wafting against him, Chance heard feminine laughter targeting him. Looking into the glee-filled shadows, he spotted two horses approaching. With each step, the riders came more into focus as the waning rim of light spread across their faces.

"Look like you've seen a ghost, Chance," Raven said from across the corral.

"Saw that, did ya?"

"And I won't forget it."

Raven's face beamed in the glow of the incandescent light. It made Chance smile, too, though his concern for her and why he was called remained.

Flint fell in line behind Raven as their horses walked around the perimeter of the corral, pulling up just shy of Chance. Raven dismounted, wrapped the reins from her horse around the middle rail of the fence, then walked over to Chance and gave him a hug.

It was a surprising greeting to Chance, but under the circumstances, it just felt right. He squeezed, then gently let go as she stepped back.

"You doin' okay, Raven?"

"Yes. I'm alright."

"An' the boy?"

"With Flint, sleeping like a baby."

Chance glanced past her and saw Flint still in the

saddle with a young boy wrapped in a jacket and cradled in his arms.

"He needs to see a doctor," Raven said, looking over her shoulder. "We did what we could, but his legs..." Raven stopped to catch her breath. Being on the ground, safe at home, sent a rush of emotion into her. She turned back to face Chance. "He was so scared. And alone. I don't think he has anyone in the world."

Chance looked on with empathetic eyes.

"I need your help, Chance. He needs your help."

"I know some people that—"

"No!" Raven interrupted. "You are not going to turn him over to social services or whatever. He's got no identification. My guess is that he was with the group we found yesterday, but they are all dead."

"Raven. There's procedure ta follow here. You know that."

Her jaw tightened and she took a step closer to Chance.

"You, of all people, know the history of the CR. He may not have set out to find the Gateway to Paradise, but I found him. That should count for something."

Chance tipped his hat back a nudge.

"What're ya saying, Raven?"

She softened her tone, releasing the building pressure between her teeth.

"I'm saying that this one..." She pointed back at the boy. "This one is my responsibility, not some stranger in a system."

"Ya know what yer saying, Raven? It's not like findin' a sick puppy to raise and rehome once it's back on its feet."

"I know. I also know that if he does have a family, it's going to be damned hard to find them."

"And if the time comes and they are found?" Chance said. "Will you be able to let go?"

Raven looked back once again at the boy in Flint's arms.

"I know that when whatever road lies ahead of him is going to be the roughest he has ever had to travel. If I can help him, I will do what it takes so long as he is safe."

Chance wiped his chin with his palm, glanced at the sleeping boy, then back a Raven.

"Let's get him in the truck. Ride with me to the hospital an' we'll get him looked at."

"And then?"

"One step at a time, Raven. For now, I'll help ya do what's right fer him as long as you understand what that means for the both of ya."

"I understand," she said with a hopeful nod.

Chance raised his arm and placed a gentle palm on her shoulder.

"*La Rescatista.*"

"The Rescuer?"

Chance chewed his bottom lip and nodded.

"The very one. Looks like the story of the Gateway to Paradise lives on."

The gaze between them marked a beginning and yet a gateway of its own that spoke of a history long ingrained in the very ground they stood upon. It was because of the Gateway to Paradise that Chance was given a new lease on life. Though he was merely an infant when he crossed through, it was the beginning of a life meant to serve where cost never stood a chance against the will of a few good people whose sole purpose was to do right by others. Now, with a new generation of Callahans overseeing the CR, the time for humanitarian intervention seemed to be greater than ever, and the life of this child meant that one more person could be saved just as Chance had been.

"Thank you, Chance."

Raven turned and walked over to Flint. She reached up, and he gently transferred the sleeping child into her waiting arms. The child stirred once, then nuzzled in against her chest. Chance opened the passenger door of his truck and held it until Raven loaded up with the child.

When they were settled, he closed the door and walked around the front of the truck, catching Flint's eye on the way. In that moment, they regarded each other with a wordless glance. Nods were shared, and then it was over. What went unsaid spoke more to their understanding of what was happening, and what it meant moving forward, and yet neither found reason to challenge the decision of the other. Like it or not, they were all in this together. With a mind full of new questions and weighted worry, Chance got in behind the wheel. The truck hummed as the engine came to life.

Raven watched as Flint stood by the horses, doused in the beams of the classic Ford truck before it pulled to the left and turned around. He gave a halfhearted wave and looked on. Raven sighed, knowing the lengths Flint had gone for her without a shred of resistance. It made her begin to wonder how a man like Flint ended up staying on the CR for so many years and why he lived his life alone. His rough exterior was thick with callouses, but underneath, she had tapped into something much deeper and pure, evident by the care he had given the sleeping child now resting peacefully in her arms.

The rolling vibrations of the cattle guard interrupted her thoughts as the truck passed over the iron bars. She stroked the child's black hair with tender fingers. His nose twitched and whistled with soft snorts. Chance remained silent. The rumble of the gravel road felt like a moment of Zen; its random crackling and padded bumps and knocks were calming. Raven sighed. Looking out the front window, she gazed beyond the headlights. Her mind drifted in and out of thought as Chance drove them into town.

CHAPTER FORTY-NINE

When I was a kid, I used to get a cluster of knotted butterflies in my stomach before stepping onto the court for a high school basketball game. It was an excited nervousness mixed with performance anxiety, the only cure of which was to see my first shot swish through the net. The same was felt before a Taekwondo match. Anticipation and planning went out the window as the match unfolded, which meant I had to think on my toes. By then, I was laser focused and the nagging butterflies had been kicked in the head.

As I sat on the end of the bed fully prepped and ready for our mission, I only felt a numbing sense of rage. It was not enough to cloud my judgment but had ample effect to overpower all other feelings any normal person would have prior to putting their life at risk for the safety of others. Oddly, it made sense. This mission was all about toppling an empire, lopping off the head of the proverbial snake, which was why Agent Zuñgia and his small corner of the FBI gave it the green light. For me though, it was a blend of justice and revenge only a father and husband with the skills and means to kill another would know.

I rubbed my thighs. The tactile sensation of pressure kneading my muscles was soothing while I replayed visions of Raven's anguish over her missing son, of his return, his vivid accounts of what had happened to him during his ordeal in the desert. I saw the mass destruction of the Brewster County Sheriff's Office, replayed the video footage of the deputies, my friends, who were brutally murdered in our house, and then painfully invited the sight of Deputy Javier Santos lying face down on the pavement following his murder on the road in south of town to enter the fray of my thoughts. I was a mess inside, but I had control. At least it felt as if I did, for now.

A knock at the door invaded my jaunt down memory lane. Ray was closest, having been in the bathroom, again, and answered through the peephole.

"Ain't got no money for Girl Scout cookies today."

A muffled grumble rose from the hall.

"Let 'em in, Ray," I said.

Ray opened the door. Agent Sharp pushed by before Ray had time to move completely out of the way. I could tell something was wrong before he vomited what it was he had to say.

"They're pulling the plug!"

I stood up as he paced by the bed and looked out the sliding glass door.

"We're this close to go time, and they're pulling the fucking plug!"

"Hold on, Sharp. What are you talking about?"

He turned and squared up to me.

"Let me spell it out for you. The *mission* has been *canceled*."

Ray and Crank joined us in the heart of the room.

"What's he sayin', Cass?" Ray asked.

"Are you all deaf?" Sharp was livid. He swung his arm around, sending a lamp from the dresser crashing into the wall. "We have been ordered to stand down and return to El Paso. Tonight."

"I received no such order, Sharp."

"Well, you're not really FBI now, are you, Detective?"

I glared at Sharp.

Watch your back.

"I don't know who you are talking to, but I am the lead on this mission, FBI or not."

Sharp pulled out a cell phone and thrust it toward me.

"Get Zuñiga on the line!"

I took the phone and tossed it onto the bed.

"You're out of line, Sharp." Our voices rose with each tick of the clock. "We were mission silent the moment we crossed the border." I looked at Ray and Crank. "We move forward as planned. Either of you have a problem with that?"

"Not a one," Ray replied.

Crank looked past me, trading glances with Sharp. His eyes told me everything I needed to know.

Turning back to face a steaming Agent Sharp, I continued, "If you lost your nerve and intend to withdraw from the mission, do it now. Nothing else changes."

"Lost my...? You son of a bitch. I want a piece of the Camargo cartel just as much as anyone."

Watch your back.

"But I will not disobey an order that might get me killed."

Who are you really taking orders from, Sharp?

I raised my hand, palm out to him.

"Hand over your weapon. Go back to your hotel or whatever hole you're staying in, and stay out of our way."

Sharp's eyes blazed a glare meant to burn me to the core. The air felt heavy in the room, almost as if we were standing underwater. Ray stood to my rear with Crank beside him. I stood close enough to Sharp to smell his breath and within range of flailing spit when he talked.

"You've been a thorn in my ass ever since I met you, Callahan. You're not taking my gun, but I am taking over."

With one swift motion, he reached for his sidearm. The feelings I had been dealing with on the bed had subsided as our encounter pressed on, but the anticipation of where I felt things were going fell naturally back into place, just as they always had, and I was laser focused.

Before Sharp was able to draw, I lunged ahead with my outstretched palm and grabbed his wrist. Balling my free hand into a steel fist, I landed a full body-weight punch to the bridge of his nose. The crack and snap of bone was quickly overshadowed by the rush of blood from his nostrils.

I sensed movement behind me, but no one intervened.

Sharp wavered once, then flinched like a hooked fish gasping for air before crumpling to the floor. I removed the gun from his hand as he fell, tossing it over to Ray like a quarterback running the option. It was all over before it started, which kept us all safe.

"That's the second time I've decked him in a month."

"You're just doing what the rest of us wanted to do in the first place," Ray said, walking over to me.

"Crank. If you've got anything to say, now is the time."

"Nope," he said. "I'm with you, boss."

We shared a nod.

"Good, let's get him up and into the bathroom before he bleeds all over the floor."

Ray helped me drag a limp-bodied Sharp into the bathroom. We slid him into the tub, then secured his right wrist to the shower pipe with a pair of handcuffs.

"Tape his mouth," Ray said. "when he comes to, it's the only weapon he'll have."

I looked at Sharp. His eyes stared off between tiny slits in his eyes. His nose drained onto his chest leaving gobs of chunky red to dry on his neck and shirt.

"We do that, he might drown in his own blood."

"We don't and everybody in the hotel will hear him scream and fuss to be let free."

Crank poked his nose in the door.

"What if we move up our timetable?"

I turned around.

"The primary window of opportunity is midnight to four a.m. Anything early might encounter more resistance," I said.

"I hear ya, boss. But if we stay here and wait for that window to open, we're either going to have to figure out how to keep Sharp quiet or untie him and bring him along. I don't think you want to do either of those things."

I glanced at Sharp while Crank spoke.

"While I understand this is your game Callahan, and I'm just a player, the way I see it is we'll be better off without the added liability. Sharp's had it out for you from the beginning. The crap I had to listen to on the way down here, you'd want to string him up right now and use him for a punching bag."

"Now that's a plan."

Ray's sarcastic timing was on point but not what the moment needed. Crank stepped forward.

"Look, it's not ideal. Hell, it may be more dangerous. But if we are going to bring this SOB Droga down, we can't afford any distractions."

He swiveled his head back and forth between us.

"Look, you said it yourself; you're going in with or without us. From the look on your face and the tone in your voice I'd say this is more of a personal vendetta than business—"

"Easy there, pard," Ray said, his words rolling slowly off his lips.

Crank lifted both hands as if in surrender.

"I don't have a problem with that. All I want is to bag the bad guy and get home."

An uncontrolled groan escaped from Sharp. The clock was ticking. The more Crank spoke, the more I considered his change of plans.

"We have to move before he wakes up. That's all I'll say."

Crank backed away from the door. A look in the bathroom mirror gave me a view of Sharp crumpled in the tub,

Ray on my six, and the reflection of my face that looked ready to go to war.

"Come on, Ray. Let's saddle up."

"Hoo-ah."

I stepped out of the bathroom and walked over to the bed where my go bag sat ready and waiting for battle. Ray followed behind me. Crank stood in front of the TV with a pack on his back and a stony look on his face. I unzipped the bag and removed three tactical earpieces. I slipped the coiled acoustic tube of one around my ear, then handed the others to Ray and Crank.

"We'll use the fire escape at the end of the balcony and head for the truck. Ray, you'll ride in the bed and keep watching our six. Crank, you're up front with me. We're going in hot, fast, and deliberate, so keep your game faces on. We stick to the plan, but if we need to improvise, stay frosty."

Ray lifted a Mk 43 Mod 0 machine gun off his bed and brought it to his chest. He kissed the barrel.

"I've got all your improvisation right here, Cass."

"Keep comms clear of chatter. Call signs only from here on out."

I looked at my men. They put themselves at great risk to be here. For that, my respect for each of them grew exponentially.

"Hulk. Dragon."

"Rowdy," they answered together.

"Grab your gear and let's roll."

CHAPTER FIFTY

The ringing in El Despiadado's ears was not bad as he had expected such side effects from the blast. On the other hand, Señor de la Droga suffered a more intense shock to his system as his wide-eyed, horrific glare, and pressed palms covering ears displayed. When the blinking red light on El Despiadado's emitter card turned amber, it marked a turning point in their evening. Fear, an emotion Señor de la Droga had forgotten that he could experience, reentered the multitude of immediate thoughts and feelings he had, taking center stage as he sat with a VIP view of his driver's torso erupting across the hood of the G-Wagon.

Bits of bone and flesh spattered the front window, chipping the glass along the passenger side at eye level. The hood was a mess of blood and mangled innards. A fractured rib pierced the metal hood of the SUV, standing erect like a tiny flagpole. A meaty mix of skin dangled from its tip like a wet flag in a rainstorm, signaling surrender. A slice of scalp, with hair still combed and fixed in place by an overabundance of mousse or gel, slid across the gentle slope of the G-Wagon's right, front quarter panel like a beaver gliding across a muddy bog. Tendrils of smoke wafted into the air. El Despiadado watched as the white, stringy haze lifted.

Another soul waiting to be collected? he thought. *But where will you spend eternity, my friend?*

Señor de la Droga's mouth opened and closed as if he were trying to speak, but the words refused to cooperate. Finally, an awkward gurgle filled with tension, disbelief, and fearful rage boiled in his chest, then shot up and out in a spray of vomit and angry words.

"*¡Te mataré! Te mataré y a todos los que alguna vez has conocido!* Do you hear me? Everyone you know will die for this!" He wiped his trembling mouth. "Everyone, Mata!"

El Despiadado tilted his head as if considering the message, then offered a rebuttal.

"Tell you what, Arturo. I think it is time to drop the whole *Señor de la Droga* title. It is not very fitting, considering your current situation. Let us continue to Casa de los Fuertes where I can help to accommodate that request. I promise, I will be very thorough. Just as you have always expected of me." El Despiadado raised his gun, pressing the suppressor to the chin of Arturo Mendez. "But first, let us step out and ride together like old times. I will drive, and you can sit next to me in the front seat. We were friends once, after all."

Arturo's eyes narrowed. His mouth snarled into an angry curl of lips and sweaty mustache.

"Whatever you are thinking will have to wait. Now, open the door and step outside."

El Despiadado opened his door and stepped out, all the while keeping his weapon aimed and ready should Arturo decide to do something unfortunate.

With pitted reluctance, Arturo opened the rear passenger door and got out.

"Very good. Now, to the front if you please."

Arturo cursed under his breath and gritted his teeth but did as he was instructed. He flung the door open and sat in the passenger seat, slamming the door behind him.

El Despiadado opened the driver's side door and peered inside. Arturo had been so focused on his discontent that he missed seeing his driver's gun sitting in plain view on the seat next to him.

"*Gracias*, Arturo." El Despiadado said as he reached in and took the gun. "I see that we have a degree of trust after all, or are you overcome with guilt that you would overlook such a thing?"

"*¡Jodete!*"

El Despiadado smiled, embracing the insult at first, then aimed his gun at Arturo and fired. Arturo grabbed his left thigh. Blood spilled from his leg, saturating his pants, and draining into the seats along the leather stitching.

"*Ahhhhh! ¡Dios mío! Hijo de puta, me disparaste!*"

"It is merely a flesh wound. You will live." El Despiadado paused, then scratched his chin. "Is there anything else you would like to say to me?"

Arturo grimaced. He bit down on his teeth to suffer the pain in his leg while holding back what else may have been on his mind.

"Good. Now, buckle up. It is important to be safe when riding in a car. So many things can subject a passenger to sudden...*injury*."

El Despiadado climbed in, clicked his seatbelt into place, pressed the brake, and shifted into reverse.

"Sit back and relax, Arturo. We will be home soon."

Before driving off, El Despiadado peeled the backing from the second explosive device and showed it to his injured passenger.

"In case you were thinking of signaling your security once we arrive."

He leaned over and pressed the small device to the side of Arturo's neck. The small, black box of death clung to his skin with the strength of a spider's web.

"Shall we go?"

With a satisfied huff, El Despiadado backed into the empty road. Arturo's eyes had followed the device as it was affixed to his neck but were now drawn to the ghastly site caught in the LED high-performance headlights.

The bottom portion of his driver's body looked intact, though covered with entrails and juicy streams of blood and bodily fluids. The rest was a morbid pile of torn skin and jagged bone, shredded muscle and mutilated vital organs. The mangled mound steamed, still heated from the blast.

Arturo looked away but could not escape the gruesome scene completely. At the furthest edge of the headlight's beam, he could see a hand in the gravel, fingers down as if clutching the ground. For a moment, it looked like it was trying to crawl away. He rubbed his eyes with one hand while keeping pressure on his leg with the other. Looking to the opposite side of what was left of his driver's body he spied his other hand lying knuckles down, its fingers relaxed, its palm inviting.

"I would hate to be the one who is made to clean that up, wouldn't you agree?" El Despiadado said as he turned the wheel and shifted into drive.

Arturo leaned his head back against the seat. His leg throbbed. His mind was ravaged. His ego stolen. But still, he held onto one bit of hope that he might survive the night.

Streetlights flickered past as the black night deepened. Casa de los Fuertes was not far, but what did it matter? It was early, and El Despiadado was just getting started.

CHAPTER FIFTY-ONE

D ressed in black from head to toe, Dragon, Hulk, and I slipped down the fire escape to the back alley adjacent to the location of the truck. I wore a nondescript tactical vest with armor plating and tightly woven Kevlar. My boots were crafted from a revolutionary microfiber compound that absorbed sound waves and dispersed vibrations from footfalls, while the high-density, viscoelastic polymer soles conformed to any surface shape, ensuring maximum contact and grip, all while minimizing noise. My pants were lightweight yet boasted a strong ripstop weave, resistant to tears. They had strategically placed pockets down each leg as well as interwoven hidden pouches above both ankles and along the right waistline. They were water resistant and flame retardant. It was overkill in the making, but better be prepared for anything than be sorry. Dragon and Hulk wore similar gear, all of which made us virtually invisible in the dark.

The truck was white, an unfortunate color that could make us stand out, but its old frame and Latin American focused make and model would blend in on any street in Camargo. We took our positions in the truck, Hulk and I in front, Dragon in the bed, and quietly pulled away from the curb unnoticed by anyone who might show concern.

The air was cool. The night was calm. With only a sliver of moonlight teasing the sky, the conditions were in our favor for a covert operation. The drive was quiet, each of us focused on the mission. This was where the angry father in me would have to take a back seat to the soldier. I had never had to consciously commit to one over the other, but with a mission objective that gave a green light to killing the cartel drug lord, Arturo Mendez, a.k.a Señor de la Droga, and anyone who got in our way, I was certain that the father and soldier would find a mutual satisfaction with the outcome.

Once the mission was over, Carlos Ruiz-Mata would be priority one and I had no intention of leaving Mexico until I faced him.

CHAPTER FIFTY-TWO

XHRPC - Radio Parral 102.5 FM blared over the G-Wagon's speakers when El Despiadado turned the audio system on as they drove. He tapped his fingers on the steering wheel to the beat of the music, though he had never heard the song before. Arturo leaned against the window scowling. He shifted his weight every few seconds to find a more comfortable sitting position, but with a bullet boring a hole in his leg, he would have no such luck. El Despiadado noticed.

"Relax, Arturo. We will be there shortly. Look out the window and try to remember what life was like when we were younger. Just coming together. Both searching for the same man. Do you remember?"

Arturo looked ahead, ignoring the question.

"Very well. I remember. How could I forget? I believe that he was to be your first? I can still see the look on your face when you discovered that I had beaten you to the task. Remember how I tossed you his head like a foot-ball?" El Despiadado laughed, acting as if their reminiscing was a solidifying moment between them. "Your face turned white, but reflexes took over and you caught it with both hands. I have never seen a man vomit and scream at the same time."

"We were only supposed to kill the man. Not chop him to pieces."

"No. You are right about that, but I wanted to have some fun. Send a message louder than I was meant to send. When I told my boss what I had done, he did not believe me. But when he heard it from another, he summoned me to him, kissed both of my cheeks and gave me my title—*El Despiadado*."

"You will always be Carlos Ruiz-Mata to me. Nothing more."

"Pity, I believe El Despiadado may be here for good."

"*No, cabrón.*" Arturo turned to look at him. "He will be as dead as Carlos before the night is through."

El Despiadado met his gaze and offered a jovial humph. "We will see, my friend."

They turned onto Calle Quinta and approached the entrance to Casa de los Fuertes.

"If you would like to die right here in the front seat of your car, by all means, make a scene. Otherwise, tell your man at the gate to let us through."

El Despiadado turned into the drive, lowered the volume on the radio, and slowed to a stop in front of the closed security gate. Looking out the window, he saw a security guard walking toward them. He wore a sidearm, but the safety strap was buckled in place. El Despiadado rolled down the window.

"Now would be a good time to speak, Arturo."

The car was recognizable, but when the guard saw El Despiadado behind the wheel, he froze in his tracks and reached to his hip holster.

"What are you doing, fool? Open the gate?" Arturo yelled.

The security guard looked past El Despiadado, then back at him again.

"*¿Quién es?*" he said, his hand still poised to draw.

"An old friend. Stop asking questions and open the gate. Now!"

"What happened to the car? It is a mess."

El Despiadado answered. "We hit a dog on the way."

"A dog?"

"It was a big dog. Jumped right in front of us. You should have seen its body explode on impact. It made *El Jefe* regurgitate his dinner, if you get my meaning."

The guard cracked a smile, then quickly put it away. He turned to the security hut and whistled. The guard in the hut activated the gate, opening it before them.

"*Gracias*, my good man."

The guard nodded and turned to walk away. Before taking a step, he looked back and asked, "*¿Dónde está Chano?*"

Arturo grimaced as he leaned over to glare at the guard. "He is still at Salón Pata Negra with the actress."

"The dog," El Despiadado added. "He should be so lucky as to catch the eye of the beautiful Isabella Constantine Salazar."

The gate clanked to a stop.

"Drive," Arturo commanded.

"You heard *El Jefe*," El Despiadado said to the guard.

The guard nodded and motioned for them to pull ahead. As they passed beyond the gate, El Despiadado whistled a tune from an old Spaghetti Western that had popped into his head. He repeated the tune once more, then said, "A fitting melody for us, don't you think? I am the good, of course. You are the bad. And what is left of Chano on the hood is very, very ugly."

Arturo grumbled. El Despiadado continued to whistle the tune over and over again as the G-Wagon slowly drove along the winding drive to the front of Casa de los Fuertes.

CHAPTER FIFTY-THREE

One of my first jobs in Dragon Company during my tour in the Middle East was to drive for our lieutenant, who just happened to be Ray Tucker. I was a young private at the time, and looked up to him, especially when under his command during missions. What I did not understand at the time was the pressure he was under to lead a successful mission and ensure the safety of his troops. Now, here I was, driving him on a mission again except our roles were reversed and I was in charge. Experience over the course of my military and law enforcement career had taught me how to handle situations, each to their own specifications, but there was never a time where I felt more responsible for the men around me than I did tonight.

As we bounced along en route to our insertion point, Hulk leaned over. "Goin' in with a smaller crew may cause us to spread out. If we get separated, watch your back."

My fingers tightened around the wheel.

Watch your back.

"We're going in tight, Hulk. That won't happen if we stick to the plan."

"Just sayin'. Anything can happen once we breach those walls."

Why are you telling me this, and now of all times?

A knock on the back window interrupted my train of thought. I glanced in the rearview mirror and saw Dragon signal that we may have a tail. I pressed my finger to my ear.

"SITREP."

"Bogey, four lengths back, right lane."

Maintaining our current speed, I looked in the passenger-side mirror and saw the square-shaped headlights of a truck or van at our five o'clock. I let off the gas, dropping our speed by five miles an hour. The vehicle surged closer for a moment, then reduced its speed to match our pace.

"Shit!" I said.

"Gotta lose 'em, boss," Dragon said.

"Hold on back there. Hulk, watch the mirror. Let me know if they make a move."

Hulk focused his attention on the mirror. At the same time, he brought his weapon, an M4A1 Carbine, to a low, ready position.

I pressed the gas, accelerating from a cruising thirty-five miles per hour to over fifty. Keeping in mind that I had a man in the back, I made calculated movements, but he was in for a rough ride.

"He's still on us, Rowdy," Hulk said.

I changed lanes as we approached an intersection, putting an old model sedan between us and our tail, then slowed my speed considerably. I watch the oncoming traffic light turn yellow. I slowed again. When the light turned red, I pressed the pedal to the floor. The engine screamed as if it were a little girl and I had just pulled her hair. We accelerated quickly and tore into the intersection between a mix of crossing cars. Tires screeched and horns blared, but we made it through without a scratch.

"Damn, Rowdy!" Dragon's voice filled my ear. "Who taught you how to drive?"

At the next corner, I diverted to a side street, cut the headlights, then turned again into a back alley that ran parallel with Calle Quinta. Slowing to a crawl, we moved through the darkness until the next cross street.

From our position, we could see the next intersection of Calle Quinta.

"Looks like we lost 'em?" Hulk said.

I raised my finger, then pointed.

"There. See that?" A black Ford Econoline van slowed at the intersection, then disappeared from view, still traveling along Calle Quinta. "That's our tail. Who the hell was on us?"

"Your guess is as good as mine," Hulk said.

"We're not keeping to our original timetable. Ain't a coincidence if ya ask me," Dragon said. "Maybe Sharp got free? Maybe he's our mole."

"Mole?" Hulk said, shooting a look at me.

Damn it, Ray, I thought.

"Yeah. The reason I changed things up last minute is because I came into some intel that suggested there was a leak somewhere in the FBI office."

"Didn't feel like sharing that info before now?" Hulk sounded disturbed.

I looked at him. "Didn't know who to trust, but I was going through with the mission regardless. Guess you're right. We all need to watch our backs." Hulk's eyes were dark so I could not get a read on how he took the last bit of what I said, but I sensed a tension in the light shifting of his seat. It was subtle, but tells often are. "We proceed as planned, but with utmost caution."

I pulled out of the alley and turned onto the side street that ran into Calle Quinta. Casa de los Fuertes was a mile and a half to our west. The clock was ticking, and with the addition of our mysterious tail, the dangers of our mission continued to mount.

CHAPTER FIFTY-FOUR

The face of Casa de las Fuertes was magnificent. Its white stone masonry gave it a smooth, silky appearance. Tall, arching windows, each decorated with hanging flower pots and lined with gold trim, looked out upon the receiving yard with palatial elegance. The roof was crowned with auburn tejas, lending it the classic charm of a hacienda while imbuing the structure with the robustness of contemporary architecture. Torchlight flickered from gas-fed sconces at the entrance, where an oversized wooden door, cut from the finest mesquite and adorned with artistic ironwork, awaited welcomed guests. Trees lined the perimeter of the yard, blocking the view of the surrounding security wall making it appear that this fortress was set in the middle of a lush countryside estate. A circle drive surrounded a massive fountain, then branched off into two separate driveways. One led to a parking surface at the foot of the house, while the other disappeared around the edge to a private drive. A series of LED lights lined the driveways at five-foot intervals.

"You see?" El Despiadado said as they pulled in. "You have made it. *Bienvenido a casa*, Arturo." He drove the G-Wagon in one complete circle around the fountain, then veered toward the private drive. "No sense in using the front door when you have other means to ensure your privacy."

They followed the lighting around to a side entrance complete with a three-car garage. To the left of the building and along the outer east side wall was a security hut similar to the one at the main entrance. Yellow light filled a window that opened up to the property revealing that only one guard kept watch, but looked more inter- ested in something in his hand than what was happening in his part of Casa de los Fuertes.

El Despiadado pulled in front of the garage. "Should I ask you to get out and raise one of the doors, or will you point out which button on the console activates them remotely?"

Arturo leaned over and pushed a digital button on the center console touchscreen, and the center garage door began to open.

"Good. It has been a month since I have been here. It is good to be back."

"You could have been here as a part of the family," Arturo said with a scratchy voice. "All you had to do was take the job that I assigned you."

El Despiadado pulled into the garage and pressed the button he had seen Arturo press, lowering the door behind them, then unbuckled and shifted in his seat to face his bleeding, angered passenger. "From your point of view, you are correct; however, the job was not ignored out of spite. Carlos, if you must know, felt that retirement might be in order. There is so much pain and suffering in the world, why continue to be a slave of those who fill the news and destroy families with such things. No, he would have rather sailed off into the sunset and enjoyed a much quieter life, but someone in this car does not take *no* for an answer."

El Despiadado shut off the engine.

"Come. We have much to do. I expect that you will have a few of your men look in on you now that you are home. Let's go into your office and welcome them together."

El Despiadado raised his gun, then motioned with the barrel for Arturo to exit the vehicle. Grunting, Arturo threw open the door and painstakingly slid out of his seat to lean against the door frame. Fresh trickles of blood seeped down his leg staining the concrete floor of the garage.

"Come. The sooner we get to your office, the sooner you can get off that leg of yours."

With a glare that would frighten a child just by seeing it, Arturo slammed the passenger door with eyes locked on El Despiadado. Never wavering his fiery gaze, he used the body of the G-Wagon as a brace and labored around the front of the vehicle.

El Despiadado met him at the grille. Chano's rib bone still stood erect, embedded in the hood, but lost its wet, fleshy flag during the drive. A sticky film covered the front end extending to the grille where bits of meat and fabric remained lodged in the openings encircling the Mercedes star. If the G-Wagon were a man-eating beast, it looked as if it had eaten its fill.

"I cannot make it without help," Arturo said with rising aggravation.

El Despiadado slid his gun into its holster within his jacket and held both arms out like he was encouraging a toddler to walk on his own. "Use me for balance. If we are seen, I will look like a hero, but remember what is sticking to the side of your neck." He lowered one hand and removed the emitter from his breast pocket. The blinking red light tortured Arturo with each tiny flash.

"Press it and you die, too, *cabrón*."

"That is true, but I am not afraid to answer for my sins. Are you?"

Having no other choice, Arturo grabbed El Despiada-do's forearm and stepped away from the vehicle. In obvious pain, he ground his teeth at each limping movement.

Together, they made their way out of the garage and into the courtyard.

"¡Qué bella vista! I am always amazed at how beautiful everything is here. The grounds are immaculate. The burning torches along the walls are impressive. But it is the statue of Jesús Malverde that I am drawn to most of all. To think that such a man may have existed is truly a marvelous thing, and the statue that you have displayed is one of a kind. May he bring you good fortune, my friend."

El Despiadado slapped Arturo on the back causing him to lose his balance. He thrust forward, jamming his full weight on his injured leg. Searing pain shot up and down his leg from the ball of his foot to the meaty hole in his thigh. Forcing his mouth to remain closed, Arturo groaned in agony.

El Despiadado grabbed him by the collar and straightened him up.

"There, there. Enough of the tour. Let's head inside for a well-deserved drink and possibly one of those Cuban cigars you like so much."

More dragging Arturo than helping him walk, El Despiadado led him to a side door that opened into the bottom floor of his private quarters. Once inside, Arturo faced another daunting task.

"Ay Dios mío. I forgot, señor. Your office is on the second floor. Is there an elevator for us to use? You look like you are becoming very weak."

Arturo's face was pale. His angered scowl hung on by only curl in his upper lip. His brow was covered in sweat. Wrought with dejection, he shook his head.

"Too bad. The stairs it is then. Come on, my friend. Up we go."

CHAPTER FIFTY-FIVE

D roplets of blood left a trail up the stairs and along the tile floor ending at the closed door to Arturo's second-floor office. Inside, El Despiadado took a seat behind his former employer's desk, leaving him to hobble to a leather couch across the room. The office was dimly lit, which set the mood for an intimate, final coming together for the two men. Next to the couch was a small bar cart stocked with tequila and clean glasses. Arturo's hands shook as he reached for a copita on the top shelf of the cart. He bypassed an open bottle of Casa Dragones, opting for a fresh bottle of Don Julio 1942. El Despiadado watched him struggle to remove the cork.

"Do be careful not to spill any on the floor. It would be such a waste," El Despiadado said, leaning forward and folding his hands on Arturo's desk.

Arturo's face reddened as he twisted and pulled the tightly set cork. After a third attempt, the cork came free with a resounding *pop*, and Arturo filled his copita to the brim. He set the bottle down and chugged half of the contents of his glass, coughing and spitting as he finally pulled it away from his mouth.

"No, no, *señor*. That is not right." El Despiadado stood up, walked over and picked up the bottle, and held it before him in admiration. He read a portion of the label aloud. "Created to honor the year that Don Julio González began his tequila-making journey, Don Julio 1942 is the culmination of decades of hard work and the pursuit of perfection."

Leaning forward, he removed a copita for himself and poured half a glass.

"Such a fitting tribute. We have that in common with Don Julio, do we not? Decades of hard work, pursuit of perfection, it says it right here on the bottle." El Despiadado twisted the label to show Arturo the inscription. "The only difference is that I have found perfection before you. How does it feel to be the lesser man?"

Arturo drank the remainder of his drink, then held the glass out for a refill.

"I was never the lesser man, Mata. I was always *El Jefe*, and you...you were just a pawn."

El Despiadado lifted his drink to his nose and breathed in the luxurious aroma. Then, with a gentleman's nod, he sipped a small helping, swirled the burning liquid around in his mouth, and swallowed. A quenching sigh escaped his lips as he pulled the glass away.

"A pawn, did you say?"

"*Sí*, a fucking pawn."

"Then that would make you the king, I suppose." El Despiadado walked back to the desk and set his glass down on the mahogany surface. Turning around, he withdrew a combat knife from a sheath hidden under his jacket. The blade was razor sharp, tapering to a fine point. Along the spine, a jagged, sawtooth pattern ran like a row of ferocious teeth, stopping just short of the hilt. The dark, blued finish of the steel provided a stark contrast to the shining, sharpened edge, underscoring the weapon's deadly elegance. El Despiadado held it before him admiring the power it had over every man that had crossed its path. "A queen, now that is where all the strength lies on a chessboard, but the king? He is the one that needs protection. He is the one who needs legions of pawns to fight his battles and sacrifice themselves so that he may continue to rule above all."

El Despiadado stepped slowly across the room. Arturo watched each movement, fighting the fury and fear that grew inside of him as the killer drew nearer.

"Funny thing though, about a king. He can plan and prepare, rule and live, smother himself with lavish riches and power, and make others suffer with the flick of a wrist, but it takes only one mistake, one simple thing to go wrong, and the life that once was can be held in check. A king's only hope is that there is someone around the moment his world collapses to keep his game alive."

El Despiadado looked down upon Arturo.

"Do you see anyone around?"

Arturo's eyes bulged. His pale face was stained with streaks of dripping sweat. He glared at El Despiadado but did not answer with words. Instead, he spit at a stringy stream across his pawn's pant legs.

"I did not think so, *señor*. That could only mean one thing." El Despiadado's face tightened. His lips curled up like a jackal. His eyes squinted so only the black remained. Looking like a true messenger of death, he leaned closer to Arturo. "Checkmate."

CHAPTER FIFTY-SIX

Parking in a secluded corner of what was once a locally owned traditional handicrafts shop, I cut the lights and turned off the engine, extending an open invitation for darkness and silence to swallow us all. A dilapidated sign with fading green and red lettering hung at a crooked angle over the dust-covered glass windows that read, Casa de Colores. I looked at the storefront imagining what dreams were lost or possibly trapped inside, left to roam the abandoned shop like ghosts in a haunted house. A tap on the roof drew my attention to Dragon standing next to my door.

"We're all clear, Rowdy."

I opened the door and exited the truck. Hulk had not moved or said a word since we parked and remained quiet as he got out.

"We've got one block to cover. Streetlights are out. I'm on point," I said. "Fall in a wedge behind me. Let's move."

Like shadows creeping across the pavement, we covered the ground between the blackened parking lot to the edge of the block. The east security entrance stood within a hundred yards of our position. The small security hut glowed with yellow light spilling out a window on the front door. I raised my HK G36 and peered through the optical site, locating the lone guard in my crosshairs.

"Target acquired. One guard. Looks to be more into his phone than his duty." I lowered my weapon and faced my men. "Hulk, you're with me. Dragon, cover us. Wait until I signal *all clear*."

Dragon moved to the side and took a covered position behind a pad-mounted transformer at the base of an electrical pole to our left, then waved us forward.

"On my six, Hulk. Let's do this nice and quiet."

He nodded and we were off again. We moved on swift feet, soundless, approaching at an angle with a clean line of sight of the target, but from a position that the guard would have to know where to look to locate us. My heart raced each beat in my chest, a reminder that I was still alive. Halfway became twenty yards, and then ten to go. I slowed our pace. With weapons raised, we advanced on the hut and slipped against the side wall undetected.

I glanced at Hulk, raising a finger to my lips, then handed him my weapon and drew a combat knife from my belt. Looking back at where we had run from, I raised two fingers to my eyes, then pointed to the hut and made a sweeping motion across my neck. I could not see Dragon, but I knew he could see me and would understand. I lowered my body to a crouched and attack-ready position and crept to the corner nearest the outer door.

The cyclical *beeps* and electronic *dings* of a game being played filtered out of the security hut. I peeked inside the glass window on the door and saw the guard's profile. He was small, had dark hair, and looked to be no older than Spencer.

Crap, I thought. Killing a kid was not how I wanted to start the night. I crouched lower, then rapped my knuckle once on the door. The noise of the game paused. I could hear feet shuffling closer, then the knob on the door twisted, its weathered metal mechanisms creaking as they turned. The door flew open, and the unsuspecting guard stepped out for a look.

With lightning speed, I grabbed the boy from the side, covering his mouth with one hand and ramming the steel handle of my combat knife down on the top of his head with the other. With a muffled grunt, the guard crumpled in my arms. I dragged him to the side of the hut and locked eyes with Hulk.

"Go."

Hulk leaned my weapon against the building then ran into the hut. I waved at Dragon, who promptly began to sprint right at me. By the time he joined me at the side of the security hut, I had zip-tied the guard's hands behind him and stuffed a rag into his mouth. Dragon shook his head when he saw what I had done.

"You know if we don't kill 'im, they will."

"We get to Droga, he may have a chance."

"It's a gamble, Rowdy."

"I'm not killing a kid."

My face said volumes more than my simple words conveyed. Dragon dropped the discussion. I dragged the guard into a patch of bushes along the foot of the outer wall, hoping he would be out for the duration.

"All clear," Hulk announced with a stealthy tone.

Returning to the hut, I grabbed my weapon and led the way inside.

"Got the video feeds running a recording from an hour ago," Hulk said. "Gives us an open window without fully disabling their surveillance. If the other guards are anything like this one, they'll never notice until we are gone."

"Roger that. Let's move," I said.

I opened the rear door to the security hut and took my first step into Casa de las Fuertes. The grounds were quiet. The service drive ran twenty yards ahead. LEDs lit the way like runway lights. The main building loomed before us; its white face displayed by arcs of landscape lighting. It looked larger than life, but that was the façade. Its long, tall walls and ornate windows gave it both the look of a villa and fortress.

Dragon and Hulk stood behind me, weapons raised and ready for anything.

"Got a wad of toe tags burnin' a hole in my pocket, Rowdy," Dragon whispered.

With a silent wave of my hand, the three of us moved out. I swept my weapon from left to right across my field of vision. Our blacked-out gear and balaclavas were perfect for the shadows but would do little under the lights except hide our faces.

When we approached the end of the service drive, I saw a three-car garage to our right. Straight ahead was a cobblestone archway that led into an interior courtyard. The building on the left was a multi-story residential suite but from the looks of it, it was bigger than my entire house and barn combined. I aimed for the door at the back of the building, quickly advancing over the blacktop drive to the entrance.

"Hulk, cover the perimeter from the arches. Use comms if you see anyone heading our way."

Hulk nodded, then took a low position near the cobblestone walkway.

"Dragon, once this door opens, sweep down the hall. I'll be right behind you."

"Roger that."

I pinched the doorknob with my fingers and gave a gentle twist of my wrist. It was unlocked, but of course it was. Who in their right mind would storm a drug lord's compound? I eased the door open making room for Ray to slip past me, then closed the door with the same care behind us. I followed as Dragon bypassed the stairs and cleared the lower hall. He motioned me forward to the edge of an open room. The far wall was made of glass so that visitors could look out to the courtyard. It was a magnificent view, but if I could see out, others might be able to see in. We moved through the room and cleared the remainder of the first floor, circling back around to the base of the stairs.

"Where is everybody?" Dragon whispered. "Don't these cartel dickheads always have an entourage or someone waiting in the wings?"

I motioned for us to go up the stairs. Dragon nodded and fell in line behind me as I took the lead. Each footfall was silent. Each step another rise into the heart of the building, and from here, there was only one way out.

At the top of the stairs, I could hear music. It was a recording of trumpets playing an eerie, yet oddly familiar tune. I was not one for traditional Mexican music, but I was sure I had heard it before.

I peered around the corner, the barrel of my weapon joining me for the look. A similar room opened out to a patio to the right of the staircase. A lamp lit a small corner table covered in magazines. A large, leather couch twice as long as any couch I had ever seen commanded the center of the room. Dragon was on my heels and saw it, too.

"Think Mattress Mac does one day delivery down here?"

"Cut it, Dragon." I pointed at a door across the room. Light outlined its frame causing it to glow. As we stepped closer, it became clear that the music was playing from somewhere behind the door.

Crossing the room, we stacked ourselves on either side of the door. I lowered my hand to reach for the handle when I froze at the crackle in my earpiece.

"Rowdy." Hulk's voice was low. "Two bogeys crossing the courtyard. Twelve o'clock."

I motioned with my head to Dragon to check it out. He slipped over to the glass and peered outside. Sure enough, two men walked and talked and were heading for our building.

"Hold your position. If they enter the building, we'll take 'em down."

"Copy."

Dragon watched until they disappeared beneath the second-floor patio. He motioned back at me—covering his eyes with his palm, then waved a hand before him signaling he no longer had eyes on them. I waved him back over to the door.

From the time I first reached for the knob until now, all I heard through the door was music. The same tune played over and over again as if set to repeat. I locked eyes with Dragon and raised my hands, giving a three-finger countdown. On go, he reached for and twisted the knob. Thrusting it open, I charged inside, sweeping my weapon left and right with my finger on the trigger and ready to fire. Dragon followed close behind. Two steps into the room we found ourselves face to face with Señor de la Droga.

CHAPTER FIFTY-SEVEN

With hands soaked and dripping with blood, El Despiadado stood on a red, crushed stone path that weaved its way in and around a vegetable and flower garden along the south rim of Casa de los Fuertes. Iron poles with curved tops ending with hook-shaped patterns were spread around the perimeter with various types of wildlife feeders dangling from each. El Despiadado reached one bloodied hand out and removed the bird feeder, placing it gently on the ground, and smiled.

"This will do nicely," he said. Looking around, he circled the same hand in the air as if attempting to summon the attention of anyone or anything that would listen. "I give you yet another option from which to draw life, my little friends. Enjoy the delicacy. It is truly one of a kind."

Growing anxious to share, he bent over and reached into the small duffel he carried and removed the treat. He stuck it on the hook where the bird feeder had been, feeling the warmth of fresh blood running over his hands. Satisfied with his slight change of plan, he whispered, "I always knew, even under your devilish scowl and greedy eyes, that you had a heart big enough to share with the world if you so desired it."

CHAPTER FIFTY-EIGHT

Señor de la Droga sat back on a couch, his arms outstretched to each side, his mouth hung open, and his eyes bulging from their sockets, covered in blood.

"Jesus H. Christ!" Dragon said, pulling down his balaclava, the shock in his voice mirroring the look on his face. "Somebody cut out his fucking heart! What is this, the Mexican version of Mary Shelley's Frankenstein?"

I walked close to the body.

"It's fresh. I mean, like we just missed whoever did this."

"But who? Is the World Cup in town? I mean, this place is a ghost town. And where is his heart? Someone just walking around, spreading the love or something?"

I pressed my hand to my ear, activating my comms.

"Hulk, SITREP."

I expected an immediate response. When none came, I asked again.

"Hulk, SITREP. Respond. Over."

Dragon cocked his head, listening in as well. Hulk failed to answer a second time. I deactivated my comms.

"Something's wrong," I said. "Let's fall back to his last

position. We'll regroup from there. It's a straight shot out of the compound if we need to fully evac."

Dragon nodded, then moved quickly to the door but was met with a flurry of rapid fire. Falling to the floor, he rolled to the side, brought his Mk 43 into firing position, and returned fire.

As he was rolling, I leaped forward, extended my arm, and tried slamming the door closed. Wood splintered as bullets tore through its solid frame. I could hear men yelling from the other room in Spanish. I activated my comms.

"Hulk! We're still on the second floor taking heavy fire. Where the fuck are you?"

My earpiece crackled. Hulk's voice filled the line.

"Doing my job, Cass."

"Call signs only, Hulk. Keep to protocol."

"To hell with protocol, buddy. Won't be too much longer now. I know how much ammo you have. We've got a lot more where this came from."

"You son of a bitch!"

"Guess Droga is dead? Thanks for that. My employer owes you one, but I doubt you'll be around to cash that in."

I looked at Dragon. His face was a mix of perplexed *WTF* and mounting rage.

"It's been fun so far, but this has to take the cake fellas. We're in a real-life Butch Cassidy situation here. We all know how that ended, don't we?"

Hulk's voice sounded relaxed, almost jovial.

"I'm gonna enjoy taking you down, big man," Ray said, his voice grim and threatening. "Should'a handled that the first day we met."

"I agree," Hulk said, almost as if reminiscing. "But then we wouldn't have gotten to have all this fun."

"Enough," I said. I was steaming, but we had bigger problems than just dealing with Hulk. Before killing comms, I heard Hulk speak, but not to us, and his words rolled off his tongue in fluent Spanish. "Ray, fuck the call-signs. It's time we show these bastards how Dragon Company responds when backed into a corner."

The anger in his face allowed a brief, and very deliberate smile to join the party.

"Unleash the blaze?"

I nodded back.

"Let's torch these motherfuckers!"

I flipped the fire control selector switch from semi to full auto with my thumb and unleashed hell.

Bullets tore through the door frame, through the wall, shattered windows and ruined expensive furniture on both sides of the door. Señor de la Droga's body jostled on the couch, catching stray bullet after stray bullet. I pulled a flashbang from my lower leg pocket, removed the safety pin, and yelled at Ray.

"Dragon fire!"

Flashbangs are designed to stun and disorient the senses using an intense explosion that results in a flash of bright light and a deafening boom. They don't throw or eject shrapnel, but the punch they pack will disorient and incapacitate anyone within close range of the blast.

I threw the flashbang out the door, then turned and pressed my hands over my ears. When the blast erupted, gunfire from the outer room stopped. Agonizing yelling and screams filled the air. Ray and I did not wait. In true Butch Cassidy fashion, we rushed through the door and opened fire, spraying the room with enough hot lead to cast an iron statue.

When the smoke cleared, three cartel soldiers lay sprawled across the floor, full of holes, and already walking with the dead.

"Where's Crank?" I said.

We scanned the room, sweeping left and right.

"Blood," Ray said, pointing toward the glass patio doors.

"Follow it," I said.

Covering each other, we moved to the door and peered out at the patio. The blood trail continued to the cement wall, then disappeared over the edge. I rushed ahead, ready to kill anyone that proved a threat but did not see Crank anywhere. What I did see, and made a cold chill rush down my spine, was a group of eight men, all running toward the building, all carrying weapons.

I raised my gun and opened fire. Ray took a position to my right and joined in the fight. We took out three of the men before the rest made for cover and began to return fire. As long as the cement wall held out, we were safe to duck behind it.

"Are we having fun yet?" Ray asked.

"Loads," I said.

"Bet you wish Sharp were here now, huh?"

"Don't get me started, Ray."

He smiled, reloaded, then turned and selectively chose targets at which to fire. I did the same, noting what ammo I had left. Crank was right about one thing, he did know what we had, and just how long it would last.

As I took aim, I saw a second group of men enter from the opposite side of the courtyard to join the fight. They came in slow, heavily armed using the building and structures in the courtyard for cover. With the number of reinforcements that were arriving, our situation was worsening by the minute. I glanced at Ray. We shared a look that said we might not make it out. That's when the first explosion rocked Casa de los Fuertes.

CHAPTER FIFTY-NINE

El Despiadado removed his fingers from the emitter that triggered the detonation.

"That should add another dimension to the party. Let's see how they like things when the rest of my little friends join in."

The south side of the residence where Arturo's body grew cold had been the target of the first explosion. It rocked the building, but the damage was not as catastrophic as El Despiadado had hoped. Relying on one charge to cripple the building was a mistake. It had worked in the past within other structures where a chain reaction of crumbled and burning debris assisted with the demolition, but Casa de los Fuertes was well constructed, which proved too much for a single blast.

Smoke blew out in a plume of heated ferocity, then settled among the flaming embers that fell into the courtyard and around the perimeter of the explosion. The garden where El Despiadado stood and watched was well enough away, but he was forced to brace himself as he felt the effects of the initial shockwave.

The gunfire paused when the blast erupted. Men in the courtyard yelled. Some looked onward in disbelief. Others advanced on the building, resuming their attack but were cut down when the men on the balcony opened fire once again.

"Who are you?" he said to himself. His curiosity piqued, but his exit plan did not allow an opportunity to stay and observe much longer. If he were seen, he might be drawn into a fight that simply was not his in the first place.

Moving quickly, and keeping his body hunched over, he left the garden and headed toward the main building. Gunfire continued across the courtyard, but El Despiadado had an entrance in sight. Before going in, and standing safely out of the line of fire, he paused to address the melee.

"It is a shame to miss out on all of this. Truly, it is not my style, but allow me to demonstrate what I enjoy when facing an unsuspecting adversary."

Reaching into the duffel, he removed a handful of small devices, then entered the building unseen.

As he maneuvered down the hall, passing through a large room complete with a full bar and rustic décor with fine leather work meant to be an area for entertaining guests, and one smaller salon staged for receiving visitors, he placed and activated each device, one after the other until he had exhausted his supply. He tossed the duffel aside as he approached a grand foyer leading to the front door. Pausing to glance back at the opulent interior of Casa de los Fuertes, he saw tiny red lights blinking throughout the lower half of the building. His charges were set. All he had to do now was step outside and enjoy the next round of fireworks.

El Despiadado slipped the emitter into his front lapel pocket, opened the front door, and went outside. The clatter of gunfire continued in the courtyard. In the distance, the shrill wail of emergency sirens pierced the air, growing louder with each passing moment. It would not be long before the authorities arrived, which meant he needed to move with haste.

At a jog, he slipped in and out of landscape lighting as he made his way along the outer wall toward the garage. It was a risky move, but he needed a fast exit from Casa de los Fuertes, and his Trailblazer was still parked at Salón Pata Negra. With a choice of vehicles parked alongside Arturo's G-Wagon in the garage, he could return to the airport in style.

As he rounded the corner of the building, moving from the grass to the blacktop driveway, the gunfire ceased. A hush fell on the courtyard. El Despiadado crouched low and moved forward until he came to the archway between the garage and Arturo's living quarters. Looking around the cobblestone arch, he saw that the statue of Jesus Malverde shielded two men with automatic weapons. They looked up at the patio balcony on his left, their gaze searching for a target while they bobbed their heads in random directions so as not to become one themselves. Dead men lay where they were shot in open sections of the courtyard.

They were not soldiers, El Despiadado thought. *None of them are. Give a man a gun and he will think he is invincible.*

He reached into his pocket and removed the emitter. The red light blinked impatiently on the device.

"It is time for the grand finale."

CHAPTER SIXTY

"What the hell was that?"

Ray's mouth moved, and I could read his lips, but the ringing in my ears from the sound of the explosion prevented me from clearly hearing him. We had both been knocked off balance from the jolt of the blast. Debris fell around us. Smoke billowed out of the far end of the building. Ray peered over the edge of the balcony, then scooted closer to me.

"Our friends in the courtyard look just as surprised. You think that was Crank?"

I gave it quick consideration, but my gut told me something different.

"No," I said. The shock to my ears began to subside, and my hearing started to come around. "The way Mendez was killed already had me thinking, but that explosion? I bet dollars to Pesos that Mata is here."

"Mata? The guy from the briefing? Your Mata?"

"The same."

"Why would he kill Mendez? What's in it for him?"

I heard voices rise from below. Ray heard them, too. He got to his knees and took another quick glance over the cement balcony wall, then recoiled.

"Looks like they're getting ready for round two, Cass."

I closed my eyes for a brief second, regrouping my thoughts, belaying my frustrations, but only one thing seemed logical at this point.

"What's the plan?" Ray asked. "I'm down to one magazine and a full load on my sidearm."

I opened my eyes and shifted onto my knees next to him.

"Time to evac."

Ray looked around, nodding in agreement.

"We ain't got but one way out, Cass, and that's just to get out of this compound. Once we hit the streets, all of Mexico is gonna be after us."

Gunfire erupted from below. We both tucked and rolled in opposite directions.

"On three, we're gonna give 'em a quick spray. Deliberate bursts. Remind 'em we're here, then make for the stairs," I said.

I held up my left hand and made the count with my fingers.

Three...two...one...

We rose together and opened fire. I took out two men on the far side of the courtyard before any of them knew what had happened. Ray picked off two more who were approaching the building, then he ducked quickly back behind the wall. The echoes of our gunfire mingled with the shouts of surprise and anger from the remaining cartel fighters.

"Let's move," I yelled.

Ray nodded, and we sprinted toward the shattered door and windows, our boots crackling on glass and bits on blasted concrete scattered across the patio. Bullets whizzed past us as gunfire erupted once again from the courtyard. We rushed into the main room, passing Señor de la Droga's destroyed office door, catching a final glimpse of his bullet-riddled body. The image of the black hole in his chest where his heart had been ripped out burned into my memory.

We entered the stairwell and descended two steps at a time, still able to hear the reports of gunfire outside. The door at the base of the stairs was solid wood. I reached for the handle and spoke to Ray before pulling it open.

"Listen. They're still aiming at the balcony. The garage is a clear shot from here. We're gonna sprint past the archway and enter through the side door. We're in for twenty seconds. Look for keys. Scan the counters, hooks, pegboards, whatever. I'll check the cars. If we come up empty, we head for the service entrance on foot."

"Copy," Ray said, crouched and ready behind me.

Taking a deep breath, I pulled the door and led the way out into the open. Ray was right on my heels as we flashed in full view past the arches. We crashed through the garage's side entrance at full speed, splintering the wooden frame with the sheer force of our momentum. Ray pulled a tac light from his belt and swept its beam across the garage.

"Whoa," he said.

Three vehicles were parked in a row. The closest was a Mercedes G-class SUV. It was posh, but it looked as if it had seen better days by the cracked windshield and debris stuck to the hood and grille. Next in line was a 2018 convertible Ferrari California painted in Blu Abu Dhabi metallic. Not a bad way to spend a cool one-hundred thousand dollars. It looked like something straight out of The Fast and The Furious franchise; perfect for a getaway, but I doubted we would fit in its cramped interior wearing all our gear. The last was a black Hummer H-1 Alpha. It was like seeing an old friend from my military days, though it was a more sleek, civilian luxury design versus the Hummers I drove in Iraq. Still, it was a beast.

Ray's light flashed away to the wall as he searched for keys. I ran first to the Mercedes and tried the door. It was unlocked. I rifled through the center console, dipped the sun visor, and trashed the glove box. No keys, but I did find the sticky remains of drying blood on the passenger seat.

Running around the front of the SUV, I leaned into the Ferrari but came up empty. Time we did not have to spare was ticking away. I rushed around the back end of the Ferrari when I heard Ray shout.

"Got 'em. Hummer."

Perfect, I thought.

His light bobbled as he ran over and handed me the keys. The Hummer doors, like the other cars, were unlocked. We hopped inside. I removed my balaclava and stowed my rifle next to me. Ray kept his at the ready. Before I had a chance to insert the key, we felt a tumultuous shake and boom as a new series of explosions rocked the compound.

CHAPTER SIXTY-ONE

One after the other, explosions ripped a path through the lower west wing of Casa de los Fuertes. Taking a moment to savor the chaos, El Despiadado leaned against the backside of the cobblestone archway and looked on as his destructive symphony played for a captive audience. Men in the courtyard ran for cover. Those who had sheltered too close to the west edge nearest the building while engaging in the gun battle had no chance of survival. Their bodies were consumed by the fire and smoke and debris that erupted from the blast. Jagged stone and razor-sharp glass soared with each ensuing explosion. Stones and cement along the exterior walls crumbled. Flashes of flame shot out like the lethal breaths from a fire-breathing dragon. One man dragged his body along the ground with his arms while the lower half of him stayed lodged under a pile of burning rubble. Another ran screaming across the courtyard, his clothing and hair engulfed in flame. No one tried to help him. It was every man for himself.

Anticipating the final blast, El Despiadado began his retreat, and turned toward the garage where the G-Wagon was parked. As he approached the door, he saw that it had been dislodged from its hinges. He removed the keys to the SUV from his pocket with one hand, pulled his gun with the other, and stepped inside.

El Despiadado's shadow grew longer with each step as it blocked the ambient light that filtered in through the open doorway. He listened as much as he looked with each step. He saw the G-Wagon in front of him. The other cars were lost in the darkness. Sliding his hand along the wall, he found the button that activated the lift for the garage door. When he pressed it, two things happened. The door began to rise, and a light turned on overhead.

CHAPTER SIXTY-TWO

The rumble and roar of explosions rattled the ground and shook the walls. Brushing away the shock, I slipped the key into the Hummer's ignition. As I placed my foot on the brake and prepared to start the engine, an overhead light turned on near the side door of the garage.

"Someone's here," I said.

Firing up the diesel beast would be a dead giveaway that we were inside to whoever flipped on the light. Opening fire would do no better, and with our depleted ammunition, we did not have enough to put up another extended fight.

"Down," I whispered.

We slid down in the seats and hid behind the blacked-out windows of the Hummer. As we settled in place, I heard the clanking churn of a chain overhead.

"Garage door's opening."

"Can you see who it is?" Ray asked.

I rose up and peeked through the window.

"Son of a bitch."

"Crank?" Ray said.

I reached for my Glock and the door handle at the same time.

"It's Mata."

Before Ray could stop me, I bolted out the door, raised my weapon and aimed. All my training, all my angst, all my pent-up rage for this man came down to this moment, yet I was unable to pull the trigger without him knowing it was me who killed him.

"Carlos Mata!" I yelled.

He moved just as quick, reacting to the subtle noises from the Hummer door, and then to my calling him out. He aimed his gun as he positioned himself behind the front end of the Mercedes, but he, too, did not fire.

"I know you," El Despiadado said. "How was it that you prefer your coffee? Black, was it?"

"You killed my friends, you son of a bitch. I could handle locking you up until the death penalty took you."

"It is true. Texas is a ruthless state, much like the cartels here in Mexico. A life for a life. Now, that is justice."

"But you also came after my family," I continued.

El Despiadado tilted his head to one side and, keeping a steady aim, thought back to all who he had killed while he was in Texas.

"Did the old man mean something to you? The boy in the canyon perhaps? Or is it the officers that you call family."

I stepped to one side, my aim center mass, my finger begging to squeeze the trigger, but still, I engaged the man who attacked Spencer.

"You tried to kill my son. My only son!"

"Tried? Oh," El Despiadado said, sounding relieved to hear the news. "The other boy from the canyon. I am glad for you that he survived, my friend. I was quite impressed with his display of skills. The way he fled. How he leaped across the canyon cliffs during his escape. But mostly—" El Despiadado paused and shook his head in an honest display of satisfaction "—when he chose to jump off the canyon wall into the murky blackness below, I thought to myself, now that is someone whom I can respect. It is because of his courage that I did not pursue him further, *señor*."

I could feel heat pulsing up my spine, filling my chest and billowing toward my ears.

"Have you come all this way for me? How did you know I would be here?"

"God works in mysterious ways," I said.

"That he does. Take me, for example. I had planned to move on with my life. Taking lives was becoming more burdensome. In the old days, killing someone was meant for a purpose, which I understood and respected. These days I have been made to kill out of necessity, or worse, for no reason except that Señor de la Droga wished it to be done. No, *señor*. I think we have been reunited for a higher purpose. Why else would we be standing here together like we are?"

My hand flexed around the grip of my Glock.

"Let me guess. You came for Arturo Mendez."

I did not answer.

"Señor de la Droga?" he said, rolling his eyes. "You Americans are too caught up with titles. The man was a cowardly piece of shit. I should know. He was my friend once."

El Despiadado kept his eyes locked on mine while stepping closer to the driver's side door of the SUV. I should have fired. I wanted to shoot, but I wanted the last word.

"But, you see? I have done you a favor. He is already dead. You must have seen him before having all that fun up on the balcony. It is too bad that poor planning on your part ruined your little mission. I am glad I have saved you from disaster. Did you see how I redecorated Casa de los Fuertes? If not, might I suggest a tour before you leave. Unfortunately, I will be unavailable due to a previous commitment. *Adios, señor*."

"You're forgetting one thing, Mata. I came to kill you too."

We fired simultaneously at each other. He grunted and ducked into the SUV, taking a bullet in the shoulder. I was knocked off my feet after being hit in the chest. Saved by my body armor, I was bruised and short of breath, but alive.

Ray jumped out of the Hummer and opened fire but was forced to alter his target when Crank limped into the garage doorway with a small band of cartel thugs behind him. Gunfire erupted in the garage, but all of it was meant for us.

"Get in the fucking car, Cass!" I heard Ray yell from behind the Hummer.

I moved slowly. Sharp pains shot through my chest. The armor protected my life, but the impact of the bullet broke my ribs beneath. Ray fired in bursts, taking out two of the cartel fighters. Crank must have had nine lives, because he continued to fire back at us.

I heard the SUV's engine start, then saw it fly out of the garage in reverse. I fired at Crank while pulling myself back into the driver's seat of the Hummer. I felt the graze of a bullet tear a layer of skin along my cheek as I pulled the door closed. Ray popped into the cab next to me.

"Let's go!"

I turned the key and the diesel engine roared to life. The clank and ding and crack of bullets on the outside of the Hummer were alarming until Ray said what I was thinking.

"Goddamn thing is bullet proof."

I glanced at Ray as I thrust the gear into reverse.

"Cartel money spares no expense."

Like a ferocious dragon, the Hummer bolted backward out of the garage. I slammed the brakes. The tires screeched leaving fresh tread marks on the concrete. Crank and two cartel soldiers ran into the driveway. One did not stop until he stood in our path to block our way. He waved his gun at us and yelled. With all the commotion and bullets flying around, a smile cracked across Ray's face.

"Let's see how scary you look with a Hummer rammed up your ass."

The design of the vehicle was not made for speed, but for its dominating, unstoppable force of sheer power and ruggedness, and with the added protection of bulletproof glass and a reinforced steel frame, nothing was going to stop us. I jammed the accelerator to the floor. The soldier opened fire but learned the hard way that trying to stop an impenetrable force such as the beast we were in meant that it was time for him to die a crushing death.

The Hummer bounced twice as we drove through and over the gunman. I caught the tail end of Mata's SUV swerving at the main gate of the compound. Ray saw it as well.

"He's getting away."

"Not this time," I yelled, squeezing the leather grip of the steering wheel like my fists were crushing an aluminum can. As we sped around the drive, Ray said something that injected a new problem into the fold.

"Crank knows everything."

In a millisecond, I processed this thought—*he knows where I live, how to find me, who my family is...everything.*

I slammed my foot on the brakes.

"Ray," I said. "Help him forget."

"With pleasure, boss."

Ray opened his door, stood on the frame of the Hummer, and raised his weapon. In one skillful motion, he located Crank and the cartel soldier as they ran down the drive firing at us and squeezed off two quick rounds. The first tore through the soldier, knocking him backward as his chest exploded in a bloody mass. The second shot stopped Crank in his tracks, piercing his forehead right below his crewcut hairline. His scalp disintegrated, but he continued to step forward, though slowing considerably and looking more like zombie from The Walking Dead. Ray climbed back into his seat.

"Hulk just got smashed," he said.

My sense of triumph turned to worry as I looked at Ray and the red pool forming in his lap.

"Ray," I said.

Ray looked down and saw the blood. He pressed his hand to his side then slapped the dashboard.

"Fuck it, Cass. Mata's getting away."

CHAPTER SIXTY-THREE

El Despiadado crashed through the main security gate and fishtailed onto Calle Quinta, tires screaming and smoking from the radical maneuver. Controlling the skid like a seasoned wheelman, he sped away from Casa de los Fuertes as the lanes were filled with approaching emergency strobes from both directions.

"You are too late for me, my friends," he muttered under his breath.

The bright, flashing lights spun through the G-Wagon as he passed by, traveling against the eastbound blue and red wave. He eased to the far side of his lane as he drove on, ensuring that the police and emergency response vehicles had plenty of room while masquerading as an upstanding citizen.

When the last vehicle screeched by and the sound of wailing sirens was behind him, he reached into his jacket pocket for his cell phone and discovered that his left shoulder was moist and warm with fresh blood. As he shifted his focus from the getaway to his apparent injury, the exhilaration and adrenaline rush of his escape gave way to a sharp, burning pain. To add to his discomfort, he probed the injury site with his fingers, wincing when his index nail scraped over the open wound.

He continued to drive while assessing his shoulder which caused the G-Wagon to swerve back and forth. He ran his hand up and over his shoulder, fingering the surface until he found an exit wound. Satisfied that there was no projectile embedded in him, and certain that he would not bleed out, he removed his hand and resumed driving with care, but it was already too late.

The chirp of a siren and the sudden reveal of flashing lights behind him put him in a precarious position. Stopping would allow his American pursuer to catch up, but running from the police would create additional problems and delay his escape.

He tapped the brakes and activated his blinker, signaling that he was willing to cooperate. Finding a suitable stopping point, he pulled into the parking lot of an auto repair shop that was closed for the day and rolled down his window. His shoulder throbbed and he could feel trickles of blood running down his arm.

The interior of the G-Wagon illuminated as if it were day when the police car shined its spotlight at El Despiadado. He watched as an officer exited his vehicle, pulled a flashlight from his belt, and walked along the edge of the G-Wagon. He stopped at the driver's side window and flashed a beam of light on El Despiadado's face.

"*¿Todo está bien?* You were swerving."

El Despiadado squinted in the bright wash of the officer's flashlight and smiled. He nodded, noted the path of the officer's gaze, and swiftly raised his right hand with waiting gun, and fired one shot. The *whoomph* of the bullet shooting out of the suppressed barrel was minimal, but the damage to the officer's forehead was extreme. His body stiffened, then toppled backward. Like a rigid board, he fell with a thud. The stop was over before it started.

El Despiadado rolled up his window, put the G-

Wagon in gear, and pulled out of the parking lot as if nothing out of the ordinary had happened.

Tragic, he thought. *But I have no time to spare, and you were just in the wrong place at the wrong time. Rest well.*

Calle Quinta was an open swatch of darkness riddled with dim streetlights and an occasional oncoming car. Most people were in for the evening, but for El Despiadado, the night was not quite over yet.

He fished his cell phone from his pocket and dialed. Tapping the speaker icon, he listened and waited for his call to be answered. El Despiadado grew more impatient with each ring, until finally, the call went through.

"*Bueno*."

"Capitán Vazquez. Be ready to take off in fifteen minutes."

"Señor Mata, I was..."

El Despiadado cut the call short as he veered off Calle Quinta. Navigating his way out of Camargo, he glanced in the rearview mirror at each turn, looking for signs that he had been followed. Leaving a lonely road behind him, El Despiadado increased his speed, racing toward the ranch where his plane and pilot awaited his return.

CHAPTER SIXTY-FOUR

Following a trail of fresh tire marks stained down the drive and onto Calle Quinta and plowing through what dangling iron remained of the security gate, the black beast roared at my command as I slammed the Hummer's accelerator to the floor. We shot out of the compound into a growing mix of flashing lights and emergency sirens, clipping the front of the lead police vehicle and sending it swirling around to crash into two more following behind it.

"Shit," I yelled.

"That about sums it up," Ray said.

I could see what I thought was Mata's SUV speeding off about a half mile ahead, but we had mounting problems in the form of a band of Camargo Police units diverting their response to Casa de los Fuertes to pursue us.

"How many are on us, Ray?"

Ray swiveled in his seat looking both in the side mirror, then out the back of the Hummer.

"Looks like four. Could be all of them. Hell, just get us the hell outta here."

"Working on it," I said.

One unit sped up, pulling next to the Hummer. Its

lights flashed, and I could see a very determined policeman leaning out the passenger window with a pistol in his hand. A quick glance in the side mirror showed the other three police cars were gaining fast.

The daring policeman fired at my window, causing a flurry of small, spiderwebbed cracks to obstruct my view.

"Sorry, pal," I said.

Wrenching the wheel to the left, I rammed the police car with the full force of our iron beast. The policeman in the window lost his balance and dropped his gun as he slipped back inside. The police car veered to the left across traffic, ramming headfirst into a food truck parked along the opposite side of the road.

Shots erupted from behind as the other pursuing units witnessed what had happened. The churn and grind of engines grew louder as they pulled closer, surrounding the Hummer. With one car on either side and one behind, I caught Ray looking at me. With his lips curled into a frown and one eyebrow raised, he shook his head.

"Did they not just see what happened if they pull that close? They're driving Volkswagens, for Christ's sake. Not too bright, are they?"

"Hold on," I said.

I switched my foot from the gas to the brakes and slammed down hard. The police cars on either side shot ahead but the trailing unit slammed into us from behind. Its siren chirped and the red and blue strobes stopped flashing as the impact crumpled the front of the car, fatally damaging its engine and sent the light bar flying from the roof.

I released the brakes and pressed the accelerator once again. The engine roared as we jolted ahead, leaving the smashed police car in a blackened wake of exhaust. As we pulled away, I saw that airbags had been deployed, which gave me hope that the officers inside the car had survived. By all accounts, I was the bad guy here, but in the real world, we were all cops. The only difference was that I was not on the payroll of a drug cartel.

The two remaining police cars slowed down. One pulled in front of us while the other positioned itself alongside the rear driver's side wheel. The trailing unit's intentions were obvious.

"PIT maneuver?" Ray said, looking through the rear driver's side window. "In that tiny piece of crap?"

On cue, the driver nudged the front panel of his unit against our rear wheel. Any ordinary car, even those with a significant amount of weight would be forced into a slide when the rear wheel is subjected to the precision immobilization technique, a tactic used by law enforcement to force a fleeing vehicle to stop. However, the width and stabilization of a Hummer H1 Alpha is much too significant to be overwhelmed by such a move, especially when performed by such a small vehicle.

Metal crunched and steel screamed as the wheels collided, but our black beast would not be denied. The driver pulled away, accelerated, and tried again.

"It's like a Chihuahua trying to hump a lion," Ray said. He turned back and faced the front. "Gotta give 'em credit for trying though."

Failing a third PIT maneuver, the driver gave up and pulled ahead. The lead police car tapped its brakes until its rear thumped against the Hummer's giant grille. I kept my speed and attention on the car in front of me, taking the size and strength and current win streak of the Hummer for granted.

As we smashed together, I heard gunfire and saw that a policeman in the passenger seat of the PIT maneuver car was shooting at us. My heart sank to my stomach when I felt the rumble of shredded rubber and heard the high-pitched screech of steel digging into the pavement.

"We're in trouble, Ray."

"Tell me about it," he said, hunched over, cradling his side.

His sudden change in demeanor had me worried. It was dark, but I could see that his face looked white, which meant his injury was worse than he had let on.

"Ahhhh!"

I pressed my foot on the accelerator with a mix of frustration, fear, and fury. The Hummer surged ahead with enough force to nudge the lead car of our bumper.

"Let's see how you like this!"

I swerved to the left, gaining on both cars. When the front end of the Hummer was alongside the lead car, I pulled hard to the right, clipping its rear wheel and sending it spinning out of control. I slammed the brakes as the disabled police car careened forward. As it spun ninety degrees to its original path, its right-side wheels dug into the pavement causing the car to roll in a series of dramatic flips. In a flash of flame, its engine exploded, and the car came to rest upside down.

The last police car held pursuit, but a glance behind us showed our problems were far from over as a new flurry of red and blue strobe lights appeared in the distance. To make matters worse, a loud, metallic crack rattled the Hummer.

"Sounds like the axel is toast," I said.

I shared a look of concern with Ray. He leaned over the expanded distance between us and patted my shoulder.

"Don't worry, pard. We've been in situations far worse than this."

His voice trailed off as he slumped back into his seat.

"Ray," I said.

No answer.

"Shit, Ray. Stay with me!"

The Hummer slowed. I had no control but to ride the wave of grinding metal and anguished emotions until it came to a complete stop in the middle of the road.

It was over. Everything was over. I watched as the last police car made a tight U-turn, and then slowed its speed as it approached. The driver parked at an angled position in front of us. I could see him in the beams of our head-lights as he talked over his radio.

"Damn it, Ray. I'm sorry I dragged you into this."

I lowered my head, looked at my rifle, and knew I had lost. I raised my head to see the policeman lower his radio. Building light showed the man's face contort in horror as his police car became engulfed in the bright beams of someone's headlights just before it smashed into it.

The two vehicles crunched together, then slid to a halt. The police car was ruined, but the van, the black van that smashed into it had shifted into reverse and was backing away.

I reached for my rifle. The van stopped near the front of the Hummer. I watched as it jostled with movement inside, then saw its side door slide open.

My mouth dropped. My heart skipped what felt like two beats. My hope, what little of it remained, found a lifeline as Agent Sharp hopped out of the van and ran over.

CHAPTER SIXTY-FIVE

T he sky over Mexico was clear and deep enough to gaze back in time, past familiar constellations, to the edge of the universe. It was an open pathway on which the opportunity to start anew aligned itself with fresh choices that encapsulated a new lease on life. El Despiadado drove on in silence, watching the road ahead, but marveled at the heavens above. For the first time, he felt tired. His sense of accomplishment pulsed with each throb of his shoulder, a subtle reminder that he was alive. His destructive demeanor began to slip into the crags of his soul. A soul that would need a great deal of repair moving forward if Carlos Ruiz-Mata was to reclaim his place. Beneath it all, it was what El Despiadado wanted. As much as he threatened to assume full control, it was not for him. If they were to survive moving forward, El Despiadado would have to resign to the more refined tendencies and pleasurable personality that Mata had mastered over a lifetime. Besides that, he loved him as much as loved himself. Even when the heights of his folly afforded him pleasures only a killer could experience, he knew Mata felt it as well, for he was a killer, too. It was his conscience that had begun to interfere in their relationship, which was why El Despiadado took the reins. Now, with Señor de la Droga dead, their ties to the cartel had been cut loose, which meant that El Despiadado and Mata were free.

CHAPTER SIXTY-SIX

"Son of a bitch," I said, opening the door.

"Ya miss me, Callahan?"

Sharp had bruising arcs of purple and green under each eye from the punch I landed on his face prior to handcuffing him to the shower pipe in the bathtub. He wore a small steri-strip across the bridge of his nose. His chin and neck had traces of dried blood, and the collar of his shirt was stained red. I stared at him, not believing what I was seeing.

"How did you..."

"Get free? Know how to find you? I am sure you have plenty of questions, but unless you want to ask them through the bars of a Mexican prison, I suggest we drop the chit chat and get the fuck out of here."

Ray opened his eyes and groaned.

"Who you talking to, Cass?" His words slipped from his lips in strings of mumbling and incoherency. "We catch up to Mata, or what?"

"What happened to him?" Sharp asked.

"Come on. Help me get him into the van. I'll tell you on the way. Mata is..."

"Mata is not the priority, Cass. He never was." Sharp

looked past me, shaking his head at what he saw. "We gotta hurry. More police are coming our way."

I looked back. A red and blue wave of flashing lights and shrill sounding sirens was getting closer. I hated to admit it, but Sharp was right. Finding Mata would have to wait. I had wanted to end it all tonight, but I had an ace in the hole that I still hoped would come through for me.

I slung the strap of my HK over my shoulder and ran around to Ray's door. Sharp pulled it open as I leaned in to help get him out of the Hummer. In his delirium, Ray took one look at Sharp and his face bent into quizzical wrinkles of confusion.

"Thought we left this ass hat back at the hotel?"

Ray slid out of the Hummer next to me, wincing in pain.

"Nice to see you, too," Sharp said. "But this ass hat is saving *you* right now."

He grabbed one of Ray's arms and slung it behind his neck. I grabbed Ray's rifle, adding it to my shoulder knowing he would literally kill me if we left it behind. Working together, we dragged him from the Hummer to the open door of the van.

By the time we got him settled inside, Ray had passed out again. The hoard of police cars was gaining ground.

"Let's roll," I said.

Sharp jumped behind the wheel while I stayed in back with Ray.

"Hold on," he yelled as he thrust the gears into drive and stomped on the gas.

The wheels spun on the pavement, screeching bloody murder before the van lurched ahead. The engine roared as we raced on. Ignoring the rules of the road, Sharp blew through intersections and ran stop signs, keeping any pursuers off our tail, then veered off Calle Quinta, weaving our way through the dark side streets of Camargo.

"There's a medical kit under the seat, and more goodies on the plane once we get to the airport."

"Airport?"

"I told you we had a plane, Cass. When you called in and changed the plan, Zuñiga cleared us to take a bird. It was the only way we were able to make up for the lost time. We landed and reported to customs that we were transporting medical supplies to La Guajira, Columbia and that we needed to layover for the day to stay in FAA compliance. The customs official that arranged our stay was quite cooperative." Sharp rubbed his thumb and index fingers together "Lucky for Ray, the plane was fully stocked in case we were subjected to an inspection."

"Perfect. I don't know how bad his injury is. The sooner we can get airborne, the better chance he has of making it. Get on the horn and alert the pilot that we're on the way."

Sharp guffawed.

"You just alerted him."

"What. *You?*"

"Yep. Looks like that's twice I'm saving your ass tonight."

I looked down at Ray, then slid forward between the front seats.

"Guess I owe you one."

Sharp glanced at me. A smug smile grew across his face.

"I'd say ya do. Let's get Ray to a hospital that won't want to harvest his organs, and then we can discuss how tightly I have you by the balls."

Sharp laughed again, enjoying his momentary victory.

"Right," I said.

I was thankful that Sharp appeared when he did and would settle up with him once we were all safe. I owed him that, but damn! He knew how to get under my skin.

As we continued toward the airport, I pulled the first aid kit from under the seat, utilizing my military field training to treat Ray's injury. I flipped on an interior light mounted above us and saw that his clothes were covered with blood. The first obstacle I had to overcome was removing his body armor. I pulled at the Velcro straps, then lifted the front part of the vest until it folded backward over his head. Next, I found a pair of surgical scissors in the first aid kit and began cutting Ray's shirt away. He remained unconscious, which helped me work quickly. Tossing the remnants of his shirt aside, I used bottled water and gauze to clean as much of the surface along his side and under his arm as I could.

"There you are," I said, locating the entry wound.

I discovered an entry wound situated approximately two inches below Ray's right armpit. My immediate concern was the proximity of the injury to his lung and that the bullet that was still lodged inside might cause additional damage. I applied gauze to the wound, taking care not to introduce any contamination, then used an ample supply of surgical tape to affix the bandages. He was stabilized to the best of my ability. Now, it was up to him to hold on until he could get him proper medical treatment.

"Almost there," Sharp announced. "Stay down and keep Ray out of sight."

"Copy that."

I felt the van slow down, then turn to the right. A quick peek through the front window showed that we were moving along a one-way concrete driveway that led us toward an inspection booth before opening up onto the tarmac where our plane was parked.

"Here we go," Sharp whispered, as he slowed to a stop and rolled down his window to greet a waiting customs agent.

"*Buenas noches, amigo*," Sharp said.

"*Buenas noches.* What is your business at Aeródromo Internacional de Camargo?" The agent sounded professional.

"Oh, just returning from a layover. Had to land this morning after a long flight or risk being flagged by the FAA. Last thing I need is to lose my license."

"*¿A dónde viajas?*"

"What was that? I only know a few words in *Español*."

Sharp laughed. The customs agent did not. Instead, he repeated himself sounding more authoritative than before.

"Where are you traveling to?"

"Right. *Lo siento*. I'm the pilot of the medical plane," Sharp said, pointing out the window. "The one heading to Colombia. La Guajira to be exact. Poor folks down there sure could use some help."

The customs agent stepped away from the van for a moment, then returned. I could hear the distinct shuffling of paperwork.

"How many of you are traveling?" he asked.

"Two. My co-pilot is still in town. I'm here early to do a preflight check. Make sure everything is in order. He'll be along shortly." Sharp raised a cell phone. "I could call him. Get him over here now if you like."

"Is there anything in the back of the van?"

"Nothing worth mentioning." Sharp lowered his voice. "Case of tequila for my boss."

This was taking too long. Ray could come around at any minute. If he made a noise, we would have a lot of explaining to do.

"Look," Sharp said. "My plane is just over there. The Cessna. I could really use a break tonight. I've got a long flight ahead of me and wonder if you could let me go ahead and pass through?" Sharp raised his left hand just above the window's ledge. A roll of American bills rested between his fingers like a homemade cigarette. "What do you say?"

The silence that followed was concerning. Either Sharp had read the man and knew he would accept a bribe, or he was gambling. Either way, it was a big risk.

I heard the beat of a hand on the side of the van, followed by the customs agent's voice.

"*Siga Adelante.* Move ahead."

"*Gracias, amigo,*" Sharp replied, then pulled forward as instructed.

Rolling up his window, he faced the front and spoke to me.

"I'm going to park so the van blocks the view of the main cabin from the inspection booth. I'll get out, do a quick preflight check, then open the rear doors of the plane and make room for Ray. When I return, have him ready to move. If anybody sees more than just me, they may grow suspicious, so we have to move fast. As soon as we have him onboard, hop up front and we're outta here like hot tamales."

"What about the van?"

"Let insurance deal with it."

Sharp parked the van just as he had said and hopped out. I laid our guns near the door and waited. It took less than a minute for Sharp to return to the van. The click of the handle, and the metallic slide of the door along its rails, thrust me into action. I hopped out, and together, we raised Ray into a sitting position, then hoisted him up and carried him the few steps to the plane.

"You gotta get him to lose a few pounds, Cass."

"Been telling him that for years," I said.

Sharp hopped into the plane and helped me get Ray inside. The rear of the plane had boxes and tubs of medical equipment, including a gurney that was tethered to the floor. Seizing the opportunity, we laid Ray on the gurney.

"We can wait to strap him in until we are taxiing. No one is going to stop us once I get this plane moving," Sharp said.

I nodded.

"Grab the rest of your gear. I'll remove the blocks from the wheels, and we can roll out."

I hopped out of the door and discreetly transferred our rifles from the van to the plane, stowing them next to Ray's gurney, then took my seat up front. I glanced back at Ray.

"Heading home, Dragon."

Sharp tossed the blocks into the van and slid the side door closed, then jogged around the front of the plane and opened the pilot's door.

"All good?" I said.

"Yeah. About that," Sharp said, pointing to the chain link fence line that ran the length of the airport perimeter.

I turned to look and saw the long line of red and blue flashing lights parading at high speed as they closed in on the airport, veering into the customs drive and heading straight at us. I heard voices shouting, and then saw the customs agent from the inspection booth running toward us.

"Lock your door," Sharp said as he climbed in.

He flipped switches and adjusted dials on the control panel, then turned a key and pressed a button labeled ignition. I heard the chug and churn of the engine start, then felt the growing vibrations in the cockpit as the propeller began to spin.

"Okay, baby. You'll have to warm up on the way out." Sharp kissed his palm, then rubbed the dashboard.

He released his foot from the brake and the plane jolted ahead. We picked up speed as we taxied across the tarmac and away from the authorities. Sharp put on his headset and spoke into the mic.

"Tower, this is 187 Alpha Mike Foxtrot, requesting immediate clearance for takeoff."

"187 Alpha Mike Foxtrot, *¿Es esto una broma?*"

"No joke, tower. Proceeding to runway for immediate departure."

The air traffic controller responded forcefully.

"Stand down, 187 Alpha Mike Foxtrot. Hold your position."

"Negative tower. Divert any incoming traffic. We're taking off. Alpha Mike Foxtrot, out."

Sharp cut the comms to the tower and headed out to the runway.

"We'll be fine," he said. "Trust me."

Trust him, I thought as I saw two emergency vehicles pull onto the tarmac and race toward us.

"Time for a detour," Sharp said, veering the plane off the taxiway and onto a grassy island between the two runways and the main airport hangars.

The plane jostled and the prop whirred in surges as if angered by the mistreatment, but we made it across the grassy patch and bounced back onto the main runway. As soon as the wheels hit the pavement, Sharp throttled up, then turned to me, and yelled.

"Get back there and strap Ray in, then find a seat for yourself. Once we're airborne you can slide back up front."

The wail of emergency sirens jousted with the noise from the plane.

"I'll give you twenty seconds, then I'm pulling the stick and we'll be off."

I rose out of the front seat and worked my way to the back of the plane. My heart pounded as we sped faster and faster down the runway. Using the straps on the gurney, I secured Ray in place. It would not be very comfortable for him, but it would keep him safe during takeoff.

"Ten seconds!" Sharp called out.

Shit! I thought.

I turned and muscled my way into the closest seat. As I reached for my seatbelt, I heard Sharp cheer as if he were Han Solo, and he had just jumped to lightspeed and felt the plane's wheels leave the ground.

The whir of the prop and the wind rushing by echoed inside the Cessna's cabin. I fumbled with my seat straps until finally clicking them into place. The plane banked left, and I found myself looking down at the colorful emergency lights scattered across the airport from the parking lot to the runway. We continued to climb, still sweeping to the left, which made my stomach sink into my crotch. I swallowed hard and held on to the armrests of my seat. When we began to level out, I saw Sharp motion to his right ear, then point to the wall of the plane. I looked left, found a headset bobbling on its mount, and put it on.

"Hear me?" Sharp said.

"Roger that."

"The fun ain't over, Cass. They'll be tracking our flight path by now. As soon as we get out of Camargo airspace, we're gonna fly NOE, nap-of-the-earth, if you know the term. If we can avoid radar, we'll be home free. It's two hours and fifteen minutes as the crow flies to El Paso. Sit back and enjoy the flight."

"Ha," I said. "Good luck with that."

"Well, they don't have our call sign, and the numbers on the plane are bogus, so if all goes to plan, we'll disappear until we reach the border. By then, we'll have Zuñiga on the line. He can coordinate with EMS to meet us at the airstrip. We'll be landing at a private FBI site just north of town. It's ten minutes max to the hospital from there."

"Thanks, Sharp."

"Don't mention it."

I looked back at Ray and held onto hope as I watched his chest rise and fall with each life-giving breath. Feeling confident, I faced the front and spoke into the mic.

"So, if they don't have our call sign, what was that back there?"

"Just my little way of saying goodbye. *Alpha Mike Foxtrot.*"

It took me a minute, but now that we were underway and my mind had settled down, I understood. I laughed into the mic. Sharp joined in.

CHAPTER SIXTY-SEVEN

Aside from the light cascading out of the airplane hangar, Rancho del Halcón was dark and looked just as deserted as when Mata and his pilot first landed. Following the entrance road alongside the blackened runway, he saw Capitán Vazquez from a distance, pacing back and forth in front of the airplane. Its running lights were on.

Good, Mata thought. *You are ready as expected.*

He turned off the entrance road, making his way around the hangar on a small, gravel service path, and pulled inside, past the Cessna, and parked. Capitán Vazquez walked over and met him as he stepped out of the G-Wagon.

"It is so good to see you, Señor Mata. I was beginning to worry that..." He stopped short of finishing the statement. Following an awkward pause, he smiled, stepped to one side, and gently extended his hands in a graceful ushering gesture. "After you, *señor*."

"*Gracias, capitán*. Before we go, I am in need of some bandages. Do you have a first aid kit onboard?"

Capitán Vazquez gave him a concerned look but hopped into action. "*Sí*, I will get it for you right away."

"Again, *gracias, mi amigo*."

Capitán Vazquez jogged back to the plane and disappeared inside. Mata's feet dragged as he followed him over. Exhaustion and pain had begun to take its toll. He had lost a fair amount of blood from the wound and was feeling a touch of dizziness. When he reached the side of the airplane, Capitán Vazquez reemerged with a small box of medical supplies.

"Here you go, *señor*. How can I help you?"

Wincing, Mata removed his jacket, letting it fall to the ground. His shirt was caked with crusted blood, yet the wound still seeped with each subtle movement.

"Open the box," Mata said. "If there is rubbing alcohol, hand it to me."

Capitán Vazquez opened the kit and removed a clear plastic bottle.

"*Alcohol Isopropílico*," he said, handing it to Mata.

"Now, help me tear the cloth away," Mata said.

The pilot reached out, looking tentative.

"Here," Mata said, removing his combat knife from his belt. "This will help."

Capitán Vazquez's eyes bulged, but he took the weapon and cut away pieces of Mata's shirt that covered his wound. As he pulled the cloth away, Mata groaned.

"*Ay, dios mio*," Capitán Vazquez said between his teeth.

Mata turned his head to one side and spit.

"Very good," he said. "Now for the worst part."

Mata removed the plastic cap and poured the alcohol, covering the wounds on both sides of his shoulder. The burn was intense but brief. For a moment, Mata's knees threatened to give way. He wavered, but Capitán Vazquez steadied him.

"Bandages," Mata said.

Capitán Vazquez removed a roll of gauze from the kit, wrapped the end over itself until it was thick enough to create a pad, then carefully wrapped Mata's shoulder. It was a crude but effective dressing, providing some pressure and protection to the wound.

"There. That should do until you see a doctor."

"*Gracias*, Capitán Vazquez. You are both a savior and a gentleman." Mata reached for the passenger door. "Take me home."

Capitán Vazquez assisted Mata into the plane, then closed and secured his door. He made one final exterior procedural check of the plane, activated a timer switch next to the hangar door that activated the runway lights for a twenty-minute countdown, then loaded up next to Mata in the cockpit.

"All set, *señor*. The night is clear, and the wind is light. We should have a comfortable flight. Please, get some rest. I will wake you when we arrive in Guaymas."

Mata nodded.

Capitán Vazquez flipped the master switch to on, opened the throttle just a touch, and turned the ignition to the start position. The engine awoke with a rumble and the prop began to spin. They sat for just a moment as the engine warmed up. Mata, ready to be on the way, lifted a hand and motioned for them to go. Capitán Vazquez released the brake and taxied the plane out of the hangar, following the track lighting to the far end of the runway.

Mata felt the power rumble through him as the plane throttled up. He heard the superstitious whispers that Capitán Vazquez recited to himself as he prepared for takeoff. He sank back into his seat as they shot down the runway and experienced a moment of euphoria when the plane left the ground. As the engine hummed and they climbed high into the black abyss, Mata leaned his head against the back of his seat and slept.

CHAPTER SIXTY-EIGHT

It was pitch black. Sharp had disabled the navigation lights on the wingtips after takeoff, making us but a humming shadow flying through the murky dark of night. Agent Dylan Sharp, as it turned out, was an excellent pilot. He was a little crazy, a whole lotta smug, but as far as his skills were concerned, I thought he did a damn good job of getting us out of Camargo in one piece.

Before moving into the co-pilot's seat, I tended to Ray. He had drifted in and out of consciousness shortly after takeoff and seemed to be in considerable pain. I searched through the medical supplies until I found a box marked *morphine auto-injectors*. Tearing open the box, I removed one of the premeasured devices.

"Enjoy the bliss, Ray,"

I tore a hole in his pant leg and administered the morphine into his thigh. It did not take long to notice the effects were taking hold. Ray settled down, falling under the spell of meds and unconsciousness. I inspected his restraints, then covered him with a silver thermal blanket before moving up front and into the co-pilot's seat.

"So, I guess this is where I explain a few things to you," I said.

"Callahan, I'm sure you had your reasons. Let's face it,

we don't get along. We're not friends. We're not planning any fishing trips. We certainly aren't sharing secrets like a couple of schoolgirls. None of what happened matters anymore." He paused and swallowed. "Fact is, you never had a chance with me anyway."

"Really," I said. "You never gave me much of a choice."

"Nope. There you were, Mr. Big Shot Houston detective doing all the right things—solving murders, bringing down the bad guys, and gaining the attention of more than just Agent Zuñiga. In fact, I know of a couple, should I say, three letter agencies besides the FBI that may be interested in your services moving forward. Needless to say, it pissed me off to no end. I've worked my ass off for years and when the time came for me to move up the ladder, I get transferred from the East Coast to fucking El Paso. That was last summer. Next thing I know, I'm sent out to oversee the investigation of some dead immigrants on a ranch in the middle of nowhere, and now here we are."

"You wore a pretty heavy chip on your shoulder, Sharp. Didn't seem you cared what you said to or about others. Where I come from, that gets a guy decked in the face."

Sharp looked over at me, his discolored eyes and swollen nose an immediate reminder of our altercation just hours earlier.

"Funny how things work out, huh," he said. "If you didn't punch me in the face, we might all be stuck fighting for our lives in Droga's compound right now, or worse."

I nodded, letting his words resonate with me.

"Since we're getting all cozy, mind telling me why you stormed in and demanded that we pull the plug?" I said.

"Got a text message; an anonymous tip that we had a rat in our group. I figured it was your guy back there. Hell, I don't know him. I barely know you. When you changed the plan, it started adding up in my book. I wasn't about to go to war with an enemy walking among us. I'd like to die of natural causes, you know, with a beer in my hand and girl's mouth..."

"I get it," I said, interrupting.

Sharp continued. "Never thought it could have been Crank."

"Tell me about it. My suspicions began just before you arrived prior to go time. I received a number of private phone calls over the past couple of days, which I ignored, until a text came through tonight from that same number. It said that you were not who we thought. After our scuffle..."

"Say it like it was, Callahan. After you punched my lights out."

"Okay, after that, and while we were handcuffing you to the tub, Crank suggested we move up the mission. That didn't sit right with me, but I went along with it anyway, especially after hearing your rant. All I wanted was to burn the palace down with Droga and Mata sitting in the middle of the fire."

"You got half of your wish, anyway. How'd you know Mata would be there in the first place?"

I glanced at Sharp and pursed my lips.

"Nothing?"

"I'll say this. I'm cashing in a favor of someone that trusted me with their life enough to put it on the line again."

"You're full of surprises, Callahan. Hate to say it, but I'm glad we're on the same team, even if we sit at opposite ends of the bench."

"Yeah," I said. "When this is over, beers are on me."

"Damn right they are," Sharp replied.

We bypassed Chihuahua, weaving a very sketchy path around the perimeter of the city while flying at levels only crop dusters would dare to fly. From there, it was a straight shot to El Paso.

I checked on Ray throughout the flight. He remained unconscious but seemed to be stable. As we approached the border, Sharp contacted Agent Zuñiga, who then orchestrated emergency services to meet us at the airfield.

The lights from El Paso illuminated the horizon in one glowing ball of freedom. Sharp communicated with air traffic control at El Paso International Airport. A quick explanation and verbal flashes of FBI credentials, followed up by a call from the FBI field office confirming our status, we were directed to proceed on to Mac Roberson Regional Airport.

Upon final approach, I saw emergency lights waiting on the tarmac.

"You gonna ride along to the hospital?" I asked Sharp.

"I don't know, Callahan."

"Come on. What else do you have to do? Let's get Ray squared away and I'll buy you the worst cup of coffee El Paso has to offer."

"Well, if you put it that way," he said.

I glanced out the window, glad to be back with the red, white, and blue as Sharp's voice filled my headset.

"MacRob regional, Cessna zero-five-one-three, final approach."

"Cessna zero-five-one-three, you're clear to land."

CHAPTER SIXTY-NINE

Golden shimmers of light cascaded across the rippling waters of the Sea of Cortez as the sun cracked the horizon, sparking a new day. For Mata, it was this freshness that filled him as he leaned against the gunwale aboard Peniel's Eden and sipped a steaming cup of Colombian coffee. He had slept only a few short hours after arriving at the boat in the middle of the night but was feeling wide awake.

He wandered across the deck to the port side of the boat, enjoying the morning as if it was his daily routine. His head was clear. His shoulder ached. El Despiadado had not resurfaced since Mata had returned, and the way he felt this morning, there would be no reason for him to surface again.

No, my friend, he thought. *Our time together has come to an end. I believe you would agree that we served each other well, but now it is time that we parted ways. It will be better for both of us, but I promise you this; should the need arise to call you back into service, I will not hesitate. We are one, you and I.*

Mata lifted his cup to the rising sun and said, "*Despedida, mi hermano. Descansa bien.*" He took a sip and lowered his head, catching the reflection of his face in the water. "Yes. Rest."

Glancing around the harbor, he took in the picturesque view. The glowing Guaymas shoreline; the marina, littered with tall clusters of masts, all various sizes, that seemed to poke at the rising sun as they towered above their ships; the pelicans that soared above the water, their wingtips creating a V-shaped wake with each touch on the surface. He embraced the call of the seagull and took deep breaths of the salt air. He felt alive.

Refreshed, he moved about the deck and began to prepare the ship for sailing. He had already decided to weigh anchor and was inclined to go wherever the wind might take him once he reached the open waters of the Pacific, but first he must head south. Cabo San Lucas was a three-day voyage from Guaymas. Located at the southernmost point of Baja California, it marked the place where the world would be at his fingertips. If he left in the afternoon, he would catch the warming winds off the distant mountains and could silently slip away.

Without concern or a need to rush, Carlos Ruiz-Mata assumed a new life where the choices he made moving forward would define who he was to become. He hummed a tune while working, a melody he could not quite recall entirely, yet its rhythm resonated with him stirring an emotion he had not experienced in a very long time—joy.

CHAPTER SEVENTY

The sterile aroma in the surgical waiting room mixed with the bland blend of black coffee I held in my hands assaulted my nose. I sat in a hard-back chair at the apex of a triangle that Zuñiga and Sharp had formed around me. We sat facing one another and held a crack of dawn, whisper-level debriefing. I had to hand it to Zuñiga, he sat there listening and did not say anything until both Sharp and I had our say.

As I heard the accounts of the previous morning roll off my tongue for what felt like the umpteenth time, I began to see how crazy my actions were, but I stood by each one without offering a shred of doubt or remorse. Sharp chimed in recalling events with him and Crank prior to rendezvousing with us at the hotel. They were insignificant to the mission, but good filler while I caught my breath and sipped my horrible hospital coffee.

I reported my version of the assault on the Camargo compound, sparing no details to the condition in which we found Arturo Mendez, Señor de la Droga, and the explosions that crippled Casa de los Fuertes.

I felt my nails dig into my palm when I explained what happened during and following our run in with Mata, drawing slivers of blood at the mention of discovering Ray had been shot. I had to give credit where credit was due though and spoke very highly of Sharp's role in our escape and ability to get us in a plane and safely back across the border.

Zuñiga sat with his legs crossed. His face was stoic, digesting every word as if Sharp and I were giving dueling Sunday morning sermons. I noted a surprised rise of his eyebrow when we corroborated that Crank had, for lack of a better word, flipped to the dark side. It was an unfortunate truth that we would all have to accept.

When we finished our debriefing, Zuñiga shifted in his seat. He leaned back, cracking a satisfied smile, then mouthed the words, "Job well done."

I shared a glance with Sharp.

"You're taking this all rather well."

"Why shouldn't I?" Zuñiga responded.

"Ah, we did some pretty hairy shit down there, not to mention the trail of bodies and destruction that isn't going to go unnoticed."

Zuñiga looked at Sharp, then back at me.

"I heard on the wire this morning that a rival cartel, led by a single foreign mercenary, raided the Camargo cartel compound last night that resulted in two things— one, Arturo Mendez was killed, and two, his empire had been destroyed. Funny how dangerous those cartels are when fighting over territory. Anything can happen on any day."

"Wait," I said.

"What?" Zuñiga replied. "I appreciate the animated story that you and Sharp just shared with me, but you might want to lay off the tequila. As far as I know, you, Sharp, and Tucker were never there."

I felt my cell phone buzz in my pocket, but it was overshadowed by a flowing sense of relief. As Zuñiga reached out to shake my hand, a doctor appeared in an observatory window and gave us a thumbs up. That was the best thing I saw all night.

My phone buzzed again.

"Gonna see who it is?" Sharp said, pointing to the rectangular bulging light coming from my pocket.

"Yeah."

I stood up, walked to the coffee counter, and looked at the screen. When I read the text message, a surge of adrenaline coursed through me like an exploding volcano. I whirled around and locked eyes with Sharp, then waved him over.

With each step, his curiosity intensified, his face exposing tells like a donkey at a poker game.

"You got that look, Callahan," he said, stopping in front of me.

"Yeah, I do," I said, raising my hand and placing it on his shoulder. "You have time for one more favor?"

"Does it involve killing bad guys?"

I smiled at him, though my eyes began to blaze.

"It just might."

CHAPTER SEVENTY-ONE

The sky was a perfect blue. The breeze had picked up since morning; a good sign for those planning a day of sailing. Music played inside Cala Costera Cantina for its early afternoon company to enjoy. A patio lined the exterior of the waterfront bar, providing an unobstructed view of the Sea of Cortez, though one section was roped off and awaiting repair. Burn marks stained the damaged wooden beams beneath the boardwalk.

Two men sat at an outside table engrossed in discussion, laughing with drinks in hand, and oblivious to everyone else around. To them, it was five o'clock somewhere, but at Guaymas's only bar with marina access and a beautiful view of the water, it was closer to one forty-five.

"There he is," I said, pointing out a man with darkened, caramelized skin, black hair, with a scar below his left ear, and the trailing ends of a black tattoo clawing its way up his neck. He held binoculars up to his eyes and was looking at boats on the water.

"Ramón," I said walking up. *"El que juega con fuego, se quema."*

The man lowered the binoculars and looked at me as

if he found offense with being interrupted. He let his scowl linger a bit too long before forming a welcoming smirk.

"You are learning. It is good to see that you are alive."

"It's good to be seen," I said. "Ramón, this is Dylan Sharp. Among other things, he's the pilot that got me down here so quickly."

Ramón gave Sharp a wary look as they shook hands. "Don't I know you?"

"Couldn't say," Sharp answered. "You know many assholes?"

They parted hands regarding one another.

"Alright, enough of the Bro-fest. What's the latest?"

"Look for yourself." Ramón handed me the binoculars. "The third boat from the left. You can see its name, Peniel's Eden."

I raised the binoculars to my eyes and twisted the lens to focus.

"Your other left," Ramón said, pointing. "There."

I swept past two boats, then readjusted my focus again as the third ship was further away from shore. Sure enough, I found Peniel's Eden. And there, at the helm, stood Mata. He wore an ugly Hawaiian print shirt, cargo shorts, and those same dark sunglasses I saw him wearing in the video footage as he left the Brewster County Sheriff's Office prior to the explosions.

"Where you headed, you son of a bitch?" I lowered the binoculars. "Is everything in order, Ramón?"

He took the binoculars from me and placed a small box in my hand.

"What's that?" Sharp asked.

I raised the box to my face and smiled.

"This is our little going away present, courtesy of my ace in the hole here." I gestured to Ramón. "You see, my friend has connections everywhere. We have some good history between us, so when I mentioned that I could use his help, he pulled out all the stops." I continued but looked directly at Ramón. "Even some that put him in conceivable danger."

Sharp scratched his neck. "I figured you for cartel, just wasn't sure at first glance. Your tat says everything I need to know."

"I left that life a long time ago," Ramón said.

"Which is why his role was so dangerous," I added. "We all know what would happen if his identity was discovered."

Ramón ran his index finger from ear to ear.

"Okay," Sharp said. "Noted. So, when did you locate Mata?"

"Only a few days ago. Cass and I had a plan in place, but when I heard from an old *compañero*, and was willing to pay him the right price, I learned that Mata was here in Guaymas."

"Tell him the best part," I said.

"My contact was Jose Vazquez, Mata's pilot. We knew where he was going, how long he was going to be away from his boat, and when he was going to return. I left the same morning as Cass, driving over twelve hours one way to get here, but I owe him my life," he said, nodding to me. "It was dark when I arrived, so getting out to Mata's boat unseen was not a problem."

I felt a tinge of ruthlessness join the bevy of emotions I was experiencing as I explained what was about to happen. I motioned for us to walk away from the bar.

Standing at the end of the marina on the docks of an empty boat slip, the three of us watched Peniel's Eden move into the deeper waters of *Ensendada Bacochibampo*, and away from other vessels. I took the binoculars from Ramón and looked one last time at the man who had murdered so many people in my life. I watched as he stood by himself, in his own little world; a world that was about to come crashing down around him.

Opening the box with my free hand, I removed a

small, black device the size of a credit card. It had two finger pads on either side of a blinking red light.

The last view of Mata saw him look back to shore, almost as if he were looking at us, though we were so far off our likeness were not discernible. He turned, then disappeared from view as he descended into the interior cabin.

I placed my index finger on the left pad, took a deep breath, and raised my middle finger over the device.

"Alpha Mike Foxtrot," I said, pressing my middle finger onto the pad. The blinking red light turned solid amber.

In an impressive plume of orange flame and black smoke, Peniel's Eden exploded with a raucous boom that seemed to never stop echoing. Secondary explosions followed the first blast causing the mast to topple over, and sent burning debris flying high into the sky, then splashing into the water. I tossed the detonator into the water and watched as what was left of the boat began to sink.

Billowing clouds of gray and black swirled in the afternoon breeze. A crowd of spectators rushed down to the docks to see. The two men who had been enthralled in a jovial conversation, sauntered over to the rail with drinks in hand to have a look.

"Come on," I said. "It's over."

The three of us turned and walked away from the growing crowd of onlookers, from their excited chatter, without taking any further looks at Peniel's Eden as it burned and sank into the sea.

As we made our way out of the marina, I heard Ramón murmur to himself.

"*No más caza de El Despiadado*."

"What's that mean?" Sharp asked.

Ramón began to translate, but I beat him to it.

"No more hunting El Despiadado."

CHAPTER SEVENTY-TWO

There had never been a time that I can remember where I was so ready for the weekend. These past few days were a marathon through hell, and the only thing I wanted to do right now was get home to Raven.

After landing in El Paso, Sharp and I parted ways. I can say that, while he still had a talent for causing the hairs on the back of my neck to prick up like the spines on a cactus, I found that underneath all the BS was a man that I could count on when I needed him. If someone had told me that just a few days ago, I would never have believed it.

I checked in with Ray at the hospital before heading out and got an ear full of how bad the food was and that he had to share a room with "Mr. Chatty Kathy" who had been admitted for a bowel obstruction.

"Get me outta here, Cass! I've heard all I can stand about him needing to 'pass gas' and that there's a bowling ball stuck in his gut. He calls the nurses every few minutes because he feels like he has to take a dump. I feel for the guy, but if I have to listen to him strain one more time over a bedpan, I might just shoot him."

"Just a couple more days, Ray, then Raven and I will come up and bring you home to the CR. You can stay as long as you like. In the meantime, I'll see what I can do about getting you some more privacy."

I reached out a hand to him. He wrapped his fingers around my palm, then pulled me close.

"You're a good man, Callahan. Aren't many like us left."

He squeezed my hand with a love only a lifelong friend could understand.

"Yeah, Ray. Thanks for always being there for me."

I fist-bumped his chest, then stood up.

"I gotta run. If I'm lucky, Raven might still be up when I get home."

Ray sunk into his pillow and closed his eyes. He was exhausted and in pain, but he was alive. That was all that mattered.

Before I made it to the door, Ray called out to me.

"Hey Cass, do me a favor, will ya?"

"You name it."

"Tell that feisty-looking Latin nurse out there I am ready for my sponge bath."

He smiled, raising and lowering his eyebrows. I laughed.

"You got it, Ray."

CHAPTER SEVENTY-THREE

The grumble of the Explorer's tires moving off the gravel road and over the iron cattle guard was music to my ears as I pulled onto the CR. I was home. The clock on my dash read 2:22 a.m. I parked in front of the house and sat looking at the front door. I wanted to rush in, grab Raven around the waist, and simply hold her. The touch of her skin, the look in her eyes, her breath on my face, it was all I wanted.

I cut the engine and stepped out of the car. A chill in the air kissed my face as I looked around the property. Moonlight washed over everything, making the barn and the corral look like the backdrop of an old black-and-white photograph.

I glanced beyond the buildings. The open range of the CR looked like a white-washed mix of ethereal showers and inky blackness that blended into a dark gray as it stretched to the Rio Grande and beyond. I thought about how strange it was that Raven and I had left our lives in Houston to move as far west as anyone could live in Texas. It was an escape, an effort to get away from the dregs of society, to focus on healing our minds and bettering our souls, and yet through it all, we found ourselves in a life where danger and mystery seemed to find us at every turn. I suppose that we had felt a new beginning meant no more problems, but we were blinded by that hope. The good news was that we were fighters, compassionate and honest, and willing to take risks for the benefit of doing what was right. We had grown during our short time on the CR and were all the better for it.

"Hey, cowboy."

I spun around to see Raven standing in the doorway wearing one of my Astros T-shirts that draped down over her thighs. She leaned against the doorframe and folded her arms across her chest.

"You just gonna stand there?" she said, her lips curling into a smile.

I smiled back.

"Well?"

Without further hesitation, I walked over to her, leaping over the porch steps, and scooped her into my arms. I twisted around as if in a dance while our lips pressed together. It was tender. Loving. It felt just like the first kiss we shared, and I wanted it to last forever. Her arms wrapped around my neck. Her fingertips caressed my back and my shoulders. When we finally parted, I set her down and our eyes met. She laid a hand on my cheek, running her fingers over the path of the bullet that grazed me. Tears formed in the corners of her eyes.

"I'm alright," I said, pulling her hand away. "It's just a scratch."

"Just a scratch?"

"Yeah," I said, tightening my grip around her waist. "You should see the other guy."

She leaned her head against my chest.

"Wanna go inside?" I asked.

Raven twisted her head so that her chin rested on my chest and looked up at me.

"I do."

I kissed her on the forehead, then let go with one hand and picked her up in my arms to carry her inside.

"Cass," she said as I closed the door behind us. "There is something I need to tell you."

"Anything, babe."

I carried her across the living room, then stopped when I saw a strange figure standing in the hallway that led past the bedrooms. It was dark, but the silhouette was clear.

I set Raven down, and the figure in the hall crept forward. Raven walked over, blocking my view, then turned around holding the hand of a small child. His brown eyes bulged with concern. His black hair fell victim to a serious case of bedhead. The legs of his pajama pants had worked their way up to his shins. He wore a matching top with a picture of Big Bird sleeping in his nest.

Raven stepped forward, hand in hand with the little boy. His steps were tentative, and he hid behind her leg as they came closer. I watched with growing curiosity. Raven led him into the living room and sat down on the couch. He cozied into her, all while keeping his gaze glued to me. She wrapped her arm around him, much like a mother bird might do when protecting its young.

"Rave," I said. "Who's this?"

EPILOGUE

The clinking of glasses and the low murmur of voices filled Ruby's Diner, a delightful restaurant located at the end of Huntington Beach Pier. Its panoramic views of the Pacific Ocean and surrounding beaches made this the perfect location for vacationers to enjoy a meal while gazing out at the beauty along the coast of Southern California. It was even more enticing during the late hours of the day when the sun descended toward the horizon, painting the water with brilliant streams of red and orange and yellow while the sky itself seemed to catch fire. The soothing crash of waves coming ashore and the chirps of seagulls were nature's simple, yet enchanting addition to the daily evening show.

As the sun lowered further, a purple haze began to overtake the surface of the water. Lights on the pier turned on, attracting fish below, and fishermen above. A sea breeze swirled around the corners of Ruby's Diner, carrying with it a flight of Double-crested Cormorants. The view, even in the waning light, was spectacular.

The restaurant was bustling, driving the waitstaff to move rapidly in attending to the needs of all guests.

Penny, a young waitress who had relocated to California with dreams of becoming an actress yet found herself caught in the daily grind of real life, grabbed her notepad and pen, and walked to serve a newly seated guest at the center, window-front table.

"Evening, sir. So sorry to keep you waiting. You've got the best seat in the place." Penny smiled and raised her pen and paper. "Are you ready to order?"

"But, of course."

IF YOU LIKED THIS, YOU MAY ENJOY:
ROWDY: WILD AND MEAN, SHARP AND KEEN

Blood, bullets, and tears bring Rowdy's world to a showdown...

Thrust to the mercy of the Mississippi river, thirteen-year-old Rowdy floats safely away as he watches the smoke rise from his burning farmhouse. His father, dead. His brother, dead. Both gunned down in front of him by a murderous gang of bandits.

Now alone in the world, Rowdy's perilous journey of survival begins, challenging and shaping him into the young man his father would want him to become. Pulled from the waters, he is given a chance by a lone river Captain and his mate. Working the trade routes between St. Louis and New Orleans, he learns to navigate safe passage. Rowdy grows strong working the river, but he must use his wit as well as his strength to confront a bullying crewman and survive a surprise attack by river pirates.

Facing life and death decisions, Rowdy's only option is to run. Survival is what Rowdy has come to know all too well. As his escape across the plains towards Lincoln, New Mexico, nearly claims his life, through a stranger's help, Rowdy recovers but is faced with questions about his rescuer's motives.

Blood, bullets, and tears bring Rowdy's world to a showdown. Fighting for what is right is his code, living life for others becomes his way, and staring danger in the face is what he must do if he can truly be Wild and Mean, Sharp and Keen.

AVAILABLE NOW

ACKNOWLEDGMENTS

Each Cass Callahan novel has had tremendous support from experts in their respective fields including law enforcement, military service, martial arts, novelists, and academics. I am continually grateful for everything I have learned from them as I create a world of believable fiction around Cass Callahan and a bevy of unique characters. I would like to thank Father Ralph Morgan of Calvary Episcopal Church for the time he took to walk me through various bible verses. His explanations helped me understand how I could effectively use words and phrases in such a way that would accentuate certain characters or settings while remaining respectful and true to the verses from which they came. I would also like to thank Dr. Ann Buchanan for sharing her vast knowledge of medications, emergency room procedures, and life saving techniques. If I ever find myself on a gurney staring up at emergency room lighting, I sure hope she's the one on service to keep me alive.

I could never close an acknowledgments section without thanking my family. They have been instrumental throughout the process of writing each novel. My sons, Ryan and Jackson, always have an open ear when I charge into their rooms and say, "Hey! How do you like the sound of this?" My sister, Julie, is a priceless sounding board for ideas and is so sharp and keen when it comes to editing. My parents, Jack and Margie, have been a trustworthy and honest audience, brutally honest at times, as I read each day's work to them over the phone. Not only am I lucky for their wealth of knowledge, but I cherish each minute spent with them as I share new adventures in the Cass Callahan novels. Finally, my wife Joellan. Without her support, Cass Callahan, and much of the Rowdy series for that matter, might not ever have had the chance to be written. 我爱你

ABOUT THE AUTHOR

Chris Mullen is an accomplished and award-winning author, recognized for his captivating storytelling and literary talent. Hailing from Richmond, Texas, he is a proud graduate of Texas A&M University.

With a career spanning twenty-three years in education, Chris has been a dedicated teacher in both Kindergarten and PreK, cultivating his passion for storytelling and nurturing young minds. In 2019, he received the prestigious Connie Wootton Excellence in Teaching Award—a testament to his commitment to education and his profound impact on students' lives, bestowed upon him by the Southwest Association of Episcopal Schools (SAES). It was during this time that the idea for his young adult western adventure series, Rowdy, was born.

The first installment, *Rowdy: Wild and Mean, Sharp and Keen*, was met with critical acclaim and earned the esteemed title of 2023 Independent Press Distinguished Favorite. Notably, the third book, *Rowdy: Dead or Alive*, stands as a 2023 Will Rogers Medallion Finalist. Garnering numerous awards, Chris's Rowdy series continues to captivate readers of all ages, cementing his place as an author in the young adult western genre.

When he's not weaving stories, you can find Chris honing his craft in local coffee shops, pizza places, or even the neighborhood grocery store. Currently, he is hard at work on an adult, contemporary western mystery series for Wolfpack Publishing.

To connect with Chris, visit his website www.chris-mullenwrites.com, where you can access updates, behind-the-scenes glimpses, and much more. Additionally, be sure to follow his Amazon Author Page and catch him on various social media platforms—Facebook, Instagram, Threads, and TikTok @chrismullenwrites, as well as on Twitter @cmullenwrites. For any inquiries or heartfelt messages, feel free to reach out directly at chrismullen-writes@gmail.com.